He hadn't changed at all in eight years,

Laurey thought. He was still as tall, as blond, his eyes were just as green, his features as perfect as ever. He was slightly broader in the shoulders, solid muscles perhaps a bit more evident, but he was as lean as he'd been before. And just as breathtaking. One would never guess that behind that beautiful exterior was someone capable of lying without a blink, of presenting a false front so perfect no one would ever suspect that underneath was a dishonest, deceitful, double-dealing—

He was gaping at her. She supposed he could be faking it, that utterly puzzled look—she'd certainly had experience with his acting ability—but it seemed more likely to be real. He didn't remember her. He'd shattered her life, and he didn't even remember her....

Dear Reader,

Once again, Intimate Moments offers you top-notch romantic reading, with six more great books from six more great authors. First up is *Gage Butler's Reckoning,* the latest in Justine Davis's TRINITY STREET WEST miniseries. It seems Gage has a past, a past that includes a girl—now a woman—with reason to both hate him and love him. And his past is just about to become his present.

Maria Ferrarella's *A Husband Waiting To Happen* is a story of second chances that will make you smile, while Maura Seger's *Possession* is a tale of revenge and matrimony that will have you longing for a cooling breeze—even if it *is* only March! You'll notice our new Conveniently Wed flash on Kayla Daniels' *Her First Mother.* We'll be putting this flash on more marriage of convenience books in the future, but this is a wonderful and emotional way to begin. Another flash, The Loving Arms of the Law, has been chosen to signify novels featuring sheriffs, those perfect Western heroes. And Kay David's *Lone-Star Lawman* is an equally perfect introduction. Finally, enjoy *Montoya's Heart,* Bonnie Gardner's second novel, following her successful debut, *Stranger In Her Bed.*

And, of course, don't forget to come back next month, when we'll have six more Intimate Moments novels guaranteed to sweep you away into a world of excitement and passion.

Enjoy!

[signature]

Leslie J. Wainger
Senior Editor and Editorial Coordinator

Please address questions and book requests to:
Silhouette Reader Service
U.S.: 3010 Walden Ave., P.O. Box 1325, Buffalo, NY 14269
Canadian: P.O. Box 609, Fort Erie, Ont. L2A 5X3

JUSTINE DAVIS

GAGE BUTLER'S RECKONING

Silhouette®
INTIMATE™MOMENTS®

Published by Silhouette Books

America's Publisher of Contemporary Romance

SILHOUETTE BOOKS

ISBN 0-373-07841-2

GAGE BUTLER'S RECKONING

Books by Justine Davis

JUSTINE DAVIS

lives in San Clemente, California. Her interests outside of writing are sailing, doing needlework, horseback riding and driving her restored 1967 Corvette roadster—top down, of course.

A policewoman, Justine says that years ago, a young man she worked with encouraged her to try for a promotion to a position that was, at that time, occupied only by men. "I succeeded, became wrapped up in my new job, and that man moved away, never, I thought, to be heard from again. Ten years later he appeared out of the woods of Washington state, saying he'd never forgotten me and would I please marry him? With that history, how could I write anything but romance?"

Chapter 1

Happy birthday to you, Gage Butler told himself as he hung up the phone.

He meant it; the warrant that gave him the right to put Mitchell Martin behind bars was the best present he could have gotten, and a few days early to boot. And Judge Aaron Partain had expressed his own pleasure in swearing it out; he was retiring early from the bench, and men like Martin were the reason why, he'd told Gage.

You won't get away with this one, Martin, Gage muttered to himself. And tried not to care that deep in his gut he knew the man had committed the same crime before, perhaps often, and had done exactly that—gotten away with it. While there was hope some of those prior victims might come forward after his arrest, Gage knew he had to settle for the fact that at last Martin would be stopped. He told himself it was enough. Sometimes he almost believed it.

"You look...grimly satisfied."

Gage turned to look at his boss, the only other person still in the detective division office of the Marina Heights police station, more familiarly known as Trinity West, at this hour. "I am," he agreed.

Sergeant Kit Walker sat on the edge of the desk and studied him for a moment, her hazel eyes thoughtful beneath her tousled blond bangs. "Martin?"

He nodded. "I just got the call. Judge Partain issued the warrant."

Kit smiled, looking rather grimly satisfied herself. "Good. What's the bail?"

Gage smiled back, but somehow his expression was no less grimly satisfied. "A million. When he heard the whole story, Partain was really pissed. And this is a hot button of his."

Kit's eyes widened in pleasure. "That's a hundred grand for a bail bond. Even Martin will have to scramble to come up with that in a hurry. Those spendy lawyers of his are going to have a fit."

"Does my heart good."

"Mine, too," Kit agreed. "When do you want to do it?"

"Friday afternoon."

Kit looked puzzled. "Not until then? Isn't he due back Friday morning?"

Gage nodded. "But his business partner is leaving that same afternoon for South America."

Kit studied him for a moment, then asked softly, "What are you plotting, Detective Butler?"

"According to the information I have, most of Martin's money is hidden in nonliquid assets in the corporation, to dodge taxes. I doubt even he's got a million lying around in ready cash."

"That's what bail bondsmen are for," Kit reminded him.

"Yes, but they're not a trusting bunch. Even with Martin, they'll want collateral for that kind of money. And he still has to come up with ten percent."

He watched as the grin spread across her face. "I get it. Even if he can manage the hundred thousand, he can't put the business or its property up for collateral without his partner's okay, right?"

"Right. I checked the incorporation papers."

"So at the least it will take him a day or two. Maybe more, because it's the weekend."

"Exactly."

Kit shook her head, still grinning. "Is there any angle you don't think of?"

"I want him where he belongs. At least for a while."

Kit's grin slowly faded. "Assuming he comes back Friday at all," she said sourly.

Gage grimaced as she voiced his greatest concern. He was still chafing over the arrogant man's blasé indifference; he'd ignored Gage's warning to stay available for further questioning and promptly taken off last week on what he called an essential business trip to San Francisco. They hadn't had enough evidence yet for the warrant, but Martin's departure had only made Gage more determined. He'd broken the man's alibi three days later.

"He'll be back. He's too arrogant to believe he'll really be arrested," he said, but he knew perfectly well that with his resources, Martin could be in Tahiti by now.

"You're still ticked at that bribery attempt, aren't you?" Kit said, her teasing tone an obvious effort to lighten his mood.

Since she'd made the effort, he tried to respond. "I'm ticked that Martin thought he could have me so cheap," Gage said wryly.

"Now, now," Kit said in an obviously mock cautioning tone, "you heard the man say he knew nothing about it."

"Right. That flunky of his just loves his boss so much, he thought up the idea on his own."

"Martin's a lovable guy," Kit said wryly. "Just ask the folks who frequent the society pages."

"The Santos family can't even afford to buy a paper, let alone make the society pages."

Kit was quiet for a moment, then, tentatively, said, "If he doesn't come back—" She stopped when Gage shook his head sharply.

"If he doesn't, I'll hunt him down. There's nowhere he can hide."

Kit said nothing for a moment, but Gage saw her mouth

tighten. She was a good cop and a better boss, but he knew she worried about him. She was only six years older than he was, but sometimes her concern seemed almost motherly. An odd thought to have about someone he'd have wondered about having a personal relationship with, if he had time for such a thing, and had she not made it quite clear very early on that that was a professional line she would never cross.

Well, he amended, maybe big sisterly; Kit neither looked nor acted old enough to be his mother, nor would she appreciate the analogy. But he was used to it; the baby face that had shaped so much of his life inspired that feeling in many. But that didn't mean he had to like it.

"I'm going to sit on his damn office all week," Gate muttered. "Just in case."

"No, you're not."

He blinked. "What?"

"You've been working eighteen-hour days for weeks now on this case. You got the warrant. That's enough. Get some rest."

"But if he shows up early—"

"I'll call Chance Buckner over at Marina del Mar. He'll have their patrol watch the office and Martin's house. If he shows up early, they'll call."

Gage knew she'd mentioned Buckner's name intentionally; the man was well-known far outside his own department. What the former Marina del Mar detective, now sergeant, said he'd do, he did. She couldn't have said anything better calculated to reassure him that the job would get done. Still, it went against the grain to trust anyone, even Chance Buckner, to do what he saw as his job.

"Look, I'll just—"

"Don't make me pull rank, Butler."

Her voice had taken on that warning tone he'd come to dread.

And she only called him Butler when he was headed for trouble. He knew just what kind, too.

"Gage..." she began.

He held up a hand. "I can feel it coming. Not another lecture, please."

"You deserve it. You've been working like a fiend, too many hours, too many days."

"It paid off, didn't it?"

"I'm not saying it didn't. We never would have gotten even Judge Partain to issue that warrant if you hadn't broken Bryant's story, blasting Martin's alibi to bits. But you can't—"

"I want this guy."

"So do I, Gage. He deserves the worst we can throw at him. More. But I don't want it to cost you too much."

"How about what it cost Diane Santos?"

Kit sighed. "Do you think I don't know that?"

Gage felt a rush of contrition; they both knew she did. Kit Walker hadn't let the difficulties of being a woman in law enforcement harden her; she'd been as furious as he had been at what had been done to the Santos girl, and she went to the mat for him—and his sometimes unorthodox methods—without fail. He couldn't ask for a more supportive supervisor. It had been instinctive, trying to divert her from ground too often trod. But that didn't excuse using a young victim's pain to do it. Sometimes he wondered if he hadn't been at this too damned long.

"Sorry," he muttered, leaning back in his chair and shoving his hair off his forehead. "I didn't mean that."

"And *that* is what *I* mean," Kit said softly. "You're on the edge, my friend. You have been for a long time, but that edge is starting to crumble."

"I'm fine."

Kit looked at him for a long, silent moment, her eyes troubled. "Someday, I hope you find somebody you trust enough to help you carry that load, whatever it is." Before he could deny it, she stood up. "I want you out of here. And that is an order. I'll meet you here at twelve hundred hours on Friday, and we'll go get the bastard."

She uttered the epithet quietly, but Gage knew there was a wealth of feeling behind it. He also knew it was a declaration of understanding, but he didn't quite know how to acknowledge it.

"Thanks," he finally said, rather lamely.

Smiling as if she understood, Kit nodded, then walked out of his small cubicle. For a moment Gage sat there, tapping the eraser of his pencil on the legal pad before him. He thought about calling Buckner himself, to emphasize the importance of knowing if Martin returned unexpectedly. But he knew it wasn't necessary. Kit would make it clear, and Buckner was the best; he'd understand.

I want you out of here. And that is an order.

He let out a compressed breath. Kit didn't often give him direct orders. When she did, there was no gainsaying her; she hadn't gotten to be a sergeant—and a respected one, at that—by being a pushover. No one did, but for a woman it was even harder. But she had done it, and any male newcomer to Trinity West who had reservations about working for a woman soon had his outlook adjusted; Kit Walker, they were told, was the one you wanted to back you up, the one you wanted on your side. She had her own way of doing things, and while it was decidedly female, it worked. She'd more than once talked a more hotheaded colleague out of trouble. And, on occasion, saved a life or two in the process.

And his life would become the proverbial living hell if she came back and he was still here.

Dropping the pencil, he stood up and grabbed the battered brown leather jacket that hung over the back of his chair. He started to put it on, then paused. He ran a finger over the time-softened leather, tracing the mended spot on the left sleeve without looking at it. He didn't need to. He knew exactly where it was. It was as much a badge to him as the gold shield he carried. But it was a badge not of achievement but of failure. The biggest, most irrevocable failure of his life.

With a sharp shake of his head, he yanked himself out of the well-worn rut. He yanked the jacket on without nearly as much effort.

He heard light, quick footsteps approaching.

"I'm gone," he yelped quickly, and headed for the door; the footsteps retreated.

"You'd better be," Kit warned from the door of her office on the far side of the room.

He grinned, threw her a salute and darted out the door. And just as quickly darted back in. Kit looked over her shoulder at him.

"I...forgot something."

He didn't bother to validate the fib by stopping at his desk, but instead headed toward the front of the office, to make his exit via the reception area. He saw Kit's brows furrow as she glanced from him to the door he'd almost used, then to the large end office, where the simple plaque like the one that labeled her Sergeant Kit Walker, Juvenile/Sex Crimes, had been replaced by a gold one elaborately declaring it the domain of Lieutenant Kenneth Robards, Commander, Detective Division, Marina Heights Police Department. He could almost see the fact that the light was still on in that office register with her. She looked back at him, her eyes widening in exaggerated horror, and she quickly dodged into her own office and shut the door.

Gage grinned and kept going, feeling a bit lighter of heart. Really, it was doubtful Martin would abscond this early in the game. He had too much at stake here, several businesses, investments, and a net worth that had enough digits to the left of the decimal point that Gage knew the man paid more in taxes than he made in a year, probably two. Martin had never had to work a day for any of it, his father and grandfather had done that, but he certainly knew how to live the life.

Yes, he'd be back. If for no other reason than that he was too damned arrogant to believe he could really be taken down.

All the more reason, Gage muttered to himself. He *would* take Mitchell Martin down, and down hard. So hard all his money wouldn't buy his way out. So hard that the Santos family would know the system hadn't failed them.

So hard that he would be able to sleep at night, without Debby's ghost haunting his dreams.

But until he did, he was in no hurry to go home and contend

with that ghost. In the parking lot of Trinity West, he sat in his car for a moment, tapping his finger on the steering wheel. Caitlin, he thought. He should tell her. She would be relieved to know that Martin would be arrested the day after tomorrow, and he knew he could trust her not to tell anyone about the warrant.

Moments later—although longer than normal, because he kept glancing in the mirrors, thinking he was seeing the same car behind him—he pulled his car to a halt on Trinity Street East, in front of Caitlin Romero's Neutral Zone. And not for the first time, he marveled at what she had accomplished here. A few months ago, this street had mirrored this east side neighborhood, beyond run-down into borderline derelict, far worse than even the worst part of Trinity West. Only the Neutral Zone had stood out as having had any kind of attention at all in the last decade, if not two. Most of the other buildings had been festooned with crisscrossed boards over broken windows. Some lacked even that much care, gaping holes yawning where windows had once been. A liquor store with heavily barred windows had been the only sign of life at one corner, the old mom and pop style grocery store the only sign at the other.

But now the grocery had been refurbished with the help of some Trinity West cops, who did it in thanks to the owner, Jorge Cordero, who had helped them in the fight against The Pack, the vicious street gang Ryan Buckhart had practically single-handedly broken up a few months ago. There was another storefront across the street, gleaming with new glass, and renovations were underway next door at the old building that was going to become Kelsey Gregerson's youth shelter. It was as if an entire block was going to be revitalized by the stubborn efforts of one gutsy woman.

As he thought of the dauntless redhead, he felt a sense of vague wistfulness; he liked, admired and respected Caitlin, and had once wondered if those feelings might grow into something more. But the arrival of Quisto Romero had settled the question before it had truly formed. Not that he could begrudge her, not when he knew how happy she was. He didn't begrudge anybody who was able to find happiness in what was too often a rotten world. Besides, if he was honest with himself, it never would have worked anyway, any more than it would have with Kit. He just wasn't the type for a serious relationship. There was no room for that in his life; his failed marriage had proved that. Just as well Quisto had come along. He even liked the guy. And Caitlin clearly loved him to distraction.

A good thing, Gage thought with an inward grin as he got out of the car, since she was very pregnant. Automatically he locked the door; the neighborhood might be improving, but it was a slow process, and there were plenty of people around who could strip down any vehicle in a matter of seconds. Not, he amended silently as he headed for the door of the Neutral Zone, that anyone would be attracted to his rather battered, ten-year-old coupe.

At this hour on a Friday night, the Neutral Zone was crowded. Gage knew there had been a drop in numbers right after word had gotten around among the street kids that Caitlin's new husband was a cop. But they'd gradually come back; Caitlin had built a lot of trust since she'd opened this place, and Quisto himself was rapidly gaining a reputation as tough but fair. And the fact that he'd risked his life to find the murderer of a street kid no one else cared about had become well-known and done much to draw the kids back.

Gage had tried back in the beginning to get Caitlin to move her club up to Trinity West, but she had insisted the need was greater here on the east side. He and a few other Trinity West cops had told her she was nuts, that nobody down there would abide by her rules of no alcohol, no weapons and no drugs, but she wouldn't listen. She had been utterly resolved. And against all odds, she had succeeded in her determination to give the younger kids an alternative to starting with the street gangs.

And now she was going to have one of her own to spend some of that love on, Gage thought.

He saw Caitlin the moment he stepped inside, her strawberry blond hair highly visible, even inside. She was standing behind the long bar, a rather makeshift affair of dark, stained wood that was nevertheless polished to a high sheen. She was pointing to the cheerful yellow wall behind the bar as someone else, on a short stepladder, was hanging a framed photograph in the spot Caitlin was indicating.

It wasn't one of the regular Neutral Zone kids on the ladder, he realized, it was definitely a woman. And she was tall enough that she didn't need much help from the ladder. Not much else about her needed help, either, he thought with an appreciative glance at long legs clad in snug black jeans and a glossy fall of hair that looked nearly as black as the denim.

At least Caitlin was being careful and not climbing the ladder herself, Gage thought as he closed the door behind him. Quisto's admonitions must have finally taken root.

"Hey, blondie, how ya' doin'?"

The cheerful hail came from a short, plumpish Hispanic girl wearing a pair of silver earrings that reached nearly to her shoulders and carrying several dirty glasses.

"Hi, Elena. How's your mother?"

"Better, she's much better."

"Good. So you're back in school?"

The girl rolled her eyes heavenward. "You gotta learn to take off the cop suit, man. Yes, I'm back in school. You know Caitlin wouldn't let me work here if I wasn't."

He knew it was true; for kids to work for her Caitlin had added one more rule in addition to her big three about booze, weapons and drugs; you had to be in school.

"You keeping her from doing too much?"

Elena smiled widely. "Sure. Gotta keep that baby happy."

Gage glanced across the room again, aware of the glances he was drawing from the other kids in the place, some of whom he knew, some he didn't. But he didn't make eye contact with any of them, partly because he knew some didn't want to acknowledge that they knew and maybe even liked a cop, and partly because he was focused on the woman who was stretching up to straighten the picture she'd just put on the wall. No, there was nothing about that lady that needed help. Nothing at all.

"Who's that?" he asked Elena.

"She's Caitlin's old friend's sister," Elena explained, eyeing him speculatively. "She's here for the baby shower."

"Oh."

"Pretty, isn't she?"

She said the last archly, with a mischievous glance over her shoulder at him as she headed behind the bar to dump her load of glasses into the sink of soapy water. Gage followed her, smiling. It was moments like this that made it all worth it, he thought. Just a year ago, Elena had been a very troubled girl, cutting school, messing with drugs, drunk as often as she was sober. Today she was back in school and doing well, despite her mother's chronic illness.

"Hey, Caitlin!" Elena called out as they reached the bar. "Look what blew in!"

The strawberry blonde turned, saw Gage and smiled widely. The welcome warmed him in an entirely different way than it used to; Caitlin was Quisto's, and he was undeniably hers, and he wasn't fool enough to stick his nose between them. But he didn't like her any less. More, perhaps, and her friendship was important to him.

The woman on the ladder turned, as well, and Gage was struck by the sensation that she seemed familiar. She looked at him, dark brows furrowed over striking gray eyes, as if she felt the same.

"Only six-thirty," Caitlin said teasingly, glancing at her watch. "What on earth are you doing away from Trinity West this early?"

He grimaced, switching his gaze back to Caitlin. "Not you, too. Kit's already chewed on me more than enough for one day."

"Good for her," Caitlin said with a laugh.

Gage glanced at the wall behind her, the yellow wall, the one where the familiar-seeming woman had just hung a whimsical photo of a baby and a gamboling puppy. The cheerful wall Caitlin had begun as an antidote to the darker, opposite wall behind him. He didn't have to look at it to remember the mass of photos there, a conglomeration of faces and names with seemingly only one thing in common: their youth. But Gage knew too well what else they had in common: they were dead. Every last one of them was dead. Some from drugs, some shot, stabbed, run down in the street. And a few suicides. The pictures were brought in by friends, brothers, sisters, cousins, anyone who wanted to be sure they weren't forgotten, these lost souls, like the way the world seemed to want to forget them. And with Caitlin's help, they never would be.

The dark-haired woman stepped down to the floor, moving with a long-limbed grace that had Gage watching with a fascination that startled him when he realized what he was doing. She was still looking at him as if she were trying to place him, and the feeling grew stronger within him, as well, that he'd seen her before.

Caitlin half-turned to the woman beside her. "I want you to meet one of my favorite people. He's half the reason this place exists. Gage Butler, meet—"

"You!" The woman's exclamation cut Caitlin off. She stared at him, recognition now clear in her face. Recognition and something more. Anger. No, Gage thought, beyond anger. Outrage. And he knew the moment she spoke again that he had, if anything, underestimated her animosity.

"It's *you!* You lying, two-faced, phony sneak!"

Chapter 2

He'd barely changed at all in eight years, Laurey thought. He was still as tall, as blond, his eyes just as green, his features as perfect. He was slightly broader in the shoulders, solid muscles perhaps a bit more evident, but he was as lean as he'd been then. And just as breathtaking. You would never guess that behind that beautiful exterior was someone capable of lying without blinking, of presenting a false front so perfect that no one would ever suspect that underneath was a dishonest, deceitful, double-dealing—

He was gaping at her. She supposed he could be faking it, that utterly puzzled look—she'd certainly had experience with his acting ability—but it seemed more likely to be real. He didn't remember her. He'd shattered her life, and he didn't even remember her.

"Are you still betraying people, lying to get them to trust you, and then—"

"Whoa," Caitlin interrupted, sounding wary as Elena, wide-eyed, scuttled away, darting for cover into Caitlin's office. "I gather you two know each other?"

"Yes." Laurey's voice was tight, tense.

"No," Gage said simultaneously, sounding as puzzled as he'd looked.

"I see," Caitlin said, eyebrows raised.

"It doesn't surprise me that you don't remember me," Laurey snapped, her eyes never moving from the tall blond man. She refused to back down, to be intimidated, not by this man. "You probably ruined too many lives to remember each one."

Gage opened his mouth as if to answer, then closed it again.

"Gage Butler," Caitlin said slowly, staring at Laurey, "has saved more lives than I can count."

"Oh, really?" Laurey said, barely managing to rein in the sarcasm slightly, and only trying for Caitlin's sake.

"Yes," Caitlin said positively. "But you obviously don't feel that way. Why?"

"I have this problem with lying, two-faced—"

"I think I just heard this song," Gage said, speaking at last.

Laurey glared at him. "I'll bet you've heard it a lot."

"Not lately," he said, then, as if something had just occurred to him, his gaze narrowed as he stared at her. "Not lately," he repeated slowly.

"Taking a break from tricking people?" she asked sweetly.

"Why don't you take a break from cryptic comments and tell me exactly what it is you think I've done?"

"Blocked it out, have you? How you lied to people you tricked into being your friends? Entrapped them? And then—"

"Laurey," Caitlin began warningly.

"Laurey," Gage said, in an entirely different tone. "Laurey…Templeton, isn't it?"

He *did* remember, she thought. And she hated the fact that, in the midst of her anger, it pleased her. It gave her voice even more of an edge.

"It is. Not that it matters. I'm just one of many who fell for your act."

"Laurey, listen," Caitlin began, but she stopped when Gage lifted a hand.

"It's all right," he said, "I think I understand. You went to Marina Heights High School, didn't you?"

Her chin came up, and she continued to glare at him.

"About eight years ago?" he asked.

"My senior year, to be exact. A year," she added bitterly, "that I'll never forget."

"Eight years," Caitlin said thoughtfully, glancing from Laurey to Gage. "Wasn't that about when you were working undercover at the high school?"

"When he was a narc, you mean," Laurey said. "Sneaky, lying—"

"You're repeating yourself," Gage said rather mildly. He looked at Caitlin and explained in a wry tone, "I think it's safe to say that your friend here got…caught up in one of the sweeps."

Caitlin eyed Laurey with interest. "Is it true? You got arrested? I never knew—"

"It's hardly something I advertise," Laurey said sharply, blushing; despite the fact that she'd later been released without being charged, the knowledge that she'd been arrested was still humiliating. "And I didn't do anything," she added quickly.

Gage's mouth quirked. He didn't speak, but Laurey could hear the words "That's what they all say," as clearly as if he had.

She glanced back at Caitlin and saw a different expression, one of understanding, or at least a willingness to listen. But then, Caitlin had always been that way. Even when she herself had been a fourteen-year-old pest, tagging along with her big sister, Caitlin had been kind. Kinder than Lisa had been, most of the time, or at least more patient. Lisa hated having her kid sister hanging around and had made it clear. It was only years later, when Lisa had graduated and moved away from home, that they had become close.

And then there hadn't been enough time. They'd wasted so much of it, thinking they had forever, never realizing…

It welled up suddenly, as it so often did, catching her off guard and unaware. Moisture stung her eyes. "Excuse me," she stammered, and turned away. She fled quickly, darting through the door at the far end of the yellow wall, into the small bathroom. She made it just as the tears spilled over.

* * *

Gage watched the door swing closed, his brows furrowed. She'd gone so quickly from anger to tears, and he swore he hadn't said anything to bring on the change. He turned to look at Caitlin, feeling a bit bewildered. To his amazement, Caitlin's blue eyes were glistening as well.

"Damn," he muttered. "What brought that on? One minute she's spitting mad, and the next… What did I say?"

"It's nothing you said, Gage," Caitlin said softly. "It's nothing to do with you at all."

"But it was me she was…mad at."

"Yes, but that's not what she was crying about."

"Oh."

He waited, but Caitlin didn't elaborate. Women, he thought. How did they do it, figure things like that out so easily? They seemed to know, somehow, when what happened on the surface was driven by something else completely different beneath.

"Did you really arrest her?" Caitlin asked.

"I…not directly. I just told the beat officers to stop the car she was in, because I knew one of the kids had just picked up a sizable stash of grass he was going to sell."

He paused, the memories the tall, dark-haired woman had wakened still stirring. And moving faster, reminding him of that time he'd all but forgotten. The time when he had first come out of the police academy and the baby face that was the bane of his existence had prompted the powers-that-be to divert him before he'd ever hit the street in uniform. They'd put him in the local high school, masquerading as a transfer student. They'd built him a rep before he ever arrived, and by the time he checked in, everyone knew he'd been in drug trouble at his previous school.

The Marina Heights students had been suspicious, as they were of any newcomer, but Gage had barely been away from the high school life for three years—he'd started the academy when he was twenty, getting special permission since he would turn twenty-one the week before he graduated—and he didn't find it too difficult to fall back into that life. The hardest part, ironically, had been purposely cutting school, skipping homework and making lousy grades on tests in classes he'd excelled in.

"But you remember her?"

"Yes." Oh, yes, he remembered her. And he was remembering more by the minute. "How do you know her?"

A shadow flickered in Caitlin's eyes. "Her sister Lisa was my best friend from school. She...couldn't be here, so Laurey came in her place." He sensed there was more—much more—to it than that, but Caitlin quickly moved on. "Lisa never told me Laurey had gotten in trouble. But we were both off to college by then." She gave him a sympathetic look. "I'm sorry she was so..."

"Yeah," Gage said dryly. "Obviously the lady holds a grudge."

"She was...young. Things are always so intense then." She eyed him pointedly. "And some people stay that way."

His mouth twisted. "And you're not? And your husband?"

She laughed. "And the Gregersons and the Buckharts and Kit...we're all guilty as charged." Then, rather briskly, she asked, "Speaking of which, what's up? You didn't just drop by to kill time."

"I didn't?"

"Gage Butler, you don't allow yourself the luxury of time to kill." She was suddenly very serious. "Do you have news? Diane's case?"

He nodded, automatically glancing around to be sure there was no one to overhear. "We got the arrest warrant."

Caitlin breathed a sigh of relief. "Hallelujah."

He nodded; he knew Caitlin was under no more illusions than any cop that the rich indeed weren't treated differently. She knew it from firsthand experience. She'd grown up in neighboring Marina del Mar, with the silver spoon indigenous to the wealthy town. It made what she was doing here even more amazing.

"Keep it quiet," he said, although he knew it was unnecessary. "I don't want to take any chance of it getting back to him and scaring him off before we can serve it."

Caitlin didn't take offense, only nodded. "I won't. I want him in prison. I want Diane and her family to know he's where he should be, locked up like the animal he is."

"He will be, by Friday evening." He explained his reasons for the timing and his hopes that Martin would be unable to make bail as quickly as he normally would.

"But he's going to make bail eventually," he warned her. "Even Judge Partain couldn't deny it. The very things that give him the wherewithal to run are the things his lawyers will say will keep him here."

Caitlin grimaced. "I hate that. It makes me think he'll somehow get away with it. That the system really can be bought."

"We both know it can be. But not this time," Gage said grimly. "I swear, Cait, not this time. He may get out on bail, but he'll be going back. He'll be going back for a long, long time."

This, Laurey told herself as she leaned against the wall papered with a cheerful yellow-and-white print, was ridiculous. Worse than ridiculous, it was stupid. It had been eight years. There was no reason for this, no reason for her to have reacted so strongly. She thought she had gained some perspective in the years since that fateful night that was so clearly etched on her memory. She thought she had consigned it neatly to the archives of youthful lessons learned.

She thought she'd forgotten Gage Butler.

So why, at the first sight of him, had all the old anger and shame welled up inside her as if it had been yesterday? Why had she instinctively lashed out? Why did she feel as if she was on the edge of some kind of fierce explosion, some eruption of temper that would make what had just happened seem mild?

She knew, of course. She knew all too well why she was so touchy, why it took next to nothing to set her off. Lisa.

"Laurey?"

Caitlin's voice came through the bathroom door. Laurey

straightened, wondering how long she had been in here. Hiding, she thought glumly. Hiding, in a way utterly unlike her.

"Gage is gone," Caitlin informed her, and Laurey felt more than ever like a child who had run away to hide from something that upset her. She let out a compressed sigh and went to open the door.

"I'm sorry," she said immediately. "I had no right to act like that here, in your place."

Caitlin stood aside and let Laurey pass back into the main room. Instead of commenting on her antagonistic behavior, Caitlin merely said "I've been told I make a mean root beer float. Will you have one with me?"

"I...yes," Laurey said, glad Caitlin didn't seem too upset by her treatment of a man who was obviously a good friend. "Thank you."

She didn't say anything else, just took a seat on one of the tall stools as Caitlin went behind the bar. The redhead opened the small freezer and took out a carton, scooped ice cream into a glass, then filled it from a tap behind her. Laurey's gaze strayed to the framed photograph directly above the root beer dispenser. A wedding photograph of the fiery-haired Caitlin and her darkly handsome husband, Quisto Romero. He had been, Lisa had told her, quite the ladies' man before he'd met his match in Caitlin. And their path had not been smooth; they had met because of the awful murder of a child, and had both come terrifyingly close to death themselves before they at last had found happiness. And they *were* happy, Laurey thought. It was undeniable. It glowed in their eyes and fairly radiated from them when they spoke of the child to come who would be the personification of that love.

Caitlin set the foamy concoction before Laurey, and she took a sip. She hadn't had one in years, and now that she tasted the creamy tang of it, she wondered why. "It's wonderful," she said.

"So my husband says," Caitlin said with a smile. "They were the way to his heart, you know."

Laurey smiled, feeling better now. "Were they?"

"He has a weakness for them."

"And for you."

"That, too," Caitlin said with a grin. She patted her belly, swelling with the child that would be born three months from now. "And it's a good thing."

"Yes," Laurey said softly. "A very good thing."

She sipped at the float again, savoring the contrast of the creamy richness of the ice cream and the bubbly bite of the soda.

"Gage is really a wonderful guy," Caitlin said quietly, catching Laurey off guard; she wondered if her friend had planned it that way. Probably. Caitlin was uncomfortably perceptive at times. She'd always been able to tell when something had upset the younger woman, and, unlike Lisa, had always seemed to have the time and patience to listen to her friend's little sister.

Laurey didn't answer. She couldn't think of anything to say.

"He helped me with this place, even while he was trying to talk me into opening it in Trinity West instead of here."

"Oh."

"He was concerned for my safety. But even he admits it's working."

"Of course it is," Laurey said, trying to change the subject. "You're great with these kids. You're going to be a great mom."

"Thank you. But," Caitlin went on, clearly not ready to be diverted, "half of these kids wouldn't be here if not for Gage."

Laurey's gaze narrowed. "Why?" she asked sourly. "Because he made it a condition of their parole?"

"No," Caitlin said quietly, "because if not for Gage, they'd be dead."

Laurey blinked. "What?"

Caitlin gestured toward a tall, lanky young boy of about fourteen, with mocha skin, wearing baggy jeans, a black football jersey and a baseball cap jammed on his head backward, who was huddled with some other kids over a video game.

"That's Dion. He nearly died in a gang shoot-out two years ago. He was only twelve, and he wasn't even in a gang, but the shooting convinced him he had to join up, for self-protection. Then Gage stepped in. He talked him out of it and got him into the gang diversion program he started a while back. It shows the kids there's another way, teaches them skills to get them out of this environment sooner. Dion is going to be a pilot now."

Laurey's eyes widened. "A pilot?"

Caitlin nodded. "Gage has a friend who flies a private jet for one of the big electronics firms in town. When Dion mentioned he liked planes, Gage arranged for him to go for a flight. He was hooked from then on. Gage is helping him study."

"How…nice," Laurey said, unable to avoid the edge in her voice, "that he's helping someone *in* school instead of arresting them out of it."

Caitlin ignored her tone. She pointed over her shoulder to a photograph on the yellow wall of four children who ranged in age from perhaps sixteen to a babe in arms. "Those are the Barton kids. Their parents were killed in an accident barely a year ago. There didn't seem to be any relatives, and they were going to have to be split up, all going to separate foster homes, except the baby, who probably would have been adopted right away. Gage spent two weeks of twenty-hour days until he tracked down a second cousin of the mother. Then he spent another month convincing her that she wasn't really ready for an empty nest yet, even though her own son was off at college. She took them all. They're still a family, thanks to him."

"You talkin' 'bout the Bartons?" Elena asked as she pulled off her apron.

"Actually," Caitlin said, "about Gage."

"Blondie? He's something, isn't he?"

"I suppose he saved your life?" Laurey asked the girl she'd met a couple of hours ago, wondering when the nomination for Gage Butler's sainthood would be made.

"Probably," Elena said solemnly, her eyes sad and old in her young face. "I was way down the road to nowhere, but Gage, he helped me. I was drinkin', smokin' dope, all that bad sh—" she broke off, glanced at Caitlin, and amended it to

"—stuff. He helped me stop, and he brought me here to the Neutral Zone, and then Caitlin, she helped me, too. And my mama, she was real sick, but Gage got her into a good hospital, even helped pay for her medicine, and she's better now."

Sainthood, Laurey thought dryly, might not be good enough for the paragon they were describing. But that paragon bore little resemblance to the Gage Butler who had torn apart her life eight years ago.

"I'm glad your mother is better," Laurey said, sure anything else she would say would not be welcomed here in the middle of the Gage Butler fan club.

"She's gonna get well," Elena said determinedly. "She's not gonna die."

"I'm sure you're right," Laurey said.

"I am," the girl avowed. "She's not old. She's only thirty-five—that's way too young to die."

"Yes," Laurey said, her throat suddenly tight. "Yes, it is." She blinked rapidly as the girl put her apron away and bade Caitlin good-night, and promised to be right on time tomorrow for her afternoon shift before Caitlin closed up the club for her baby shower.

"I can't pay much, but it's more than she'd get at the local hamburger stand, and she's safer here," Caitlin said after the girl had gone. "And her mother rests easier, knowing she's here instead of in that gang hangout. Want another float? I could finish off the last of the ice cream myself, except that I already feel like I weigh a ton, and…"

Laurey didn't even hear the rest of Caitlin's prattle. She knew that was what it was; Caitlin never just chattered on like this. She was doing it to distract her, Laurey was sure. Too bad it wasn't working.

She fought the tears that threatened. She'd been sure she was past this stage, when the moisture welled up at the slightest reminder. Apparently not.

Then she felt a gentle hand on her shoulder.

"I miss her, too, honey," Caitlin said softly. "So very much."

"It was just so stupid!" The words burst from her as if she hadn't wailed them a thousand times before.

"And worse, because there's no one left to blame," Caitlin said.

Laurey knew exactly what she meant; the carload of drunken, stoned kids that had plowed into Lisa's little compact had died just as she had, leaving no one for Laurey to vent her rage upon. No one to cry out to see punished, no one to rail at when the fury rose in her. She could hardly take it out on the families, not when she looked in their eyes and saw her grieving self looking back at her.

"I'm sorry," she said, swiping at eyes that were about to overflow. "I thought I was over this."

"You'll be over the instant tears someday," Caitlin reassured her, "and even the anger." Then she added sadly, looking over at the dark, far wall of the club, "But the pain never goes away, it just changes. To something you can live with."

Laurey followed Caitlin's look, staring at the mass of photographs, knowing that among them were Caitlin's own cousins, dead from their own bomb back in Ireland. She knew that was the common element of all the young faces in those photos; all had died before they had really lived. Caitlin had started the yellow wall—the bright, cheerful wall of life and love and successes, of puppies, babies and graduations—as an antidote to the other, so that her kids could see that good things were possible, that it wasn't all death and misery. But it had a long way to go before it would match, in numbers or in impact, the dark, grim wall that held all those young faces that would never grow older.

"Such a waste," Laurey murmured.

"Exactly. And it's that kind of waste that Gage fights so hard against. And the brutality. He takes on the worst rape cases, the ones no one else has the stomach for, even though it tears him apart inside. He's the most dedicated cop I know, and that includes my husband."

Caitlin's voice rang with conviction, and Laurey knew she meant every word. "If you say so," she said, "but if he's still using the same methods, I still don't think much of them."

"It was his job, Laurey. But he didn't ask for it. The brass just took one look at that baby face of his, found out he hadn't gone to school around here so no one would know him, and grabbed him for it. They planned it from the minute he made it through the first phase of the academy with flying colors. He never had a choice."

"He could have said, 'No, I don't want to trick kids into thinking I'm their friend and then bust them.'"

Caitlin didn't advance the argument Laurey half expected, that if the kids hadn't been breaking the law in the first place, they wouldn't have been arrested. Instead, surprisingly, she agreed.

"Yes, I suppose he could have, although it would no doubt have damaged his career. But instead he chose to try, to try and stop the drugs and guns before they got to the kids, before more of those kids wound up on that wall."

Laurey looked away from the grim photographic chronicle, not wanting to see it, not wanting to think about all those young lives snuffed out.

"I can name you at least a dozen kids who would be up there if not for Gage. And two dozen more who would be behind bars."

Laurey sighed; Caitlin seemed determined to convert her. And she herself was equally determined not to be converted. Although she had to admit, the things Caitlin was saying were having an impact; Caitlin, she knew, had few illusions left and generally saw things as they were. If that included Gage Butler, if he was indeed everything Caitlin said he was, then perhaps he'd changed on the inside, if not the outside. Maybe he was no longer the lying, deceitful—

You're repeating yourself....

Gage's words, uttered as if that were his only concern, not the fact that she was calling him all sorts of nasty names, echoed in her head. Of course, maybe that was because he was used to being called such names.

She felt Caitlin's gaze and looked up. Suddenly it was as if she were twelve again and had just said something silly. Lisa had always just rolled her eyes; it had been Caitlin who had gently pointed out the error in her assumption or logic. And her tone was the same now as it had been then.

"The bad guys have weapons the police can't afford and wouldn't be allowed to use if they could. More, they have no compunction about using those weapons. And they don't have anyone, especially people who have never faced death, watching their every move, second-guessing them. You try looking down the barrel of a Mac-10 in the hands of a gangbanger high on crack, knowing that to him your uniform makes you a target, part of a rival gang all of them hate."

"But—"

"What is it you expect, Laurey? That the cops go out on the street armed with nothing but Boy Scout honor? That they always play fair and honest when nobody else does?"

Irrationally, Laurey knew her instinctive cry would be yes. She bit it back; it seemed so foolish now. But Caitlin didn't relent.

"Quisto once talked an armed, barricaded suspect with several hostages into giving up without a shot, and he had to lie in the process. Is that wrong, lying to a criminal who is threatening innocent people? Is it wrong when it saves a half-dozen lives?"

Laurey lowered her gaze, feeling utterly confused now.

"I know," Caitlin said sympathetically. "It would be a lovely world if everybody told the truth, if no one ever hurt anyone, if no one took the easy way out by stealing instead of earning. If everything came out right and fair." Caitlin looked at her wall of remembrance, at the photos of those who had learned the hard way. "But it's not that kind of world, is it?"

Laurey couldn't argue with that. If the world was fair, Lisa would still be alive. And she felt a sudden burst of shame that she'd let an incident so long past matter so much. It seemed so petty, compared to the stark, unrelenting reality of the world. To the reality of her sister's death, at a time when she should have been living life to the fullest.

Time to grow up, kiddo.

Lisa's teasing words, which had once made her so mad,

rang in her mind, and Laurey wished fervently that she were here to say them again. She'd been so tired of always being the little sister, always being the one behind, the one who could never be first at anything because her sister had always been there already.

And now she would never be there again.

Time to grow up, kiddo.

She was almost twenty-seven years old, but she suddenly felt as if she had never grown up. She'd gotten her childish wish: she was no longer the little sister. But she'd never dreamed Fate would grant her that wish by making her not a sister at all.

Be careful what you're dreaming, 'cause it someday may come true....

The words to an old, loved song came back to her with a pang; the songwriter had been even wiser than she knew.

Chapter 3

Gage nearly laughed at himself when he realized he was skulking down the hallway long after hours, as worried about running into Kit as he was about running into Robards. The latter was a fear common to all the Trinity West detectives, although for him it was for a different reason than the others. But Kit was usually greeted with boisterous welcome; she'd made her way in a tough job that was mostly a male domain with grace and style and humor, and she'd gradually won over anyone who worked with or for her for any length of time.

The only reason he wouldn't be glad to see her as well was that she'd ordered him out of here until Friday. Well, not in so many words, but that had been the implication, and he knew pleading that she hadn't actually said it wouldn't get him very far if she found him here long after he was supposed to have gone.

He wondered, as he sat down at the single, sadly outdated computer terminal that graced the now-deserted detective division office, if the fact that the reason he was here had nothing to do with the Martin case would cut any ice with her.

That he himself wasn't sure what it *did* have to do with was something he hadn't quite dealt with yet.

He tapped in the records system access code, then his personal password. The inquiry form popped up, and he quickly filled in what blanks he could. He hit the Enter key and settled back in his chair for the wait; the antiquated machine took its own sweet time as it sent the command to search through the files held on the overtaxed system. Places like Marina del Mar had computer terminals on every detective's desk, but it would be a long time before such modernity reached Trinity West. Chief de los Reyes was a miracle worker when it came to wringing things out of a strapped budget—he ought to be mayor, Gage thought, except they couldn't afford to lose him—but even he could only do so much.

He listened as he waited; he didn't really expect Kit to be here, but he wouldn't put it past Robards to show up. Everybody knew he came in at odd hours in an effort to catch somebody at something, or to search desks for anything he could use against his subordinates. Someday, Gage thought, the bastard was going to go too far. He was going to give the chief enough rope to hang him with, and Gage could only hope he was around when that day came. He would truly like to see Miguel de los Reyes take the pompous, arrogant Robards down. He wouldn't mind doing it himself, of course, but he was sure de los Reyes would reserve the pleasure for himself; Robards had made it too clear too often how he felt about taking orders from a man of de los Reyes's heritage.

A faint beep brought his attention back to the computer screen. When he saw the response, Gage thought he'd made a mistake, the entry was so short. But when he sat up to read it, he saw why.

It was her, he was sure of that. It gave her name, her date of birth—she would be twenty-seven in three months, he noted—and her address at the time of the contact. Below those unhelpful details, most of which he'd already known, were the words "Juvenile Record Sealed."

He stared at the glowing amber letters that spelled out *Templeton, Laurey Lee* and wondered what he'd expected to find out. Even had the record not been sealed, it would have told him little more, unless she'd gotten into trouble again, which he doubted. Besides, his memory had been stirring rather actively since the encounter at the Neutral Zone, and just looking at her name glowing on the screen completed the job.

He must have been better than he'd expected to be at quashing the less pleasant memories of that time. Much better, he thought, for him not to have recognized her immediately. He'd certainly wondered about her often enough, even after he'd finished the assignment. So often he'd finally made the decision to try to forcibly stop the memory of the tall, gangly, earnest girl with the huge gray eyes that made him think of the sky when a storm had begun to ebb and the sun was trying to break through again.

Except, judging by her reaction last night, this storm wasn't going to pass. Apparently what had happened back then had made a tremendous impression on her. He tried to console himself with the thought that because of it, she had probably never even been close to being in trouble again, and that was, after all, the point, wasn't it? So why did it bother him that she was so angry still?

Probably, he told himself as he flipped off the computer and stood up, because anybody who can hold a grudge for that long makes you nervous.

It was a valid answer, and comforting. Far more comforting than admitting that Laurey Templeton had had such an impact on him. Far more comforting than admitting she had made his job back then harder than it already was, simply by her presence. He'd known she was flirting with him, or trying to; her innocent attempts were somehow infinitely more appealing than the more practiced efforts of others, although there'd been no shortage of that. That there was no question of him pursuing her attempts somehow didn't make them any easier to ignore.

He'd begun to have trouble focusing on the task at hand when she was around. He'd tried to ignore her, telling himself there was nothing the least bit attractive in her long, gangly frame or her innocent naiveté—obvious to him at the ripe old age of twenty-one—but had instead found himself thinking that when Laurey Templeton finally bloomed, she was going to be something to behold.

He'd been right.

He leaned back in his chair. She had more than fulfilled the promise he'd seen in her back then. She was no longer coltish and gangly, she was a tall, slender, graceful woman who moved in that undeniably feminine way that drew male eyes from every direction. She'd indeed grown up.

Well, he amended silently, on the outside, anyway. He wasn't sure she'd matched it on the inside, if she was still carrying such a grudge. What had happened to her hadn't quite been worth that kind of long-term rancor. Idly, he wondered if, thanks to the job he hadn't really wanted, she now hated all cops, or if she reserved her resentment for him.

Not that it mattered, he told himself. What mattered was him getting out of here before somebody found him and reported back to Kit that he'd been here. He didn't want her mad at him. She had a long fuse; he'd only seen her blow up once or twice, but when she did, it was something to see.

He headed out to his coupe, not remembering until he was almost there that he'd probably been safe from Kit discovering him all along; tonight was Caitlin's baby shower, and she was to help Lacey Buckhart, who was even more pregnant, and Kelsey Gregerson do…whatever it was women did to prepare for such things, he thought, a vague image of birthday decorations in soft baby colors forming in his mind.

He felt an odd pang. What women did was something that had long been absent from his life. Ever since Trish had made it clear she was through playing second fiddle to his job, or what she called his obsession, and walked out, his social life had been so close to nonexistent that the difference hardly mattered. For the first couple of years he'd been able to write his isolation off as the normal reaction to the end of his marriage. But after that, the habit had become so ingrained that he hadn't quite been able to break it. And wasn't sure he wanted to.

It wasn't just that his job consumed him, although he admitted it was the primary focus of his life; it was also that the effort it took to begin and maintain a relationship seemed too much. Even when he'd thought about it, with Kit or with Caitlin, it had been more in the nature of thinking he should than that he truly wanted to.

And even that, he thought wryly, was mostly due to the continual chiding of male friends who worried about his neglected libido and were always urging him to accept the offers so regularly thrown at him. He'd thought about doing just that now and then, but he knew it was solely his looks, those damned, pretty boy looks, that attracted most women, and once they found out what trying to have a relationship with a cop was really like—especially, he admitted ruefully, a cop like him—they quickly went looking elsewhere. And after a while he'd grown weary of the seemingly inevitable circle and quietly withdrawn from the fray. He'd found that he didn't miss it, not really, found that the longer he went without, the easier the urges were to ignore. It was a lonely life, he supposed, looked at from outside, but it worked for him.

If only his friends would give up their campaign. And then there were the female friends who wanted to set him up with their sister, cousin, or old school friend.

Old school friend...

Had things been different, he could be saying that about Laurey Templeton. Had things been different, she could have been looking at him as she had then, shyly yet avidly, her attraction to him glowing in those silver-gray eyes, instead of glaring at him in near-loathing.

He sighed as he yanked open the door to his car. He loved his job. It was the only thing he'd ever wanted to do. And he was rarely bothered by those who were uncomfortable with that choice, and less so by those who flat out disliked anyone who carried a badge. He was a cop, and he did his job as well as he could. Resentment and enemies came with the territory, and they didn't bother him. Usually.

But Laurey Templeton bothered him. For the first time in a very long time, he wanted to say, "It's not fair." He thought he'd long given up on fairness in this life, and he wasn't happy with the fact that this woman he'd never quite forgotten was making him feel this way.

And he resented the fact that anything was detracting from the satisfaction he should be feeling right now, when for once things were going as they should.

"It's been quite a year at Trinity West," Kit said. "Caitlin and Quisto married, Lacey and Ryan back together, Kelsey and Cruz married—"

"Guess that makes it your turn," Caitlin quipped, making Kit roll her eyes.

"Not likely," the blonde said. "My social life makes Death Valley look like the Garden of Eden. The only person I know who goes out less than I do is Gage."

"Now *there's* a man who needs a life," Kelsey said. "I thought Cruz was bad, but he's a slacker compared to Gage. I've never seen anybody work so hard, even on poofs."

"Poofs?" Laurey asked, hoping to change the subject.

"Runaways. The ones you never find," Kelsey explained, her green eyes troubled. Laurey knew from Caitlin that Kelsey was dedicated to helping runaways in whatever way she had to, even if she ran afoul of legalities. That was, in fact, how she'd met her husband. "Cruz says they call them that because they walk out the door and *poof*, they vanish. Never seen again. But that doesn't stop Gage from looking for them. Nothing does."

"Ryan says he's driven," Lacey said softly. "He doesn't know by what, but it's not the job."

"And Ryan would know, wouldn't he?" Kit said, reaching over to squeeze one of the very pregnant Lacey's hands as Lacey pushed back her long, sandy brown hair with the other.

Laurey watched the other women silently, her thoughts rather chaotic. They were all so nice and had made certain she felt welcome, although she knew only Caitlin among them. She watched as Lacey smiled at Kit's gesture. Caitlin had recounted Ryan and Lacey Buckhart's story, of how they had lost each other after the death of their first unborn child, but had found themselves and their love again after Ryan had risked his life to break up The Pack, and gone to Lacey when he'd been shot.

Laurey glanced at Caitlin now. She hadn't realized all the aspects of Caitlin marrying Quisto Romero, but she did now. It was amazing how quickly these women had become close. It was as if the one common bond they had, being married to cops, was as strong as any blood relationship. She supposed it was true, that no one who hadn't been there could truly understand what it was like. And more than once tonight, one of them had made comments she couldn't help but think were aimed at her, about how each of them had had many misconceptions about cops to work through.

Laurey eyed Kit then, wondering what made an attractive and very feminine woman want such a job. And what it would have taken for her to become a sergeant in such a world. A sergeant who had men like Butler working for her.

When Lacey spoke again, Laurey yanked her mind out of what was rapidly becoming a well-worn groove: thoughts of Gage Butler.

"Yes, Ryan knows what it is to be driven. But he faced it. *We* faced it. He doesn't think Gage ever has."

"I wish I knew what it was, whatever is prodding him," Kit said. "But he's been that way since I've known him, and every time I bring it up, he just…avoids the question." She sighed. "Sometimes I think he'd be better off in another line of work."

"Sam says he's like her animals," Kelsey said, toying with a lock of her dark auburn hair thoughtfully. "That he can't tell you that he's hurt, but it shows in his eyes."

Laurey felt her breath catch. What a perceptive thing for a child to say, she thought. Cruz's little girl must be quite something.

"I just hope it doesn't push him over the edge someday," Kelsey went on, her tone concerned.

"I gather you're part of the Gage Butler fan club, too?" Laurey asked, not liking the jolt of feeling that had gone through her at Samantha Gregerson's too-wise assessment. She thought she'd managed to keep any sarcasm out of her voice, but Kelsey looked at her almost sharply. Laurey's gaze flicked to Caitlin, wondering if she'd told the others of her distaste for the man they all seemed so enamored of. Caitlin lifted her brows and shrugged in negation; she hadn't said anything. Apparently even the slightest hint of a lack of appreciation wasn't welcome. The man was clearly a favorite among these women in a way Laurey had to reluctantly admire, since there was nothing but friendship involved; it was clear Kit considered him off-limits, and the others were all deliriously in love with their husbands.

"If it hadn't been for Gage, Cruz and I might not be together," Kelsey said. "He helped us, risked his job, just because Cruz asked. He knew I…wasn't telling him the whole truth, just like Cruz did, but he did it anyway. No questions asked."

"Gage is his own man," Kit said with a nod. "And he has strong ideas about loyalty to his friends."

Except when he's about to arrest them, Laurey thought, but wisely held her peace; this was obviously not the place to voice anything negative about Gage Butler. Apparently nowhere was.

Now if she could just control her thoughts as easily, she told herself ruefully as the conversation shifted to the inevitable talk of the soon-to-arrive babies. But everything she'd heard since she'd arrived seemed to be tumbling around in her head.

Half of these kids wouldn't be here today if not for Gage…they'd be dead…and two dozen more who would be behind bars.

I was way down the road to nowhere, but Gage, he helped me.

He helped us, risked his job…no questions asked.

I've never seen anyone work so hard.

He's driven…

She knew too much about that kind of man. Far too much. She'd grown up with one. Her father had been a living stereotype of the classic workaholic. Was that what Butler was, too? It certainly sounded that way. She knew why her father was the way he was, but what drove Butler? What was it that Lacey's husband said he'd never faced?

Even eight years ago, he'd seemed utterly confident, so sure of himself that she couldn't imagine him ever being out of control about anything. Or perhaps it had been simply that he stood out among the less certain boys around him. Of course, she reminded herself, stirring up her anger anew, he'd been years older, too. He'd been young, but he'd been a man among those boys and, she supposed, toughened by the police academy he'd only just left.

She wondered if that had been what kept drawing her back to him, that difference between him and the boys her own age, boys she found ridiculous most of the time. That and the fact that he never laughed at her, never teased her about her height or about the brains that got her good grades with remarkably little effort. And she would have thought he would have; students who flunked more tests than they passed usually showed great disdain for those who got *A*'s and *B*'s. Of course, that had probably been part of the act, too, his troublemaking and bad grades.

And as quickly as that she was back wrestling with things she'd never resolved, back wondering how much of it, if any, had been real.

Stop it!

She nearly snapped it aloud, and probably would have if she hadn't been among so many people.

"So, Laurey, Caitlin says you work for a magazine in Seattle. Do you enjoy it?"

Grateful for the distraction Lacey was providing, she nodded. "I miss the sunshine down here, but it's lovely up there. And I love my job." She meant it, she did love her job as an advertising coordinator for the slick publication that focused on the beauty and style of the Pacific Northwest. "I get to talk to people from all over the world."

"And wonder of wonders," Caitlin put in teasingly, "actually use that college degree."

They all laughed, and Laurey nodded. "I was lucky to get

a job in my field so quickly. But it was thanks to you, you know," she said to Caitlin.

"Me?" The redhead looked startled.

"Sure. If you hadn't talked me into taking that internship, I never would have gotten the job. The experience I got on that magazine down here was what made them decide on me. And I don't think I ever thanked you for that."

"You're welcome," Caitlin said.

"I'm very glad they rebuilt Marina Heights High School when they did," Laurey said softly. If the old school hadn't been torn down when it had been, its students temporarily displaced to the newer—and admittedly much wealthier—halls of Marina del Mar High, Lisa—and Laurey—never would have met Caitlin Murphy.

"Me, too," Caitlin agreed, understanding perfectly.

They left it at that in silent, mutual agreement; neither of them wanted to intrude sad memories on what should be a happy occasion.

She talked about her job a little more, then listened with interest as Kelsey enthusiastically detailed the plans for her new runaway shelter and Lacey regaled them with absurdly funny anecdotes about life at a fancy resort hotel. She even dropped a notable name or two, after swearing them all to secrecy about the antics of the rich and famous.

Kit contributed, as well, relating a few of what she called "war stories," tales that amazed Laurey; she hadn't realized what silly fixes people got into and then expected the police to get them out of. She was sure Kit was carefully telling only funny stories—and some of them were uproarious, especially the one about the burglar who tried to get into a restaurant via a vent, and ended up dangling upside down over the stove until a startled cook found him in the morning—but she couldn't help thinking of what Caitlin had told her about cops' "gallows humor," that crucial knack of finding something to laugh at in the most dire situations.

"If they didn't," she'd said, "the suicide rate would be even higher than it is, and it's already one of the highest in the world."

Laurey had known that. She supposed she'd read it some-where, but she'd never thought much about it. Perhaps because until Caitlin had married a cop, there hadn't been anyone to make her think of such things. Or care about them. Her thoughts of cops had been limited to what she'd seen on the news, which usually brought on resentful memories about the one cop she'd had personal contact with.

And there she was, back to Gage Butler again. Why did everything seem to lead back to him? Was it just that she was here among people who knew—and admired and re-spected—him? Or was it the shock of seeing him again that had started all these thoughts stirring?

It didn't matter, she told herself firmly. After tonight, she would take the week's vacation she'd planned here in the Cal-ifornia sunshine before she headed back to face a Pacific Northwest winter. Hopefully she wouldn't run into him again. And she would put Gage Butler out of her mind. She *would*.

Even unspoken, it sounded too vehement for comfort.

She sighed. Okay, she told herself as she helped gather up the plates that had held a luscious chocolate cake Kelsey had laughingly assured her was low fat, so she was impressed. Whatever he'd once been, Butler was apparently a heck of a guy now, the kind of cop they should all be.

What is it you expect, Laurey? That the cops go out on the street armed with nothing but Boy Scout honor? That they always play fair and honest when nobody else does?

Caitlin's gentle but chiding words rang in her head, and she felt the sting of them again, realizing more than ever, after having spent the evening with these women, that perhaps she'd been a bit…naive. Maybe Butler hadn't really had any choice, maybe they'd made it a part of the job he couldn't say no to.

As she left the kitchen and went back for more dirty dishes, she passed a framed photo of Caitlin's husband and paused for a moment; Quisto was charming, suave, and in love with his wife as only a former ladies' man could be. Sort of like an ex-smoker becoming the strictest of nonsmokers, she thought, trying to joke herself out of this silly mood she seemed to have fallen into. But she had to admit, he was nothing like she'd expected a cop to be. Then again, her expectations were based on what she'd sadly learned at eighteen.

Had her view been so skewed back then?

Possibly, she acknowledged grudgingly. To be fair, she had to admit that a big part of the reason she'd been so furious all those years ago was that she'd had quite a crush on the new boy in school. She'd been a late bloomer, only growing into her tall body in her early twenties, and had never dated in high school. But Gage Butler had awakened every suppressed urge she'd never let herself feel before. She'd flirted with him, in some of her first, tentative efforts at the task, and his seeming ignorance of her had hurt her fledgling pride. Then she'd learned in the worst way that he was a cop, that his very presence had been a deception from the beginning. Her humiliation had stemmed as much from her embarrassment as from anything else.

Did her hostility stem from the same source, as well?

If so, it was a childish reaction she wasn't very proud of. For the first time she looked at her outburst yesterday from a step back, saw and heard it as Caitlin must have. And she blushed at the realization that she had indeed sounded like a petulant child still clinging to a wrong done them long ago.

Time to grow up, kiddo.

Or maybe past time.

Chapter 4

Mitchell Martin's shouts of outrage had one result the arrogant man could never have expected—the louder he got, the wider Gage's smile got. That infuriated the man even more, and the circle continued. And it enabled Gage to easily refrain from the urge to tell Martin his alibi had vanished; no sense in tipping off the defense before they had to.

This was it, he thought, the payoff for the long days and longer nights, for the hours spent walking the streets, talking to people, calling in favors, searching endlessly for something, anything, that would break what appeared to be a rock-solid alibi. A something he had finally found, proof that Martin hadn't been where he said he had.

This was the payoff for the hours spent getting Diane Santos to trust him enough to tell him every grim detail of that harrowing night and ugly morning after, and the memory of the traumatized girl's weeping story was enough to make Gage relish every bit of Martin's rage and bluster. His high-powered attorney was finally able to shut him up, telling him that he'd be free in no time, and already speaking ominously of lawsuits against the department, and Gage in particular. Gage wondered about the coincidental presence of the lawyer, curious whether the mouthpiece was always with Martin or was along for a reason. Such as knowing this was coming. He would have to check into the possibility of a leak.

Both Gage and Kit wore expressions of grim satisfaction as they stuffed the haughty man into the back of a police car with perhaps less care than they could have used. They hadn't bent to the lawyer's insistence that he not be handcuffed, either.

"Rape is a felony, counselor," Kit said coldly. "He goes cuffed."

"And in back," Gage added, before the man had the chance to make his next move, which Gage was sure would have been a request to have his client at least have his hands in front of him, where it would be easier to hide the cuffs from the press who, in the nature of sharks scenting blood, would no doubt be waiting when they arrived at Trinity West.

At the lawyer's vociferous protest, Gage glared at him and said softly, "Maybe you should talk to his victim about restraints."

"Gage," Kit said warningly, and he turned his back on the protesting attorney and ignored Martin's ever increasing threats.

Yes, this was what it was all about, Gage thought as, back at Trinity West, they went through the booking procedure. He knew it was going to be a battle to get this man convicted. A war, really. But just because there was a good chance you were beaten before you started didn't mean you didn't try. He hadn't reached that point. Yet. It was still a war worth fighting. Even if he had to work a little harder to convince himself of that lately.

It was about putting slime like this away, about getting justice for victims like the innocent Diane; it was the idea that a poor man could get the same fair judgment as a king in a courtroom. Not, he thought sourly, that he believed what had once been an ideal was still true. But that it had been corrupted in practice didn't diminish the ideal itself, and giving up was not the way to get it back to where it should be. He was sure of that, even if he wasn't sure how much longer he could keep going.

But he'd finally gotten Mitchell Martin where he should be. And God would just have to forgive him if he took a certain pleasure in divesting the man of his Gucci belt, his Rolex watch and the three heavy gold-and-diamond rings he wore. And if he took longer than was necessary to do the booking of the property, well, he was, after all, not a jailer, and it took him a while to figure out the forms. Besides, with such a lot of valuable items, he had needed a witness for the booking, to waylay any later claims of theft. Two would be better, considering who they were dealing with. And everybody else was busy, so it was going to take a while. A long while. Just long enough to be sure that Martin's partner was long gone on his trip out of the country.

Martin was soon yelling again, demanding his phone call. Gage looked at him blandly.

"Your lawyer already knows where you are and why," he said.

Martin swore, loud and crude. Gage stepped aside, giving the video camera aimed at the booking cage a clear view of the man. He knew what the monitor would show, an expensively dressed, smooth on the surface man who was rapidly losing his polish.

Yes, he thought as he watched the jailer take the furious Martin away. This was what it was about, this was why he'd gone into law enforcement. To do this, not to snag unsuspecting young kids and toss them in jail when they were in many cases victim as much as suspect.

Whoa, he thought, *where did that come from?*

He stopped in the middle of stapling the fingerprint card to the booking form, something normally done by the jailer, but Gage had wanted to do this one all by himself, just for the sheer pleasure of it.

He hadn't liked the high school undercover assignment, but he'd never questioned the rightness of it. He still didn't; every kid that had been picked up as a result of his investigations had broken the law or been about to, and he'd cut the few who were teetering on the edge some slack, hoping that they'd been scared enough to come down on the right side of that narrow fence. As Laurey Templeton had.

He put the stapler down sharply, the thump echoing hollowly in the jail office. Darn that woman, but she'd stirred up a nest of stinging old memories. It was that, those memories, that were nagging at him, he was sure, not she herself.

Maybe she did hate him for what he'd done back then, but he had only to look at her now, to know what she'd gone on and done in her life, to know he'd been right. She'd needed her cage rattled, because she'd been headed for dangerous territory. He'd done the rattling, she'd obviously awakened and seen the danger and had changed her course. She didn't have to like him for it, or even thank him. No cop expected that, or, if they ever did, they soon learned that the old axiom was true: If you want love, be a fireman, not a cop.

"How about a drink? I think we need to celebrate."

Kit's cheerful invitation yanked him out of a reverie he'd been spending far too much time in lately. More than ever, since he'd walked into the Neutral Zone and seen Laurey on that ladder.

"I'm buying," Kit added.

He smiled but began, "Thanks, but I need to finish this and then pull the file—"

"That's what the jailer gets paid for, let him earn his salary. I'll make it an order," Kit said, sounding half-serious. "You deserve a break. You *need* a break."

He could see she wouldn't take a refusal gracefully; she might just follow through on her threat to make it an order. He gave in; maybe he *did* need a break.

"If you're buying, you're on," he said, grinning at her.

"Good. You can drive. I plan to have a very large beer."

"Okay."

Gage didn't question her assumptions; Kit knew quite well that he didn't drink, and she knew why. He suspected she had, long ago, spread the word, because the initial ragging on his refusal to drink even beer had faded much quicker than he'd expected. And for that he owed her a stint as designated driver anytime she wanted. It wasn't often—she drank rarely, and not all that much—but she knew that made her more vulnerable—and dangerous behind the wheel—than if she drank regularly, and she never took the chance. He was glad she was so careful; he liked and respected Kit, and would hate anything to happen to her.

Once in the bar in the back of the small restaurant that had become a department hangout because it was run by an ex-cop from upstate New York who'd moved here for the weather, Kit lifted her foamy glass.

"Here's to the good guys winning one…for the moment."

Gage raised his glass of cola. "Amen."

They both sipped, then lapsed into silence. Gage knew Kit was as aware as he was that Martin would be out no later than Monday morning, and probably before. But for now, he was in jail, the kind of humiliation the proud, imperious man would not bear well.

You took what you got, Gage thought as the bartender came by to check on their drinks. He watched as the middle-aged and very happily married man flirted shamelessly with Kit, who returned the favor with a sparkle in her hazel eyes.

"All the good ones are married," Kit said with a sigh as the bartender went off to another patron after refilling their glasses.

"Thanks," he said dryly.

She grimaced at him. "Okay, married or off-limits," she amended.

Gage chuckled. "What about that karate teacher of yours?"

"He's sweet. Charming." She sighed. "And there's not an ounce of chemistry between us."

"Better than that stockbroker," he teased.

"Oh, yeah." Kit grimaced. "Hot stuff. Too bad he stood in the sex appeal line twice and skipped the integrity line altogether."

"I keep reading the business section, figuring he'll show up in the headlines someday."

"He will," she promised. "Along with the words 'SEC Investigation.'"

Gage laughed. So did Kit, and he waited until she stopped before turning serious. "Er, you are...being careful, aren't you?"

"Careful?"

"I know it's none of my business, but...it's scary out there these days, and—"

"Why, Gage Butler, are you giving me advice on my sex life?"

"Well...yeah," he said sheepishly.

She patted his hand in mock patronization. "Sweetie, if it makes you feel any better, it's a moot point."

He blinked. "Oh."

"Yes, oh. My sex life is about as active as yours."

His mouth twisted up at one corner. "That bad, huh?"

"Speaking of which—"

"Uh-oh."

"Yes, uh-oh. My social life may not be the hottest around, but at least I *have* one. Unlike you, my friend."

"I don't have time for a social life."

"Exactly my point. But I'd settle for you even having a sex life."

"Haven't we had this discussion before?"

"Repeatedly," Kit said. "For all the good it does."

They *had* had this discussion before, and Gage didn't really see the point in having it all over. "Then let's skip it this time around."

"Let's not," Kit said, sounding determined enough to make Gage sigh inwardly. "You can't keep on like you always have, nothing in your life but your work."

"If I didn't, Martin wouldn't be in jail right now," he said pointedly.

"I know that. You're a good cop, Gage. The best. But you've got to find some balance. You're bordering on obsession here." She hesitated, then added, "Some people think you're already there."

His gaze shot to her face; he knew Kit was genuinely concerned, but he wasn't sure just how far she would go. He also knew her opinion was universally respected by everyone—

well, except for Robards, and he hardly counted, since no one respected him—from the chief on down.

Would she have spoken to de los Reyes about her concerns? They had a good relationship, he knew. The man had an open door to anyone who worked for him; it was one of the things that had won him the unwavering regard of most of the force. Again except for the blowhard Robards.

"Gage," Kit said softly, "you know it's true. You're too smart not to see it, even from the inside. You don't let anything else into your life, it's—"

"Look, just because I haven't been on a date in a while—"

"I'm not even talking about that. You don't let *anything* in, Gage. Or anyone. You don't hang out with the guys, you don't do anything on your own, you have to be ordered to take even this much downtime," she said, gesturing at their surroundings.

"My caseload has been—"

"I know what your caseload is, Butler. I give it to you, remember?"

Uh-oh. He was suddenly Butler again. And that told him what was coming. Told him she meant what she was about to say, and strongly.

"It's got to stop," she said, her voice quiet but still somehow fierce. "You're using your job to hide from life."

"When did you get your psychology degree?" he asked, knowing it wasn't a fair shot, but unable not to make one last effort at stopping her.

"Same place you did," she snapped back at him. "On the street. And don't try diverting me, Butler. You need to face whatever it is that's driving you. And since you mention it, maybe Dr. Walters is the answer."

He shook his head as she mentioned the name of the department-affiliated psychologist, the man officers were referred to in the aftermath of traumatic incidents, such as shootings.

"Just drop it, will you? I'm fine."

"You're not fine," Kit insisted. "You're putting on a good front, but someday it's going to catch up with you. Nobody can put in the hours you do, pour the mental energy into the job that you do, and not pay a price. A big price.''

"You have a problem with my work?" he asked stiffly.

"You know I don't. I said you're the best. But you're also running on overload, and you have been since I've known you."

"I'm fine," he repeated, feeling a bit battered. He knew Kit. She was never this insistent on a personal matter unless it mattered to her. She'd never been so insistent with him before, and it was wearing on him. And wearing him down.

"I don't want you getting killed because you hit the wall at the wrong moment," she said. "Do I have to go to the chief and have him make it an order before you get some help?"

Damn, Gage thought. She would, too. He'd never seen her quite like this before.

"I'm your friend, Gage," she said softly. "You have to know that, know that I'm not blowing smoke here. I'm worried, damn it. I don't want to lose you."

He let out a compressed breath. She *was* his friend. The best kind of friend.

"Maybe…maybe I have been pushing a little," he said at last. "I've been…a little edgy." He gave a wry chuckle. "Even been feeling a bit paranoid lately, thinking somebody was following me." Kit frowned, and he waved a hand at her. "Just imagination. So maybe you're right, I need a break. And I'll take one."

"Hallelujah," Kit muttered.

"It's going to have to wait, though. We need to have a watertight case against Martin, and that's going to take a lot of preparation."

"You know it'll be months before it comes to trial."

"But there are things I have to prepare."

"You'll have time. Plenty of it, once his lawyers start kicking the system around."

He had no answer to that; it was absolutely true. "Okay, okay. After we have a trial date set, I'll take a break."

Kit eyed him skeptically. "Should I ask for that in writing?"

"I promise, Kit."

She studied him for a moment, then nodded. "All right. But I'm going to hold you to it."

He lifted his glass and drained the last of the soda. "I have no doubt of that."

After another exchange with Henry, the bartender, in which she declined a refill, Kit got to her feet.

"Let's stop by the Neutral Zone," she said. "I want to let Caitlin know Martin's spending the night on her tax dollars."

Gage opened his mouth to instantly protest, remembering the last time he'd set foot in the Neutral Zone. But Kit didn't know about his confrontation with Laurey. At least, he didn't think she did, unless it had come up at the baby shower last night. But Kit probably wouldn't have been able to resist teasing him about it if it had.

And he was driving, he remembered belatedly, so there was really no way out of it unless he explained exactly why he didn't want to go. And even to himself, avoiding Laurey Templeton sounded too silly a reason to be believed. So with an inward grimace, he pulled out his keys and led the way back to his car.

You need to face whatever it is that's driving you.

Her words echoed eerily in his mind. It wasn't true, he told himself. He knew what was driving him. The fact that he didn't talk about it didn't mean he didn't know what it was.

And he ignored the nagging little voice that was telling him that knowing it and facing it were two very different things.

"Quit pacing, Gage. You're making me nervous," Kit told him lazily from her seat at the bar, where she was sipping one of Caitlin's famous root beer floats.

"Sorry," he muttered. He knew he was restless, but he couldn't help it. It wasn't anything in particular—certainly not the things Kit had said—he was just…antsy. And the noise level in here, with music blaring, kids jabbering and video games whooping, was getting to him. He thought of the kids' standard joke, "If it's too loud, you're too old." He hadn't expected to be old before he was thirty, but he felt it right now. If he was honest about it, he'd been feeling it for some time.

"Okay, I give up for now on teaching you how to relax. Go ahead and go," Kit said. "Quisto will give me a ride to the station to pick up my car when he comes for Caitlin. I'll be fine to drive by then."

He stopped his transit of the floor, turning to look at the two women. He knew Quisto was working the evening shift, not getting off until midnight, and that Caitlin usually waited here for him after the Neutral Zone closed, which was a bit later on Fridays, to keep the kids off the streets on the more dangerous weekend nights.

"You're sure?" he asked.

"Sure, we'll get her back to Trinity West," Caitlin answered. "Or Laurey said she might stop by, and if she does, she can take her sooner if Kit wants."

An instant knot formed in his belly. It scared and irritated him at the same time. He resented the fact that he wanted to dodge out of here before Laurey arrived, yet was grateful for the chance to do it, at Kit's suggestion, without being obvious.

And he didn't like the way Caitlin was looking at him, as if she knew exactly what he was thinking.

"All right," he said abruptly and set down the half-full glass of soda he'd been nursing since Caitlin had poured it for him in celebration of their news about Martin's arrest.

"See you Monday," Kit said. "Bright and early, I'm sure."

"Unless Martin or his lawyers manage to pull together a hundred grand, or find his partner, or a bondsman who will take a chance without signed papers before then."

"If it happens, it happens. We knew going in he'd be out in a hurry," Kit said.

"Yeah," Gage muttered. "Have money, will travel."

"But Judge Partain made it as tough as he could, setting the bail high."

"Let's hope it's high enough to keep him eating jail food for the weekend," Gage said.

He gave Caitlin a quick, brotherly kiss on the cheek and turned to go. He made his way out of the Neutral Zone, nodding to those who waved to him, smiling at those who looked at him hesitantly, and overlooking those who looked away. He knew Kit was right, Judge Partain had done all he could. Maybe because he was a friend of Chief de los Reyes's, but also probably in part because of Kit. He liked her. Said she had changed his old, set-in-his-ways viewpoint about women in law enforcement. She followed the rules and still got the job done, he'd told Gage once, leaving him to wonder if there'd been an implication in there for him.

He started toward the car he'd had to park a block down, thanks to the busyness of the Neutral Zone, thinking idly he was going to have to get that tune-up soon. Yet another thing he'd skipped in his passion to become a cop had been learning anything much about cars. He supposed that made him an anachronism, a guy who didn't know or care much about the quintessential guy thing, but as long as the thing got him to work, that was all that mattered.

All that mattered.

He ignored the way the words seemed to echo in his head. He wasn't obsessed, he was just...involved. And he knew sometimes his methods weren't by the book, but when it came to dealing with confused kids and the victims of the ugliest of crimes, it was results that counted in *his* book. Getting runaway kids home or at least help, getting kids in deeper trouble on a better path, getting rape victims what justice the system would allow, that was what mattered. It was all that mattered, to him.

All that mattered.

You're bordering on obsession, here. Some people think you're already there.

He wasn't obsessed, he repeated silently as he neared the blue coupe and dug into his pocket for the keys. Obsessed meant something else controlled you, and it was he who controlled what he did and when, and how much. He was very conscious of controlling it, knowing that it was partly because there was so much he *couldn't* control that he so tightly controlled what he could.

But there was nothing wrong with that, he told himself as he unlocked the driver's door and pulled it open.

You've got to find some balance.

Balance. It was clear Kit thought he could find it in a relationship, but he wasn't convinced. He'd never known a woman strong enough to deal with him, or that he was drawn to enough to counterbalance his commitment to his work.

An image formed unbidden in his mind, of a woman with misty gray eyes and silky dark hair, who had the strength to face him down with a passion that had startled him. And bothered him, he thought, in more ways than one. She was—

She was walking toward him. He stopped dead, his fingers curling around the keys he'd just removed from the door lock, inanely feeling how warm they were. From his body heat. Which had suddenly gone soaring upward, he thought a little dizzily as he watched her. She was wearing jeans, possibly the same black ones she'd had on before, and a silky gray blouse that was nearly the shade of her eyes. She also wore boots with a heel, making her legs appear even longer and herself even taller. He liked that, that she was no longer trying to hide her height by slumping over, as she had in high school.

And he didn't like that it meant something to him.

She saw him then, and when her steady stride faltered, he realized his last thought had made him frown. Or maybe it was just that she hadn't expected—or wanted—to see him.

Of course it was, he told himself ruefully. She'd made her feelings clear enough. So clear, he half expected her to keep right on walking without even acknowledging him. But instead she stopped, a safe couple of feet away, but still close enough to show that she wasn't going to simply ignore him.

No, she was probably going to chew him out again, and he was in no mood. He'd had enough of heavy emotional discussions for one night. Maybe from her point of view she'd had reason to be angry once, but it had happened years ago, and it was time to move on. Past time.

"Hello…"

She said it tentatively, and he had the distinct impression she'd stopped there because she couldn't decide what to call him. The best he could hope for was Butler, he supposed. The worst... Well, she would have to go some to top what she'd said the other night. But he supposed she could.

"About the other night," she began, then paused.

"Don't start in on me again," he said. "I don't need it."

"I was angry—"

"No kidding," he said, cutting her off. "And over something that should be ancient history. Tell me, do you hold a grudge over every little thing that long?"

He saw color tint her cheeks. "It wasn't a little thing to me."

He thought of all the kids he'd tried to save but had lost, kids who lost the battle to stay safe and alive in a world that seemed to have no place for them. Kids who had faced abuses of the worst kind, who had battled drugs, violence and the betrayal of those who should have loved them the most. Kids to whom a street shooting was a little thing, because it happened every day.

"I'll bet it wasn't," he said, unable to stop himself. "I'll bet it was the worst thing you've ever had to deal with in your entire sheltered life. But you'll have to excuse me if I don't have much sympathy or patience with your idea of tragedy. Grow up...Miss Templeton."

Her eyes widened, and the blush faded as she went strangely pale. He was surprised at the apparent depth of the nerve he'd struck. For an instant he felt guilty, but the memory of her verbal attack on him assuaged it quickly. If she couldn't take it, maybe she should think twice about dishing it out.

After a visible effort to shake off her reaction, she said very coldly, "I know quite enough of tragedy, thank you. I buried my sister six months ago, after her car was demolished by a truckload of drunken, stoned kids."

Her sister Lisa was my best friend in school. She...couldn't be here, so Laurey came...in her place.

Caitlin's words came back to him, and he felt a chill sweep through him. God, he hadn't known. No wonder she'd broken up when Elena had spoken of dying too young.

"I didn't—"

She cut off his apology as quickly as he'd earlier cut her off. "And I deal with it every week at the youth rehabilitation center I volunteer at." The look she gave him then was icy. "I started that job to help keep kids from getting busted by sneaky cops."

He let out a weary breath. "Look, I'm sorry. I didn't know about your sister. Caitlin only told me you came because your sister...couldn't."

She looked away, and he saw her blinking rapidly. It was obviously still very close to the surface for her.

"I'm sorry," he repeated. "I...know how you feel."

"Oh, sure you do," she muttered, starting to turn away from him.

"I do," he said, surprising himself. "I...lost a sister, too."

She glanced back at him then, a startled look in her eyes. She didn't speak, as if waiting for him to elaborate. He wouldn't—he couldn't—and he wished he'd never said the words he so rarely did. He couldn't quite believe that he had. It was something he usually kept buried deep, so very deep....

He shook his head sharply. "I didn't mean to...probe a raw wound," he said rather lamely.

Still she didn't speak, and he supposed he'd managed to make her hate him even more. And once again he hated the fact that that mattered to him.

"You'd better get inside," he said brusquely, ignoring the odd hollowness he was feeling. "Caitlin may be a miracle worker around here, but this still isn't any neighborhood to be standing out on the street."

She gave him an odd look that was strangely intent, then nodded sharply and began walking toward the Neutral Zone's front door. He watched until she reached it safely, a habit so long ingrained he doubted he would ever break it. After she'd pulled it open, she glanced back over her shoulder toward him. He quickly got into the driver's seat and started the coupe, wanting to get away from here and the fiasco that seemed to occur every time he encountered Laurey Templeton.

He pulled away from the curb, ordering himself not to look in his mirror to see if she were still standing there.

He drove down Trinity Street East, thinking he would take it all the way until it turned to West, then turn off at—

Something caught the edge of his vision, and he looked to his left, toward the alley he was passing. He had a couple of seconds to register that the van was brown and had no front license plate before it hit him.

Chapter 5

She'd meant to apologize to him, Laurey thought as she glanced into the bustling Neutral Zone. She really had. She'd meant to apologize for what she'd finally had to admit was true, exactly what he'd just said, that it should have been ancient history. She wasn't quite sure how she would have explained it without confessing to her silly crush on him all those years ago, but—

The sound of an impact and the screech of tires froze her fingers on the doorknob, stopped her foot in the act of stepping inside. She jerked around and saw a bulky dark van careening down the street, listing as if it had blown a tire. The car it had obviously hit sat at an angle in the street, the driver's side ominously crumpled.

She recognized the car. She had just been standing next to it, remembering that Caitlin had told her Gage drove the old, beat-up coupe because he spent too much of his own money helping people to buy a new car. Without another thought she began to run toward it, vaguely aware of shouts as someone near the grocery store on the corner yelled that they had called for an ambulance. There were a few kids on the street, but they were watching warily, apparently not moved to help. She nearly skidded and went down when her booted feet hit a puddle of some liquid leaking from the car, as if it were bleeding.

Her heart was pounding; she'd seen pictures of her sister's accident, and the very sight of a crumpled car made her ill. But something kept her there, and she held her breath as she peered through the window. The safety glass was shattered, making it difficult to see, especially in the darkness of this neighborhood, where as many street lamps were shot out as were intact. But she thought she saw the sheen of light on blond hair, oddly, on the passenger side.

Quickly she ran to the other side of the car; there had been no hope of opening the driver's door anyway. But she was able to yank open the passenger door easily and saw that Gage was sprawled sideways, his head and shoulders in the passenger seat, his torso bent awkwardly across the center console, his legs still on the driver's side. She would have thought he'd been thrown there were it not for the seat belt that was still tangled around his legs.

She sucked in a breath, then made herself reach out, terrified of what she would find. She hadn't been at the scene of her sister's death, but in the nightmares that had plagued her for weeks afterward, she had seen every grim detail. Every bloody, awful, grim detail. And she was afraid she knew, from those gory images, what she would find now.

Before her trembling fingers could touch him, he groaned. Then moved.

Her breath escaped her in a rush; he was alive. She nearly wept her relief; she might not like Gage Butler, but she would never wish such a thing on him. Not after Lisa. If someone had been there for her...

"Gage," she said, aware that his name felt strange on her tongue even as she decided that calling him anything else at this time would be colder than she could manage. He was hurt and needed help, and this was no time to be detached.

He shifted so that he could turn his head and look up. He

seemed to see her, his brows lowered, and he said quietly, almost wonderingly, "Laurey?"

"Help is coming," she said. "I heard somebody say they'd called an ambulance."

He moved sharply then, raising himself up on one elbow. "The van..."

"I saw it. It kept going—" she gestured down the street "—that way."

She saw the sudden change in him, alertness pushing aside the dazed look he'd had. The quickness of his recovery amazed her. "Did you call it in?"

"Somebody already called an ambulance," she repeated, thinking he'd been too shaken to take it in the first time she'd said it.

"Not that, the hit-and-run. The van description. Did you give them that?"

"No," she said, a little bewildered. "Someone else called. I thought I should—"

"Damn," he muttered, and began to twist around until he was almost sitting up.

Laurey heard rapid footsteps approaching from the direction of the corner grocery but didn't look toward them. "I'm sorry," she said, an edge creeping into her voice now that she saw he obviously wasn't seriously injured. "I thought you might be hurt and that that was more important."

He had the grace to look chagrined. "That wasn't aimed at you. Just...the situation."

"The paramedics are on the way."

The breathless words came from behind Laurey, and she turned to see a small man with a fringe of gray hair edging his bald pate. He was the one she'd heard shouting, she realized as he bent over to peer into the car.

"Are you all—Gage?" the man interrupted himself in startled recognition. "Oh, no, I did not know it was you! Are you all right?"

"I'm fine, Mr. Cordero. Just a little rattled."

"But you are bleeding."

Laurey's breath caught. He was? She hadn't seen any blood.

She crouched back down to look again at Gage. He was gingerly touching his neck, where now she could see a dark rivulet staining the collar of his shirt.

"Just a little flying glass, I think," he told the old man reassuringly. "Thanks for calling it in, but I don't need the paramedics."

"They should check you," the man said sternly. "You will sit here and wait."

"Yes, sir," Gage said, so meekly Laurey couldn't help smiling.

"I told them to look for that maniac in the van. I did not see the license, though," the man said regretfully.

"Didn't have one," Gage said, wincing as he pulled himself totally upright. "At least, not in front. No make, either."

Even the old man had thought that way, Laurey mused. Just like Gage, one of his first thoughts had been to catch the bad guy. Perhaps she was the one who was out of step here, putting his welfare above catching the hit-and-run driver, she thought wryly. It seemed that her attempt to help hadn't been much help at all.

She heard the wail of sirens approaching. Gage grimaced. "I don't need anybody code three," he muttered.

"I'll go get Caitlin," she said, beginning to straighten up, thinking that having a good friend around would be more help than her own presence.

"No," Gage said quickly. She stopped, looking down at him questioningly. "We're a couple of blocks away, and with the noise level in there, they probably didn't hear anything. Let it go."

"But she—"

"She'd be upset. She worries about her friends. And she doesn't need any extra stress right now, not when she's pregnant."

"You are right," Mr. Cordero said, nodding approvingly. "A woman and her child should be protected at this time."

"But she'll find out anyway, won't she?" Laurey asked.

"I'll have Quisto tell her. Tomorrow, maybe. So long after the fact that it will be pointless for her to get upset."

She found it oddly touching that he was so concerned. And Caitlin *did* worry about her friends. She worried a lot. So perhaps he was right and it would be better if she didn't see him now.

"I will go flag down the paramedics," Mr. Cordero said as the sirens neared, and he strode off with a briskness that belied his apparent age.

"She'll want to talk to you personally, you know," Laurey said, remembering how Caitlin had insisted on talking to her every time she'd called her parents' house after the funeral, to hear for herself that Laurey was hanging on in those dark days. Laurey had never forgotten how, in the midst of her own pain and at a time when she was just beginning her marriage, Caitlin had never forgotten the others who had loved Lisa.

Gage nodded. "I'll stop by and see her tomorrow." He grimaced then, shifting with obvious discomfort. "Or maybe call. I have a feeling I'm going to turn some interesting colors by morning."

"At least you'll be here to do it," she said.

He looked up at her, and she saw a dark swelling over his right temple where one of those bruises he'd mentioned would no doubt appear.

"Wishing you could trade?" he asked.

There was no mistaking his implication, and color flooded her cheeks.

"No!" she exclaimed, horrified that he could believe she would think that. Not that she wouldn't trade just about anything to have Lisa back, but she would never wish death on anyone else to do it.

"Sorry," he muttered, rubbing at his head in a way that told her he must be hurting pretty badly. "That was a cheap shot."

She steadied herself. "You're entitled, at the moment," she said, glancing over the damage. "When I saw the car, I thought you were going to be…"

Her voice trailed away; she was unable to say it. And then the paramedics were there, and a bustle of activity began. One of the assisting firefighters ran a flashlight over the driver's side of the car and let out a low whistle.

"Boy, if I didn't see you sitting there talking, Butler, I wouldn't believe it. Why the heck aren't you dead?"

Laurey fought the chill that came over her at the grim joke. Apparently gallows humor extended to the fire department, as well. She supposed it was as necessary for one as for the other.

"Too stubborn, I guess," Gage quipped back.

"Yeah, well, if you were a cat, you'd be down to about three lives on this alone," the man returned. "What happened?"

Gage gestured toward the alley. "Van came out of there. Never stopped. But I saw him in time to dive for the passenger side. Barely."

"Good reflexes saved your ass, then," the paramedic poking at Gage's temple said.

"Cops are looking for the van, but you know how that goes," the other medic said as she ran through the standard pulse, respiration and blood pressure checks.

"Yeah, I do," Gage said, his tone a bit sour.

At that moment a marked police unit pulled to a halt a few feet away. Laurey instinctively turned to look as the officer got out and scanned the wreckage, and an instant later she saw his gaze narrow sharply and saw rather than heard a low oath escape him. Only then did she realize that it was Quisto Romero. He took off at a run toward them, slowing only when he saw Gage sitting upright and obviously alive on the passenger seat of his ruined car. Gage looked up and saw who the officer was, and his mouth twisted into a wry grimace.

"I heard the location come out on the air, so I came over," Quisto said, "but I never expected it to be you." Concern showed in his darkly handsome face, and Laurey thought once again that even their wedding photos didn't do Quisto Romero justice.

"Neither did I," Gage said, wincing as the paramedic pressed on one of those tender spots a bit too hard.

Instinctively Laurey winced in turn and drew Quisto's sharp, dark-eyed gaze. "Laurey?"

"Hi," she said, rather awkwardly.

"She was the first one here," Gage said, then glanced at her. "Thank you for…checking on me."

"Yes," Quisto agreed, his eyes never leaving her. "I know your instinct was probably to…avoid an accident scene."

Laurey looked away swiftly, unable to deal with the gentle perceptiveness in his steady regard. As he pulled the handheld radio from his belt and notified Trinity West that it was one of their own, she tried to calm herself. It was to be expected, she supposed, that he would know. Caitlin would have told him. Lisa had been her best friend, and who else would she have turned to for comfort? Who else would she have shared the grim details with?

"Damn."

It was low and heartfelt, and Laurey looked up in surprise when she realized it had come from Gage.

"I didn't think of that," he said to her softly. "After your sister…"

Laurey jerked back. She didn't want him feeling sorry for her. Not him, of all people. Not the man who had—

She broke off her own thoughts, a little startled at how quickly she'd fallen back into blaming him for that ancient history. It had, apparently, become routine. And it seemed quite out of place now, when he was hurt, when he was looking at her with such gentle compassion.

Compassion? Gage Butler? Rattled, she looked away from him, and found herself confronting Quisto's interested gaze. Finished with his broadcast, he shoved the radio back into its belt holder before he spoke.

"How'd you end up here?"

"Just passing by on my way to see Caitlin," she said quickly, glad for the diversion. Quisto drew back, a furrow creasing his brow, and she hastened to add, "She doesn't know." And then, because he deserved the credit for his thoughtfulness, she gestured at Gage. "He didn't want to upset her, so he wouldn't let me go get her. He said you could tell her later, when it seemed right."

Quisto's gaze switched to Gage, who met his look steadily.

There was an oddly tense moment as something almost electric passed between the two men. Then Quisto nodded.

"Thank you, my friend," he said quietly.

Gage smiled, nodded in turn, then shrugged, wincing as the movement clearly caused some pain. "I'd just as soon you kept it quiet at Trinity West, too. I don't really want everybody hovering."

"I won't put out an all-points bulletin," Quisto agreed with a grin. "But I'll have to tell the chief. You know how he is when one of his people gets hurt."

"Yeah. But…can you wait until I get through at the hospital? So it doesn't turn into…a big deal?"

"If it doesn't, I'll wait," Quisto agreed.

"Thanks," Gage said, wincing again as he inadvertently turned his head too sharply. Then he quickly changed the subject before Laurey could voice the suggestion that he shut up and go to the hospital. "Anything on the van?"

"Not yet. Although," Quisto added, eyeing the mangled coupe, "with the amount of damage it must have, it may not be as hard to find as we thought. Did you get a look at the driver at all?"

Gage began to shake his head, but stopped when the paramedic ordered him to be still. Another police unit arrived, this one marked Accident Investigator, and after the officer came over and satisfied himself that Gage was functional, he began to make notes on his metal clipboard.

"Not much." Gage directed his answer to both Quisto and the traffic officer Laurey guessed would be taking the actual accident report. "Dark clothes. Gloves, too, I think, from the hands on the wheel."

Quisto's brow rose. "Interesting. It's cool out, but not cold."

He was right, Laurey thought, but she didn't quite see why it was interesting.

Gage closed his eyes, and Laurey leaned forward, afraid he might be feeling worse. But when he spoke again, she realized he'd only been trying to replay the scene in his mind.

"Odd," Gage said, sounding puzzled. "It was so close, I should have been able to see more, but it's all...dark."

"Maybe it'll come back later," the investigator said, then went off to make some measurements on the street and alley-way as Quisto and Gage tried to estimate the extent of damage to the suspect vehicle.

What a contrast, Laurey thought as they talked about what was obviously most important to them. Quisto's dark beauty against Gage's blond perfection. Yet she knew from Caitlin that both of them considered themselves alike in the most important way; they were both defined much more by the gold of their badges than their looks.

"I told them which way it went," Mr. Cordero put in help-fully. Quisto turned to look at the older man he apparently hadn't yet realized was there in his concern over his friend. And the escaped hit-and-run driver.

"Señor Cordero, gracias para su ayudan. ¿Como esta su esposa?"

"Mejor, Quisto," the older man said. *"Gracias."*

She knew just enough Spanish to know that Quisto had thanked him for his help and inquired after his wife. It was interesting, Laurey thought, that both Quisto and Gage allowed this diminutive old man the familiarity of first names, yet ac-corded him the respect of being addressed as Mr. Cordero. But not surprising, she supposed, when she remembered what Quisto had told her about the part Cordero had played in the breaking up of The Pack, allowing the police to stage a mock arson attack on his store both to further Quisto's own murder investigation and to lure the vicious street gang deeper into the undercover net Ryan Buckhart had been weaving.

The paramedic who had been checking Gage's temple straightened up at last.

"You got off easy, it seems," he said. "But I'd recommend an X ray of that granite skull of yours. That's a nasty whack you took there."

"I noticed," Gage said dryly. "I think I hit the door han-dle."

"Since it's you, they'll let us cancel the ambulance and run you in to the hospital," the man said. "Let them take a look."

"I'm fine. I don't need—"

He paused when the paramedic shook his head. "No joking, Gage."

"He's right," Quisto added. "You don't mess with head injuries."

Laurey waited, expecting Gage to continue to brush off the recommendations. She was surprised when, after a silent moment, he nodded. Somehow she had expected him to be more stubborn about it, although she wasn't sure why.

The paramedics nodded and began to pack up their gear.

"I'll go over with you," Quisto offered, but Gage shook his head. Gingerly.

"I'd rather you find the idiot in the van," he said.

"You'll need a ride home," Quisto said pointedly.

Gage glanced at what was left of his car; what hadn't been bent was covered with the foam the fire department had used to be sure no fire started. His mouth twisted.

"Yeah," he muttered. "But you know how long this'll take. I'll worry about that when they're done poking and prodding and telling me what I already know, that I'm okay. Just find the jerk, all right?"

Quisto hesitated, and before she even thought about it Laurey said, "I'll go. My rental car's right there, and I can take him home."

After an instant of consideration, Quisto nodded. Gage, on the other hand, looked utterly startled. Shocked, in fact. No more than I am, Laurey thought, wondering where the offer had sprung from. Strictly out of common courtesy and the urge to offer help where needed, she told herself. Nothing more.

"That's good of you," Quisto said. "Now I'll get out there and rally the troops. Maybe we can scare this moron up."

"Do I get a say in this?" Gage asked, his tone teetering on the edge of sarcasm. Laurey knew it was directed at her and couldn't stop the heat that rose to her cheeks.

"It's the perfect solution," Quisto said, his brows exaggeratedly raised. "Don't you agree?"

Gage's eyes were fixed not on Quisto but on Laurey. "Only," he said pointedly, "if *she* stops referring to me in the third person when I'm right here."

Laurey wished the night had been cold enough for those gloves he'd said the driver wore; it might cool her now flaming face. She *had* been talking that way. She hadn't even realized it.

"You called me Gage when you first got here," he said quietly. "Do you think you could manage it again?"

Had she? The image of those first moments when she'd seen him lying so still swamped her. And the memory of his name escaping her as more plea than anything.

"I...thought you were dead," she stammered.

"Thanks," he said, sarcasm creeping back into his voice. "I guess I know now what it would take."

She nearly moaned aloud; she truly hadn't meant it to sound that way. Quisto backed up a step, his quick, dark eyes flicking from Laurey to Gage and then back again, speculation dawning on his face.

"I'll leave you two to work it out," he said. "And I'll check on you later, buddy."

He was gone before either of them could react. Laurey didn't know what Quisto had been thinking, to bring that speculative look to his face, but she was fairly sure she didn't *want* to know. It was too much, when placed on top of the obvious need to apologize to Gage for her unintentional rudeness.

She couldn't even look at him, so she looked down at her hands instead. And saw that they were shaking, rather fiercely.

"God," she moaned under her breath, closing her eyes. She was reacting as if she'd been the one hit and nearly killed.

She felt a sudden warmth on her chilled fingers. Startled, her eyes snapped open. She stared down at her hands and saw Gage's big, strong hands cradling them. His heat surprised her. That he'd done it at all shocked her.

"Your sister...were you there?"

The quiet, gentle question was the last straw that broke her already shaky composure. She barely managed to stifle a sob.

"I...no. But the pictures...we saw them. All of them. And her car, after, at the tow yard."

His hands tightened around hers. "I'm sorry, Laurey."

There was no doubting the sincerity of his words. And the irony of it hit her suddenly. He was the one who had nearly died tonight, he was about to go to the hospital to find out just how badly he was hurt, yet here he was comforting her.

Maybe that nomination for sainthood was in order after all.

Chapter 6

He was going to be as sore as he'd ever been, Gage acknowledged glumly.

He shifted on the narrow gurney. It creaked beneath him. Or at least, he thought it was the gurney; it could just as well have been his aching body.

Tentatively he ran his fingers over his bare chest to the sorest spot along his ribs. His best guess was that his dive sideways away from the impact had gotten him just far enough for the seat belt to snap tight across his ribs at that spot. But he could hardly complain; had he not moved, he would have been in a lot worse shape. He'd seen how the driver's door had buckled into the interior, how the raw, torn metal would have ripped at his flesh. As it was, he was lucky the damage, thanks to the height of the van that had plowed into him, had been mostly above his legs after he'd dodged to the side. He'd seen enough accidents in his career to know it was a small miracle he'd walked away from this one relatively unscathed.

And that wasn't the only small miracle that had happened tonight, he thought, still not quite able to believe that Laurey

Templeton was really sitting outside in the emergency room waiting area. For him.

Of course, she might have changed her mind by now; it had been over an hour. Perhaps it had just been shock that had brought on her unexpected offer in the first place, some lingering need grown out of the memory of the accident that had taken her sister's life. He wouldn't be surprised if she'd left him to find his own way home.

In fact, he expected it. It was the opposite he had trouble with; he'd never quite gotten used to people being concerned about him, even his friends. He never lost that little jolt of surprise when someone, the Buckharts, Caitlin, or even Kit, expressed worry about him. And he was afraid he didn't react in the best of ways; he tended to brush off their concern rather than accept it with any kind of grace.

But if he was surprised when his friends worried, he was astonished that Laurey Templeton had cared enough to even think about staying with him at the hospital. She'd made it quite clear what she thought of him, and he'd been more than stunned when he'd looked up from the seat of his mangled car to see her staring down at him, her eyes wide with fear.

She'd just been afraid she was going to be confronting a body, not a living person, he told himself. Disturbing for anyone, but especially to someone who had lost a family member in similar circumstances. That was what had upset her so, not any concern about him. And her offer to help had surely come out of courtesy, the kind any decent person would show in such a situation. That was all it was, and to read anything more into her generous action would be foolish. Worse than foolish.

But he couldn't help admiring the fact that she had braved what had to be a scenario fraught with awful memories to help someone she didn't even like. He could hardly blame her if she bailed after the shock had worn off and she had time to think about it.

The ER physician, a young black woman he'd met frequently when his job brought him here, returned, waving at him with a gloved hand.

"Get outta here, Butler," she said with a grin, "and take those cops that keep coming in and out of here with you."

He let out a relieved breath; the way his head was pounding, he'd been afraid something was going to show up on the X ray that would keep him here.

"Thanks, Roxy," he said as he carefully levered himself upright.

"That's Dr. Roxanne to you," she said. "And next time, be more careful who you drive in front of."

She accompanied the teasing comment with a stern waggle of her finger, and Gage grinned at her.

"Yes, ma'am," he said, swaying slightly as he slid off the gurney and his feet hit the floor. The woman in hospital greens watched, and he steadied himself quickly, knowing that if he didn't, Dr. Roxanne Cutler just might change her mind and book him into this expensive hotel for the night.

"Get some rest," Roxanne told him, her voice now serious. She held out a small white envelope the nurse had also brought. "And take these, even if you don't want to. They'll help with the pain, and any swelling later."

"I'll be good, I promise."

"See that you are. And you aren't driving," she added in a commanding tone.

His mouth twisted ruefully. "I don't have anything left to drive."

"Good." She eyed him pointedly. "Straight home, Butler. And to bed. Preferably alone."

"Easy enough," he muttered, reaching for his bloodied shirt. He spent almost all his nights alone anyway.

"I mean it, Butler. Your lady will just have to do without your…attentions tonight."

He froze. "My…what?"

She lifted a dark, arched brow at him. "The young lady who's been haunting our waiting room, asking repeatedly if you were really okay."

Gage gaped at her.

"Tall, dark hair, gray eyes?" Roxy said dryly. "Ring any bells?"

"I..." He stopped, swallowing rather thickly. Ring any bells? He didn't want to think about it. "I just didn't think she'd stick around this long," he finally said.

"Why? You haven't been treating her right or what?"

There were times, he thought, when he wished Dr. Cutler had a more formal bedside manner. Something of his thoughts must have shown on his face, because the doctor laughed.

"Oh, honey, I want to hear this story," she said, "but not tonight. It's shaping up to be a busy one, so get out of my way."

"Gladly," Gage muttered, but he gave her a lopsided smile as he said it; she was one of the best doctors around, and her cheerfully personable manner was part of the reason why.

When she left, he pulled on his shirt, a task that took three times as long as it should have thanks to various twinges and aches. He fumbled, then gave up on the buttons as he walked out into the waiting room, his steps careful but steady. At least, they were steady until he saw her.

Even with Roxy's teasing, he hadn't really believed it, yet there she was, still there, not reading a magazine or pacing in irritation at the long wait, but rather sitting quietly, elbows on the arms of the chair, her hands steepled before her as if in prayer.

She looked up as if she'd heard him, and when she saw him, undeniable relief flashed across her face. She stood up with that easy grace he'd noticed before, so at odds with the gangly awkwardness he remembered from eight years ago, when she'd been taller than all the girls in her class, and many of the boys, as well.

She walked over to him, stopping a bare two feet away. He caught a whiff of some sweetly spicy scent, a luscious counterpoint to the strong, antiseptic smells of the emergency room.

"I didn't really expect..." His words trailed away uncomfortably, and he had to try again. "You didn't really have to wait all this time."

"I said I would," she answered simply.

"I know, but...I know you didn't really want to."

She blushed. "I... I know I was..." She sounded as uncomfortable as he had, and when she went on, it was in a rush. "Look, can we talk about that later? I'm under orders to get you home. Fast."

"Roxy," he guessed.

"Dr. Cutler," she said.

He nodded. "She's used to giving orders."

"And you're not?" Laurey said, but in a teasing way that made it impossible to take offense. She was trying to keep this light, he saw, and he wasn't going to be the one to make it harder on her. It was kind enough of her to have stuck around to give him a ride home.

"Just let me call Trinity West and—"

"Uh-uh. She warned me that you'd want to do that, and she said the phone's off-limits. Home, take your pills and to bed."

Gage blinked. "But—"

"Besides, I already called."

He blinked again, really startled now. "You...called Trinity West?"

"I did. They didn't know who I was, of course, so they wouldn't tell me anything. But I had Quisto call here. They found the van."

For the moment, he set aside his surprise that she'd done it in favor of the more important fact. "Where? Any driver? Did they—"

He stopped when she held up her hand. "They found it over on Trinity East, abandoned. That was as far as it got, with all the damage. No driver."

"And let me guess," he said tiredly. "When they called the owner, they said they were just about to report it stolen."

It was her turn to stare. "How did you know that?"

"Because that's the standard story. Sometimes it's true, most times it's to try and cover up the hit-and-run."

"Oh."

She looked almost chagrined, like someone confronted with something they supposed they should have realized before. And she also looked almost let down, as if she'd thought she had good news that had fallen flat. It made him feel bad about his reaction.

"Thank you for finding out," he said.

She gave him a half smile that seemed almost shy. "I thought you'd want to know."

As a peace offering, it might not be the largest, but to Gage, it was enough for the moment. He was too tired, aching too much, to resist, anyway.

"I did. Thank you," he said again.

"Let's get you home," she said, and he found himself nodding and quietly following her as she walked out through the automatic doors. He watched her walk, wondering how he'd known, all those years ago, that she would someday have this delightfully feminine grace.

And telling himself that if he'd known a mere traffic accident would change her attitude so much, he might have been tempted to have one sooner.

It really wasn't very flattering, Laurey thought, that he'd been so completely surprised that she was still there when the doctor had finished with him. She had, after all, offered to wait. Did he think she would go back on an offer to an injured man? Any man?

No, just him.

Her breath caught, her fingers tightening around the steering wheel. She hadn't looked at it from that angle before, but now that it had hit her, she couldn't deny it. Why wouldn't he think that? Why wouldn't he believe that while she would do such a simple thing for almost anyone, she wouldn't go out of her way to spit on him; hadn't she virtually said as much? And for the first time she realized just how she must have appeared to him since they'd met again after all those years.

No wonder he'd thought her childish and naive. It was true. Only a child would bear such a grudge over so little for so long. She remembered her mother saying, after she'd graduated college, that she wanted to send Gage Butler a thank-you for getting her back on the right course. She'd been furious, of course, and angry with her mother for tainting her proud day with even a hint of those ugly memories.

Her parents had, annoyingly, laughed at her, seeming startled that she still harbored such anger about the long-ago incident. Her father—a week after the graduation he couldn't be bothered to attend—had said she was selfish, only remembering her humiliation, not theirs, while her mother had told her they had feared that their daughter was slipping away into dangerous territory, and that someday, when she had children of her own, she would understand.

Of course, they hadn't known she had been well into teenage love with the boy—the man—who had betrayed them all. No wonder it hadn't made sense to them.

No wonder it hadn't made sense to Gage.

She glanced in her rearview mirror, at the quiet street where she'd dropped him off. Nothing fancy, it was an older but still tidy neighborhood. When he'd directed her to the house on the corner, a modest Spanish style with a red tile roof like many in the area, she'd pulled into the driveway carefully, trying to stay on the twin, narrow strips of concrete and off the grass. She had exclaimed in surprise at the profusion of flowers that grew around the small front porch—that was something she missed about southern California, flowers all year round—and had found herself smiling when Gage disclaimed responsibility and told her to thank his gardeners, he didn't have time to keep up the garden. The place had been his family's, he told her, and he'd kept it after they'd left Marina Heights.

"It's a cute house," she had said.

His mouth twisted. "Funny, that's what my wife said."

She'd stared at him then, barely managing to remember to apply the brakes. "You're…married?"

"I was." He'd opened the car door, put one foot out slowly, then looked back at her. "I was eight years ago, too."

He'd gotten out before she could react, leaving her sitting there wondering why he had said that, if there had been some kind of implication she was supposed to understand. But then he was thanking her for the ride, and for waiting, and the moment to ask passed.

He had graciously thanked her again when she'd helped him gather up the personal items that the accident investigator had thought to take out of his car before it was towed. The man had dropped them off at the hospital, just one of several uniforms that had appeared as word got around that one of their own had been involved in the hit-and-run. Some had glanced at her, one or two had smiled, but none had let anything slow them on their quest to check on Gage.

And now, as she turned into the parking lot of the Marina del Mar resort hotel she was staying at—where Lacey Buckhart worked, when she wasn't nine months pregnant—Laurey let out an audible sigh. Caitlin had suggested the place because of Lacey, and Laurey had agreed because it was close to the beach and far enough from her old home not to be a constant reminder that the carefree life she'd once known was gone forever. The life she'd never appreciated enough when she had it.

After she parked the car, she sat for a moment, staring down at her hands on the wheel. They weren't shaking now, but the memory was still clear. He'd been hurt, had barely escaped dying, yet he'd had the discernment to sense what had upset her to the edge of hysteria, and the grace to comfort her when she'd done nothing but berate him for something she was sure he saw as simply doing his job. When, for all he knew, she still hated him.

For all he knew? Didn't she still hate him?

She searched within herself for the anger, the loathing she had always carried, but all she could find was a vague sheepishness. Could it have changed so quickly? Could those feelings have vanished in a matter of days after existing in that corner of her mind for years?

She was now willing to admit that she had taken out on him all her hurt feelings from back then, when he'd ignored her efforts to gain his attention. She should have been above screaming at him as if she were some hysterical child. And for that, she admitted ruefully, she did owe him an apology.

But did that change what he'd done? Did that make his betrayal any less? Did it alter the fact that he'd pretended to be something he wasn't, in order to trick kids into thinking he was their friend and to be trusted?

What is it you expect, Laurey? That the cops go out on the street armed with nothing but Boy Scout honor? That they always play fair and honest when nobody else does?

Again Caitlin's words came back to her. And more.

...he chose to try, to try and stop the drugs and guns before they got to the kids....

She couldn't remember ever feeling so torn. Except the day she'd found out that the beautiful golden boy she'd loved was a narc. A plant, a spy, a traitor.

She ran the old litany through her mind, wondering if she could stir up the old fire. Perhaps even hoping she could. It would be much easier if she could just continue to hate him, if she could hang on to that image from long ago.

But she couldn't. The one-dimensional picture she'd always had in her head had changed now. Gage Butler was real, not some cardboard cutout villain she could vent her anger on. There was nothing one-dimensional about the man so many others loved and admired. There was nothing one-dimensional about the man who had helped all those kids on Caitlin's wall. There was certainly nothing one-dimensional about the man who, in the midst of his own fear and pain, had taken the time to ease hers. Even thinking she would most likely not welcome it, his instinct had been to try to help.

And there was most certainly nothing one-dimensional about the man who had walked out of that emergency room, his unbuttoned shirt revealing a strong chest and flat belly that even the reddened areas that would no doubt soon be bruises of varying colors could detract from. Her reaction had startled her; she'd hated him in her mind for so long that she had managed to forget why she'd been attracted to him in the first place. And when she'd seen him again, seen that he was indeed the same golden boy he'd been then, she'd been moved not at all; Gage Butler, she'd thought with satisfaction, was an affliction she'd been cured of permanently.

So why had her pulse speeded up at the sight of him tonight? Why had she found it suddenly hard to breathe as she watched his careful walk, and why had she felt that odd quiver in the pit of her stomach as her gaze had strayed to the bloodstains on his shirt? When she was eighteen, she might have thought he deserved it, simply for being a liar and a sneak. In fact, she'd thought she was being extremely fair by not hating all cops, just him. Had her reluctant admission that she owed him an apology turned her head to mush? Was she buying all the pro-Butler propaganda that was being tossed at her?

She didn't know. Right now, she didn't feel like she knew anything. Except that, once again, Gage Butler had turned her ordered world on its head.

Chapter 7

"It's better to just get it over with," Laurey repeated for at least the tenth time since that morning.

She rehearsed the words she'd worked out in her head as she'd lain awake long into the night. "You were right, it should be ancient history, and I should never have said those things to you. I'm sorry."

How hard could it be? It wasn't as if she had to explain *why* she'd reacted so strongly. She wasn't going to have to admit to that silly, long-ago infatuation. She wasn't going to have to say "The reason I went so crazy now was because I was crazy about you then."

No, she wouldn't have to explain how hurt she had been, how he'd trampled all over her fledgling feelings, already tenuous because of their very newness. She wouldn't have to tell him of the nights she'd spent in helpless longing, praying he would give her any little sign that she stood out for him at all. She wouldn't have to tell him of the hours she'd spent trying to make herself over, trying to mask her height, her awkwardness, trying to become what she could never be—the petite, pixieish cheerleader type, one of the confident, poised girls who were secure in their appeal and therefore not at all hesitant to turn their charms loose on the gorgeous new transfer student. She'd taken some small comfort in the fact that, although he flirted right back, he never took it any further with them than he did with her, which meant nowhere. It hadn't been much, but it had been all he'd left her then.

She'd better be careful, she thought as she turned off of Trinity Street West and slowed, trying to remember the directions he'd given her last night and reverse them. She'd better be careful, or she would be back to hating him again.

Maybe she should thank him, she thought ironically, for at last giving her something in common with those confident girls; they'd been fooled by him, too. Somehow she didn't find much comfort in the fact. Nor, now that she could look back, did she feel much regret that she hadn't had much in common with those girls; too many of them had slid by on their looks, and when they had to rely on something else in the real world, they'd had nothing to turn to. There was something to be said for having had little to do in your spare time except study, she supposed.

As she turned the corner, breathing a sigh of relief as she saw the house and knew she'd found her way back, she found herself wondering what kind of student Gage had been when he had really been in high school. Not the slack-off, uncaring type he'd pretended to be, she guessed. He wouldn't have been able to pull off what he had if he'd been stupid.

Don't let the fact that you're here to apologize inspire you to admiration, she told herself as she negotiated the drive once more, more easily in the daylight.

She'd waited until now, nearly noon, figuring he would be sleeping late after the battering he'd taken last night. She noticed the curtains at the front window were closed, but she thought they had been that way last night; he'd probably just left them that way.

As she went up the three steps of the porch, she took a deep breath of air tinged with some sweet smell that had to be coming from one of the plants by the front porch. Amazing, that there were blooms this late in the year. Only in California, she thought. She'd gotten used to winters in Seattle.

Had his wife originally planted those flowers? she wondered suddenly.

He'd been married eight years ago. That boy who looked young enough to pass for seventeen had gone home to a wife at night. Was it that that had kept him from cashing in on the more obvious offers he'd gotten from some of the senior girls? Or had it been simply that he was on duty? She knew cops weren't supposed to drink on duty, but did that extend to…other things?

For the first time she thought about what a fine line he must have been walking then, trying to balance the facade with the reality.

"So now you feel sorry for him?" she chided herself. "Just apologize and get it over with."

That got her to the door, and she rapped her knuckles on it smartly. She waited, then knocked again. When a couple of minutes passed, she looked around and spotted a doorbell half-hidden beneath a vine Gage's vaunted gardener needed to pay some attention to. She pushed the button, heard the distant chiming, and waited again.

Still nothing.

A furrow creased her forehead. He could still be asleep, she supposed. She knew the doctor had given him some pills; the doctor had mentioned it, and she'd seen him take the small white envelope inside last night.

He was probably only asleep, she told herself. But then a memory of that dark swelling above his right temple came to her, and she felt a creeping shiver. What if…something had gone wrong?

You don't mess with head injuries, Quisto had said. And wasn't it true that sometimes people went to sleep and never woke up? The doctor had said he was fine, no concussion, but mistakes were made sometimes, everybody knew that.

She stood there on the porch, uncertain of what, if anything, she should do. Just leaving occurred to her, but she didn't know if she could do it. What if she did and later found out he'd died or something?

The thought made her shiver again, and she told herself it was only at the thought, that it was nothing personal, nothing to do with Gage himself.

She would look around, she decided. Maybe she would be able to see something in the back, or maybe he just couldn't hear the knock or the bell from wherever he was.

She went down the steps and walked slowly, carefully over to the driveway that led past the side of the house to the garage. There was no sound except her footsteps. No sign of life, except the occasional yelp of a dog somewhere down the block.

She hesitated, then went through a back gate, wondering if she was setting off some kind of alarm that would have Gage's colleagues swarming over her in moments.

There was a small, tidy backyard, a patch of grass bordered by more flowers, and a patio with a wood cover and some furniture scattered around, plus what looked like a well-used barbecue to the side of a sliding glass door. Seeing that the drape was partly open, she crossed the cement deck to the door and peered inside.

The house looked utterly deserted, no lights on, no sound from within. She could see a sofa that looked cushy enough to sleep on, and a couple of overstuffed chairs that looked nearly as comfortable. A television and stereo sat in a shelf unit in one corner, a bookcase crammed with books in the other. There were a few magazines scattered on a low coffee table and what looked like the bloodied shirt tossed across the back of one of the chairs. The rest of the room was neat, including the corner of what seemed to be a dining table; all she could see from where she stood.

She knocked on the glass door. It rattled slightly in its track, but nothing else happened. No movement, no response. That chill started up her spine again. Could he be inside, unconscious—or worse?

"Gage?" She called his name tentatively, then repeated it more loudly. Still nothing.

Now what? she muttered under her breath.

For a long moment she stood there, thinking. What would she do if she were home and this had happened? If it had been her friend Sandy, or someone else she knew?

I'd call somebody with a key, she answered her own question. But she didn't know anybody with a key. Should she call Caitlin? What if Quisto hadn't told her yet? Maybe she should just call him? She glanced at her watch, wondering what time he left for the evening shift. She couldn't call the house; if Caitlin answered, she could hardly ask to speak to him without explaining.

Maybe she should just call the police, period. The accident must be general knowledge by now; Caitlin had told her that Trinity West had a grapevine that put any other to shame. It wouldn't be like she was spilling the beans or anything.

And really, did any of that matter if a man was lying hurt and helpless on the other side of the door?

Decided now, she ran back to her car. There had been a phone at that convenience store a few blocks back, she thought, and moments later was pulling into the busy parking lot. She found the phones, hesitated about calling 911, then decided she wasn't sure enough to tie up an emergency line, and looked up the nonemergency number in the rather ragged directory hanging below the phone. She dialed quickly and got a helpful voice asking how she could direct her call.

"It's about one of your officers, Gage Butler," Laurey began.

"Did you want to speak to him? I can put you through."

Laurey blinked. "You mean…he's there? On Saturday?"

The woman chuckled. "He's almost always here. He hasn't taken any extra time off that he wasn't ordered to in his entire career."

Laurey felt a bit foolish now, over her panic. She'd been envisioning him unconscious or dead in his house, and all the time he'd been at work. She thanked the woman, declined another offer to connect her to Gage's office and hung up.

He was at work. It was the weekend, he'd nearly died in a

traffic accident the night before, he had to be stiff and sore, and he was at work.

Dedicated, she thought, wasn't the word for it. Driven, maybe. But there was a fine line between driven and obsessed, and nobody knew that better than she did. She'd lived her childhood with a man on the wrong side of that line; her father's compulsion had left his family as alone as if he'd been merely a distant relative who occasionally visited.

She tried to veer away from old, tired thoughts that accomplished nothing. Her father was who he was, and he would never change. She didn't know if a man like that *could* change, even if he wanted to. And her father had certainly never given any indication that he wanted to.

It doesn't matter, Laurey told herself as she got back into her rental car. They'd gotten along just fine without him, her and Mom and Lisa....

She started the car quickly as the ugly memories threatened to swamp her once more. She pulled out of the parking lot, driving with fierce concentration, thinking through every move in her head, fighting to block the ugliness with the mundane.

What her father was didn't matter, and if Gage was like him, well, that didn't matter, either. Certainly not to her. And even if he was the worst kind of workaholic, she still owed him that apology. And she wanted to get it over with, so he would quit hovering in her mind like this, so she could quit thinking about him all the time, so she could quit feeling guilty about how she'd acted, nursing that long-ago grudge like a little girl clinging to some childish slight.

She found her way back to Trinity Street West, the main road back to her hotel, and sat at the corner for a moment, waiting for the light to change.

The Marina Heights police station was on Trinity Street West, she thought, remembering that was how the building had come to be called Trinity West. In fact, she'd heard the cops who worked there called Trinity West cops more often than anything else, despite the formal name of the department. She'd already been in Seattle when all the big news had happened, when the Marina Heights police chief had been murdered in a drive-by shooting that had left two other men injured, including the man who had succeeded him as chief. She'd sarcastically hoped that one of them had been Gage, although she'd had the grace to feel a qualm of unease even as she thought it.

At least he didn't know that, so she didn't have to apologize for that, as well, she thought now. This was going to be bad enough.

So get it over with, she ordered herself yet again.

"All right," she muttered, "no time like the present."

She'd never voluntarily gone to a police station before, but then, she'd never had to apologize to a cop before. She'd never even talked to a cop, not since that awful day she had never forgotten.

"And if you don't quit thinking about that, this is going to be impossible!"

That exclamation got her around the corner, and she drove the few blocks until she saw the large, plain building ahead. It sat boxlike on a corner, overlooking a large lot that had been vacant for as long as she could remember. It was from there the windows had been shot out, she thought, the childhood memory stirring; her father, on one of his rare evenings at home, expressing outrage at the idea of a sniper taking aim at the police station. She'd been shocked, as well; she'd been raised to respect the police.

She still did, she told herself as she signaled, then made the turn into the visitors' parking lot in front. It was just an individual member of the group she didn't care for. And what she'd felt last night had been only a natural concern she would have had for anyone under those circumstances. That was the first thing she'd convinced herself of this morning, after she managed to blot out the memory of how he'd held her shaking hands and comforted her, when by rights it should have been the other way around.

She parked and went up the front steps, wondering if the front doors would be open on Saturday. They were, and when she stepped inside, she had an instant to realize that it seemed as bustlingly busy as any weekday here before the rush of memory hit her. The last—and only—time she'd been in this lobby was when she'd been released from custody here.

She made herself move before the swamp of painful memories made it impossible. She got in the line at the front desk, wondering what exactly to say. How did one get to see a detective? Did you just ask?

There was a young man who looked as if he was barely out of high school behind the raised counter. He wore a light blue uniform shirt, which she guessed meant he wasn't a street cop, but he wore it with a tangible pride that made her wonder again what made people choose a line of work that forced them to deal with ugliness on a daily basis.

There had been a time when she would have said it was for the power, that they got off on being able to mess with people's lives, but Caitlin's Quisto had cured her of that. He was charming, a pure gentleman, and loved Caitlin more than she'd ever seen any man love a woman. And in his job, he wanted only to make things better for people.

She listened to the people ahead of her, marveling at some of the petty things people seemed to expect the police to solve. For every routine request for a copy of a report or legitimate small crime to report, there were two of the other kind, the "my neighbor parks in front of my house, lets his leaves blow in my yard, mows his lawn too early in the morning" kind of complaint, and she wondered at the young man's composure; she would have been laughing at the absurdity by now.

There are murders happening, people, she thought. *Get a grip.* She'd never really thought about this side of police work, never realized they really had to deal with this kind of thing so much.

Apparently there was a lot she hadn't realized, she thought with an almost weary sigh.

When she got to the front of the line, she realized she'd been so lost in thought that she hadn't really decided what to say and ended up blurting out a quick question.

"I understand Officer Butler is here today?"

"Detective Butler?" The young man corrected her politely before he nodded. "Yes, he is. Did you want to see him?"

Was it that easy? "Yes, if it's possible."

He gestured to her right, to a pair of double doors. "Detective Division is through there, first door on your left." He gave her an apologetic smile. "I'd take you in, but I'm kind of busy here."

"I can see that," she said, rolling her eyes at him as the woman behind her began to chatter about the stray cat that was terrorizing her.

The young man—cadet, she saw now on his uniform beneath the Marina Heights Police patch on his shoulder—started to grin, then covered it discreetly by pretending to cough.

"Give me your name and I'll let him know you're coming back," he said, reaching for the phone.

She hesitated, wondering if Gage might just say, "Don't let her in." But she didn't see any way around it, so she gave her name.

The cadet nodded, waving her toward the doors. As he dialed, he also pushed a button that apparently buzzed open the locks, and she pushed on the right-hand door. When it opened, she waved a thank-you at him and went through.

She found the door on the left as the cadet had indicated, but the lights were out in what was obviously a reception area, and she hesitated. A moment later Gage came through a back door from what appeared to be a huge single room with several cubicles. She only had time to see that he had on the same battered leather jacket he'd been wearing every time she'd seen him before he flipped on the lights and stopped dead, staring at her in surprise.

"It really is you," he said unnecessarily.

"Didn't he give you my name?"

"Er, yeah, but…"

He shrugged, then winced; he was definitely feeling the aftereffects, she thought. Although his eyes looked shadowed with something other than simple pain, something darker, something that made her think of Sam Gregerson's words about hurt animals.

"Pretty sore?" she asked.

"I've felt better," he agreed with a wry twist of his mouth. "And...thanks again for sticking around last night."

"You're welcome."

"What are you doing here?"

It sounded rather abrupt, and Laurey began to question her wisdom in coming here. Something must have shown on her face, because he spoke hastily.

"I didn't mean it like that. I was just wondering... I mean, I guess I didn't figure you'd ever come back here if you didn't have to."

"I wouldn't. But I was looking for you."

He blinked. "You were?"

She nodded.

"Why?"

There it was, the logical opening. *Tell him*, she ordered herself silently. The words wouldn't come. "I...wondered how you were feeling," she said instead, it was partly true, but it sounded false, even to her own ears.

Gage's blond brows furrowed. "I'm okay, just a bit stiff. And sore in spots. A little headache. Nothing serious."

"I'm glad," she said, relieved to hear she sounded more genuine that time.

"How'd you know I was here?" he asked.

"I...called," she stammered; not for the world did she want to admit to him what she'd done.

His eyes narrowed then, and she thought with a sinking certainty that he knew she was lying. Or at least not telling the whole truth. Was this some sixth sense cops were born with? Did having it somehow guide them in to being cops, or did they learn it on the job?

"Laurey," he said, and to her ears his voice sounded ominous. Her common sense told her it was her imagination, that he didn't really sound almost threatening. She was reacting to this place, she thought, and the bad feelings she had about it—and him—that was all. But still, her words came out in an uncomfortable rush.

"Look, I wanted to apologize, all right? And it's not easy for me, so can we please get it over with?"

He drew back slightly, his face suddenly impassive. "If it's that hard, then maybe you should just skip it."

"I can't."

"But you'd rather."

His voice was flat, as expressionless as his face. And it made it even harder for her to go on, but she did it, doggedly.

"I was rude, and I'm sorry. And you were right, it should have been—should be—ancient history. It's childish to hold a grudge so long, and I apologize."

"Pretty speech. Been rehearsing?"

She flushed. Stung, she backed up a step. She'd said what she'd come to say, now she could leave. She drew herself up to her full height, which wasn't as imposing next to Gage as it was with many others; he still had a good four inches on her five foot nine.

"It doesn't really matter if you accept my apology. I had to make it," she said stiffly.

An audible breath escaped him, and his head lolled back on his shoulders. The thick, blond hair fell back, starkly revealing the rapidly developing bruise on his temple. A little headache, he'd said, but she would be willing to bet it was a bit more than that.

"Now *I'm* sorry," he said, raising his head to look at her again. She hadn't really realized just how green his eyes were. There was no touch of hazel or brown in them; they were simply, purely green.

"I'm afraid I don't get...apologies like yours often enough to know how to deal with them gracefully. But...thank you." His mouth quirked. "Even though you still don't like me much."

"I don't like what you did," she said, the correction small, but important to her. "Or the fact that you did it so easily."

He went very still, his eyes fixed on her. "I did it *well*, but it was never, ever easy. Do you think I liked having kids who thought I was their friend look at me like...you did? Do you think I liked it when even the kids who didn't get involved hated me? Hell, half the teachers who knew hated me being there, and I felt like I was being pulled apart by them, by my boss, by the kids, and by the slime that was channeling drugs and guns in by the truckload.''

She didn't want to think that it had cost him emotionally just as it had cost her and the other kids who had gotten caught up in the dragnet he'd started. She didn't want to think he had been torn by what he was doing. She didn't want to think that he'd hurt, just as she had. Because if she admitted that, she might start forgiving him, and while she'd felt she had to apologize, she didn't think she was ready for that.

"I never saw all that much of drugs, and I never saw a gun at school," she said, because it was the only thing she could think of to say.

He gave her an odd smile. "Of course you didn't. That wasn't your crowd. Or hadn't been, until you started hanging out with Chadwick."

She gaped at him. How on earth had he known—and remembered—that? "You knew I...started being friends with Curt?" she said, sounding as astonished as she felt.

"I knew he was always trying to suck in the straight kids. And I saw you with him a couple of times. Made me move him up on my timetable a bit."

She was still staring at him. "Why?"

"I didn't want you in any deeper than you were."

He'd been...protecting her? Was that what he was trying to say? That he'd had her arrested for...for what? Her own good?

"Curt was one of the prime distributors," Gage said, as if in answer to her skeptical look. "Anything from grass to coke to heroin. And if you didn't see him with a gun it was only a matter of time. He had a small arsenal."

"He...did?" she asked weakly.

"Automatic pistols, revolvers...when you're dealing, you have to protect your inventory, not to mention the cash."

"I...knew he was into pot, but..."

Her voice trailed off, and she shivered. It had been Curt's car she'd been in that night, his car the police had found the bag of marijuana in. Only days later the rumors had been flying that it had been Curt's arrest the cops had been waiting for, but that had seemed so wild that she hadn't put much credence in it. And besides, everything else had been driven out of her mind a few days later when it had come out that they'd pulled it off thanks to the narc they had on the scene. Gage.

She didn't realize how long she'd been standing there, her thoughts whirling, images from the past engulfing her, until she felt a touch on her elbow. She came back to the present abruptly, to see Gage looking down at her in apparent concern.

"I was about to go get some lunch," he said. "Come with me? You look like you could use a stiff cup of coffee or something." She hesitated, and he gave her a lopsided smile. "Peace offering?" he suggested. "For my lousy reaction to your very nice apology?"

She didn't know if she was just too numb to protest, or if some part of her had made a subconscious decision, but a few minutes later they were walking eastward down Trinity Street West, toward a small restaurant Gage said had the best coffee around. He'd offered to check out a department car, saying he'd ridden his bicycle in, figuring it would help keep him from stiffening up any more, but when he told her it was just a few blocks, she had opted for the walk.

"If you ignore the cheesy decor," he said as they turned onto a small, narrow side street and neared the restaurant, "it's not a bad old place. They have good food, anyway."

It was old, Laurey could see. It was on the edge of the older part of Trinity West, just before the change into the east side, where buildings of this era were the norm.

"If the food is good," she said, "the decor doesn't—"

Gage choked off the rest of her words, grabbing her, shoving her hard into the small alcove of a shop doorway. Her face was pressed against glass. A store window, she thought inanely, full of secondhand clothes and costume jewelry. His body, tall, lean and frighteningly powerful, was pressed against her back, as if he were trying to smother her.

She opened her mouth to scream. Whether he'd suddenly

gone crazy and decided to exact vengeance for her treatment of him, or this was just an absurdly heavy and utterly unexpected pass, she wasn't about to—

The sound of a racing car cut off her scream.

The sound of gunfire cut off her breath.

Chapter 8

The window Laurey was pressed against exploded. Shattered, the shards falling with an odd tinkling noise like crystal rain. She nearly fell forward against the razor-sharp fragments that stayed in the frame. Gage grabbed her as the store's burglar alarm blared. He pulled her hard and tight against him, shuddering at the mere thought of what those jagged edges could have done to her.

For the first time in his career he paid little attention to the suspects in a crime. He'd caught a vague glimpse of a small blue sedan, noted that it had a brown primered right front fender, that there had been at least two occupants, but beyond that, his well-trained powers of observation had failed him. He was aware only of the woman trembling in his arms.

"God, those were gunshots." Her voice was as shaky as she felt.

"Yes," he said, tightening his grip on her. She seemed to welcome it, pressing herself against him, tremors still shaking her.

Get back to business here, Butler.

He stayed hunched over her, keeping his body between her

and the street. With one hand he reached under his jacket and pulled out the small, plainclothes revolver he carried while in the station, wishing he'd changed to the larger semiautomatic that was in his desk; it wasn't unheard of for drive-by shooters to make a second pass, and the little two-inch lacked the fire-power he would have preferred. He craned his head as far as he could without leaving Laurey unprotected. There was no sign of the car on the narrow side street, although the usual traffic rolled by out on Trinity Street West.

Not, he thought, flicking an irritated glance at the clamoring alarm bell, that he could hear it. Or anything else, over that racket.

After a long moment when nothing happened except that damn bell making his head ache, he released her and started to turn. She made a tiny sound of protest that he miraculously heard. He squeezed her arm reassuringly.

"Just stay here." He had to put his mouth practically next to her ear to be heard, and he caught a whiff of that sweetly spicy scent he'd noticed before.

"No!"

"I'm just going to take a look, make sure they're gone."

She shuddered violently, her eyes widening at what obviously hadn't occurred to her. And when he took a step away, she made a convulsive little movement after him.

"All right," he said, conceding she had a right to her fear, and her reluctance to be left alone, under the circumstances. "Just stay behind me."

She nodded, still a little wild-eyed. And just then, merci-fully, the alarm shut off.

"Hopefully that scared them off," he said.

He moved carefully out to where he could see the street. It was still empty. One of the parked cars had a shattered back window, the hole at the center of the starburst of cracks om-inously large. Still cautious despite the silence, he edged the two-inch around the corner, ready to fire. Then he moved his head so he could see. The sidewalk was empty in both direc-tions.

He could see some people huddled in the entrance to the

restaurant, staring out with frightened faces. But there was no sign of the car, or of anyone else who looked suspicious. He let out a long breath. But he didn't holster the two-inch. Not yet.

When he turned back to Laurey, she was staring at him.

"It's okay now," he told her quickly. "They're gone."

"Who...what...?"

"I don't know. Most likely a random drive-by, although they're not frequent this far west. Or maybe it was for whoever owns this—" he gestured at the shop "—and we just got in the way."

"You did, you mean," she said, her voice steadier now. He had to give her credit for that, he thought; she'd just seen an incident that would leave most people terrified for days, yet already she was pulling herself together. She was still pale, and her eyes were still wide, but the trembling had already lessened.

"I got in the way?" he asked, puzzled.

"You got in between them and me. And you stayed there."

She said it so wonderingly, sounding so amazed, that his mouth quirked upward at one corner. "What is it, Laurey? Did you think that 'to protect and serve' was just lip service? Or that it only goes for the people who like us?"

Color flooded her pale cheeks. "I...I don't... But you could have gotten hurt. Or killed!"

His smile gentled then. "That's what the job means, Laurey. It means you stand between the bad guys and the people you're sworn to protect. And sometimes it means it... literally."

"But... I never thought..."

"Most people don't. They've never dealt with things like this firsthand. And part of our job is to see that they don't have to. It's what we get paid for."

"Nobody gets paid enough for *that*."

He grinned at her. "We've been saying that for years."

Her gaze flicked to the weapon he still held, then back to his face. "How can you joke like that?"

His grin faded. Old memories stirred, of the man who had

helped so many of them, yet been unable to help himself as his life had crumbled around him. The man who had become a legend, not only at Trinity West, but throughout the county, even the state. The quintessential good cop, Clay Yeager had been the first to tell him that you had to see the humor in the darkness or the darkness would overwhelm you.

As it had, eventually, overwhelmed Yeager himself.

"Because," Gage said softly, "if we don't joke about it, it'll eat us alive."

Before she could respond he heard the sound of an engine approaching. His fingers tightened around the two-inch. Then he caught the reflection of a black-and-white in the surviving glass window and relaxed his grasp.

"The cavalry arrives," he muttered, and stepped out to flag the unit down.

Laurey leaned against the hood of the police car, grateful for the warmth rising from the engine. Not because it was particularly cold—what would have been an Indian summer back in Seattle was just normal fall weather here in California, sunny and bright—but because it helped her stop shivering.

Despite his own seemingly unshakable cool, Gage had told her she had every right to be rattled. And she *was*. But not so rattled that she hadn't noticed that Gage was handling her with care, being solicitous and understanding, and so gentle it nearly brought tears to her eyes. If this was his standard demeanor as a cop, it was no wonder everybody thought he walked on water.

And if it wasn't…

She didn't want to think about that. She didn't want to think that there might be anything personal in his tender care. Because not only was she aware of how he was treating her, but she had realized with a little shock that she liked it.

The remnants of that long-ago crush, she told herself, that was all. Besides, it was unlikely that he meant anything by it. One apology from her was hardly going to turn things around that much.

Another little shock jolted her. What was she thinking? That she *wanted* things to turn around?

No, she insisted silently, of course she didn't. She was just…rattled. That, plus those old, never-quite-forgotten feelings, had combined to leave her in this state of confusion. That was all it was.

As if to prove it to herself, to prove she could do it and feel nothing of the little thrill that had always gone through her back then, she lifted her head to look at him.

He was talking to the officers in uniform, explaining what had happened. One of them left and began walking up and down the block, studying the ground, although she had no idea what he was looking for. The other was listening to Gage intently, only once glancing up at the shattered store window. Gage had told her that he would have to write a report and she would need to give a statement, but that they would go back to Trinity West for that.

Now, standing there beside the man in uniform, he looked tall, strong and remarkably unscathed in snug jeans and a white long-sleeved shirt under the brown leather jacket. No less beautiful than he had been when he had fueled her adolescent fantasies and been the focus of all her youthful heart's dreams.

Really, she thought, he had changed very little in the past eight years. He had the same leanly muscled body, the same smile, the same thick, golden hair that still fell thickly over his forehead, the same vivid green eyes.

The same eyes.

They *were* the same. She'd thought when she'd first seen him today that they were shadowed, haunted somehow, she had even thought of Cruz's little girl's surprisingly astute assessment, but only now did she realize that they had been that way even eight years ago. Why hadn't she seen it then? It seemed so obvious now, that darkness, that sadness, how had she not noticed those old, old eyes in the young face? Had she truly been so unobservant, so callow? Or had she just been young, too wrapped up in her own dreams to truly notice such things…even in the object of those dreams?

He glanced over at her then, as if in continued concern for her. She gave him the best smile she could manage, and he smiled back. And even though it was clearly genuine, that smile didn't quite take all the darkness away.

She wondered what it was. They had obviously been with him for a long time, those shadows. What was it that he carried within him? What made him look like this? What had made his eyes, in the baby face that had enabled him to masquerade as a boy, look like that even at twenty-one? Was it the same thing that made him nearly obsessed with his work?

She didn't know. And she wasn't at all sure she wanted to.

She saw the officer who had been walking along the street bend to look at something, then shift his gaze to something else a foot or so away, and then something else. She saw the glint of metal on the asphalt in the instant he raised his head.

"Got them," he called out. "Looks like nine millimeters."

"Great," she heard Gage say. "That narrows it down to half the weapons on the street."

She realized then what the man had found. Shell casings, she thought they were called, whatever was left after guns like that were fired. She shivered again as she thought of Gage placing himself between her and the deadly barrage. Yet he'd done it automatically, instinctively, as if no other thought had crossed his mind. She wondered yet again what drove him.

And then he was coming toward her, and with an effort she reined in her thoughts, telling herself she had no interest in Gage Butler's past, in what made him spend his weekends working, or in what made his eyes look haunted.

Yet, as they began to walk—back toward Trinity West, both of them having agreed they'd pretty much lost their appetites—the first words out of her mouth made a liar out of her.

"Why were you working on Saturday, anyway?"

He looked startled by her choice of subject, perhaps having expected some further comment on his decision that they should walk back, since he guessed she wouldn't have much fondness for riding in a police car. It took him a moment to answer.

"I had to call some...people, and their phone numbers were in my desk."

She wondered what the hesitation had meant. "People? You mean like...what do you call them? Snitches?"

His gaze narrowed, and she supposed he was wondering whether there had been some particular significance to her question, given her feelings about the past. She truly hadn't meant it that way, but before she could say so, he was answering.

"Actually, no. Bail bondsmen."

Puzzled, she asked, "Don't...people who are arrested call them to get out?"

"Yes. That's why I called them."

"Oh," she said, although it made no sense to her.

"I just wanted some warning if a guy we arrested gets one of them to post his bail."

"They'll...tell you that?"

"Some of them. They like to stay on our good side. And it's not like we stop them from doing it, it's just that in some cases we want to know if somebody's about to get out. If nothing else, so we can...notify the victim."

"Oh." That did make sense to her, and she wondered what this particular person had done that made such notification necessary. And what it was like to deal with such people on a daily basis.

This time she was treated, although she hardly thought it was the right word for it, to a visit to the inner reaches of Trinity West. The long hallways were mostly empty, minus, Gage told her, the brass, detectives and support personnel who normally worked only on weekdays.

Gage got her a cup of coffee and, with a warning about the vending machines, offered her a snack, which she refused. He took her into what he called the report writing room, furnished with several long tables, each with a phone, and a wall full of shelves that held phone books and what appeared to be dozens of different forms. Waiting there was an officer who didn't look much older than the cadet she'd seen at the front desk—did this mean she was getting old at almost twenty-seven?—who said he would take her statement. Gage promised her a meal soon and retreated to his cubicle to begin his own report.

The young officer was businesslike but polite, and it was relatively painless, especially since she didn't have much to say. No, she hadn't seen the car at all, nor had she seen who or how many were in it. Yes, she'd heard shots; no, she didn't know how many; yes, probably more than three but less than ten. Yes, they'd been quick, but she knew nothing about such things, so she had no clue if they had come from an automatic weapon of some kind.

"No problem," the young officer said agreeably as he stood up. "I'm sure Gage will know. He never misses a thing."

The admiration in his voice was unmistakable. Everyone, it seemed, was a dues-paying member of the Gage Butler fan club.

"You're welcome to sit here, if you like, or there's a coffee room at the end of the hall," he said as he gathered up his things. "Or, if you want to see Gage, Detectives is down the hall that way."

She nodded as he pointed, and he thanked her nicely for helping, then left. A very polite young man. And eager. And obviously thrilled to be doing what he was doing. What *was* it about this job? Laurey wondered.

She finished as much as she could of the rather overwhelming coffee, then got up and tossed the cup into a wastebasket near the door. More of that brew was out of the question, she thought, or she would be up all night.

Mildly curious—and not feeling any of the distaste now that she was in a totally unfamiliar part of Trinity West—she wandered down the hall in the direction the young officer had indicated. The door labeled Detective Division was propped open. She hesitated, but the other officer had seemed almost to expect she would go looking for Gage, so she didn't see the harm and stepped inside. She could hear the murmur of voices and headed toward them. As she got closer, she recognized Gage's voice, but the other, and even deeper, one was unknown to her.

She was so intent on deciding that she didn't know the second voice that it took a moment for the words themselves to register. When they did, she stopped, wondering if she should retreat and leave them alone.

"—feeling all right?"

Gage, Laurey thought with certainty.

"She says she's fine, but…"

"You can't help remembering last time she was pregnant."

There was a pause. Pregnant? She knew it wasn't Quisto's voice, so, perhaps…Ryan? Lacey's husband? It had to be.

Then the other voice came again, low now, harsh and strained. And his words confirmed her guess. "I almost lost her. I couldn't…take that again. She's my life, Gage."

"I know," Gage answered softly.

Perhaps because she couldn't see him, Laurey was even more aware of his voice, of the timbre of it, the tone…and the undertone. Not envy, not jealousy, but a sort of…wistfulness. As if he didn't quite believe in the kind of love the other man was speaking of, yet couldn't deny it, either, not when it stood right there in front of him. And it was the sound of his voice that kept her rooted in place, despite the qualm of guilt she felt at eavesdropping.

"There are times," Gage said, that wistful tone replaced now by a strangely flat note, "when I'm glad…"

His voice trailed off. Laurey wondered what he was glad about, because his voice certainly didn't sound glad. A moment later, Ryan's low, gentle rumble came with the answer.

"Glad there's no one who owns your heart?"

She heard a low sound that could have been a word or just a grunt.

"Always invulnerable, aren't you, Gage?" Ryan asked. "Don't ever give the world a lever to use against you."

"At least then the world can't take them away from you."

"So you think it's better never to have anyone?"

"Isn't it?" Where Ryan had sounded merely curious, Gage's voice was oddly fierce. "You nearly lost Lacey. You did lose your son. Can you really say it wouldn't be better?"

Laurey's breath caught in her throat. This was more than

just a rather dark, philosophical discussion in response to Ryan's worries about his pregnant wife. If Gage's words hadn't told her that, his tone of voice would have. No, this discussion was grimly founded in reality. For both of them. Did Gage really believe it? Did he really think it was better not to have a family than to have one and lose it? She found the thought both poignant and intriguing.

"I'm sorry," Gage said suddenly, and Laurey wondered what Ryan's face must have looked like. "I didn't mean to bring back...painful memories."

"I haven't got the corner on those, it seems," Ryan said, gentle commiseration clear in his voice.

Gage didn't speak, and after a brief moment, Ryan went on. "I've been there, buddy. I grew up without having a human being in the world who gave a damn about me. And I'll tell you, it's a damn cold way to live."

She had to leave. This was too much, too private, and she had no right to listen to these old friends speak of such personal things. Moving with exquisite care, she edged away, knowing she would surely die of embarrassment if she was caught eavesdropping.

When she thought it was safe enough, she turned to hurry back out into the hallway. And ran hard into something soft and squashy feeling. She stifled a yelp and jumped back. The backs of her knees came up against a chair, and she sat down abruptly, thinking it was better than falling while trying to stay upright. She stared for a moment at the rotund belly beneath a shirt whose buttons were straining at her eye level.

"Well, well, well," she heard from above her, the words accompanied by an odd sort of chewing sound. "What have we here? Hello there, little lady."

Little lady?

Laurey nearly laughed. She hadn't been called little in a very long time, and never "lady" in such a blatantly patronizing tone. She looked up.

The first thing she saw was the reason for the chewing sound, a rather disgustingly wet cigar stub was clenched between the teeth of the man who had spoken. Teeth that were yellowed evidence of a lifelong acquaintance with such cigars.

She'd never seen anyone quite like him. He looked to be in his mid to late fifties, but in other ways seemed caught in a time warp, as if he'd never quite made it out of a previous era. With buzz cut blond hair and heavy jowls, a polyester suit and a tie that wore the remnants of his last meal, he looked like a caricature to her, something out of some screenwriter's nightmare vision of an old-boy cop.

"If I'd known the other witness was such a good-looking broad, I'd have been here a lot sooner," the man said around the cigar.

Laurey stared at him. He looked back expectantly. It took her a moment to realize that he thought that had been a compliment. He was mired in another era in more ways than one, it seemed.

"Laurey?"

Gage stepped around the corner of the cubicle, his gaze flicking swiftly from her to the older man. She thought she saw irritation, then wariness, flash across his face in short order.

"Hello, Lieutenant," he said.

"Butler," the man said, sparing Gage the briefest of glances before he looked back at Laurey, who still sat in the chair, staring upward in amazement at this walking visit to the past. "Glad to see you didn't get hurt, missy. I'd hate to see that pretty face damaged."

She supposed she should be outraged, but she found herself stifling a laugh instead. It was all she could do not to turn to Gage and ask incredulously, "Is he for real?"

And then she saw someone move, stepping past Gage. The man came to a halt, crossed his arms over his chest and stared down at the older man. Laurey gaped, stunned. She'd been told about Ryan Buckhart by just about every female connected to the department who had been at the shower, but hearing about him was obviously, as Caitlin had warned her, quite different than seeing him.

Ryan Buckhart was everything Caitlin had promised. And

more. A couple of inches taller than Gage, he was tall enough to make even her feel small. And broad-shouldered, solidly strong, with long dark hair, bronze skin and high cheekbones. He was exotically striking, and powerfully, uncompromisingly male. Even more than Quisto, he was a dark foil to Gage's golden looks, and the two of them together created a dramatic contrast she knew she wouldn't soon forget.

She remembered what Ryan had said, in that low, strained voice, that his beloved Lacey was his life. What must it be like, to have a man like this so madly in love with you? A man who could literally stop traffic: female because of his looks, male because of his aura of sheer power? In that instant she didn't envy Lacey Buckhart one bit.

Ryan fixed the man Gage had called lieutenant with a steady glare.

"And of course you're delighted to see your detective in one piece, aren't you, Robards?"

Laurey was a little surprised; weren't cops supposed to be like the military, respect for rank and all that? But there was no respect at all in Ryan Buckhart's hard-eyed gaze.

She was even more surprised by the older man's reaction.

"Er, of course," he sputtered. He backed up a step, eyeing Ryan warily.

Deciding on a whim to add what she could to his discomfiture, Laurey stood up. Slowly. And as she'd known she would, she stood a good two inches over the cigar-chomping other man, something she doubted he'd noticed in the instant she'd collided with him. She made sure she stood tall and close as she smiled down at him.

"Thank you so much for your unnecessary concern," Laurey said sweetly. "I accept it in the exact spirit in which it was rendered."

He gaped up at her in turn, muttered something about Gage getting his report finished and turned in immediately so he himself could go home, then spun on his heel and retreated. The instant after she heard a door close, she heard choking laughter from behind her. She spun around to see Gage nearly doubled over and the imposing, intimidating Ryan nearly howling with glee.

It took both men a moment to recover. When Gage straightened up, he gave her a grin that warmed her in a way she'd never known before.

"That," he said, "was worth a hundred apologies."

Her cheeks flushed, but this time in a pleasant way.

"You haven't met Ryan yet, have you?" Gage added when the big man finally wiped his streaming eyes and seemed to be under control again. "Laurey Templeton, Ryan Buckhart."

Laurey gave him a tentative smile, unsure how she should greet this living prototype. But he took any unease away when he took her hands in his and said with utter sincerity, "Ms. Templeton, it is truly a pleasure to meet you."

"I...Laurey, please."

"Laurey," he agreed with a smile that made him even more recklessly handsome. "I've rarely seen anyone size up our illustrious division lieutenant so quickly and accurately."

Laurey wrinkled her nose. "He's really your...boss?"

"To our dismay," Gage said. "He's a dinosaur who does his best to make life miserable for everyone."

"But not you, my friend." Ryan's voice was clearly teasing. "You're his fair-haired boy. Literally."

Gage grimaced, as if he didn't care for the joke. Or didn't think it was a joke.

"Literally?" Laurey asked, her gaze flicking to Gage's nearly platinum locks. "I assume that means something besides the obvious?"

"It means," Ryan said, his earlier laughter completely gone now, "that neither I nor Cruz Gregerson, nor Quisto Romero...nor the chief, for that matter, have the right skin coloration to be on Robards' good side."

Laurey's stomach turned; the way Robards had treated her was bad enough, but this, too? She looked from Gage back to Ryan in shock. He gave her a shrug, as if it meant little, and spoke quickly to lighten the sudden change of mood.

"If Gage here didn't work so hard to get on Robards' bad side, we'd all hate him."

"Just trying to level the playing field," Gage muttered.

"You mean you intentionally…provoke him?" Laurey asked.

"Fortunately," Ryan said, "it doesn't take much."

Something occurred to Laurey then. "What about Kit?"

Ryan chuckled. "Ah, yes. She does put a kink in his bigotry, doesn't she?"

Gage echoed the chuckle. "She does that, all right. She's got the right skin color, but she's a woman in a man's job. And with rank, yet. Confuses the heck out of him. So he pretty much leaves her alone."

As if their talk had conjured her up, the subject of the discussion walked in at that moment. Dressed in snug jeans and a sweatshirt emblazoned with the name of a local concert venue, her blond hair tousled, she looked trim, fit and none too happy.

"Just can't stay away, can you, Butler? Hi, Laurey, Ryan."

Laurey returned the greeting as Ryan nodded.

"Sorry you got caught up in this," Kit said to her.

"Me, too," Laurey said, shivering, knowing she would never, ever forget the sound of those bullets being fired.

Kit glanced at Ryan. "Working?"

He shook his head, his raven black hair flowing with the movement. "Just checking on Gage."

"Chief here yet?"

Ryan shook his head again as Gage sighed. At the sound, Kit turned her attention back to Gage.

"He'll be here, you know. He doesn't like his people getting shot at."

"I know."

"Neither do I. That's why I need to talk to you."

"Report's on my desk."

"Later. That's not what I want to talk about."

Gage looked puzzled. "What, then?"

Kit gave him an exasperated look. "What? How about the fact that somebody's trying to kill you?"

Chapter 9

"Come on, Kit, nobody's trying to kill me," Gage said for at least the third time. He knew he sounded a bit fervid, but he had to convince her. If he couldn't, his life would degenerate quickly.

"Butler, I swear, for a really smart guy, sometimes you are so darn stubborn."

Rather than deny it, he said mildly, "I didn't realize the two were mutually exclusive."

He sensed rather than saw Laurey smile, but he didn't dare look at her; he had to concentrate on talking Kit out of this idea that he was in mortal danger.

"Stubborn," Kit repeated in frustration.

A phone rang. Ryan, who was leaning against Gage's cluttered desk, leaned over and picked it up.

"Detectives, Buckhart." A pause, then, "Okay. Thanks." He hung up and glanced at Kit and Gage. "Chief's here."

Gage winced. "Head him off, will you? I don't want him buying into this theory Sergeant Walker here has come up with."

"Do you really think it won't occur to him on his own?"

He knew it would; de los Reyes was a very smart man. "It might, but I can talk him out of doing anything as long as you don't tell him you think it, too."

"Look, Butler," Kit began.

"Kit, listen, please," Gage said. "If you get him into this, you know what will happen. He doesn't mess around if he thinks somebody's in danger."

"Exactly," Kit said.

"Why don't I introduce Laurey to him," Ryan said, "while you two...work this out?"

"Great," Gage said fervently. Then, as Ryan ushered Laurey—who gave him an oddly intent look over her shoulder as they left—out of the office, he turned back to Kit. "Look," he said patiently, "the accident was just an accident, and this was just a random drive-by, or a hit at that shop. That's all."

"You really believe that?"

"Dispatch got hold of the guy, the owner. He said he's had a few problems with some east side kids, probably gangbangers."

"That's true of just about any business in the neighborhood."

He couldn't argue with that, so he tried to turn it to his advantage. "And that's what it runs to. Since Ryan took down The Pack, there just isn't anybody left around who'd take the risk of going after a cop."

"You think there aren't gangbangers out there who'd love to make their bones offing a cop?"

"Sure there are.... In the heat of the moment, if they're cornered, they'll react like any other rat. But this wasn't like that, and the bottom line is still that killing a cop brings more grief than it's worth to just about anybody."

"Even Martin?" Kit suggested, her tone sour.

"Well, almost anybody," Gage reluctantly admitted as she said the name he knew had been in her mind from the first moment. It had been in *his* mind since the moment she'd first broached the idea. Silently he admitted the possibility, but he continued to play it down, both because he didn't really believe it and because he couldn't allow the limitations it would put on him if she convinced the chief.

"Murdering a cop is a bit extreme, even for that slime."

"I'm not so sure." Her tone was even more acid. "He's got a lot to lose, and you're the prime reason he might lose it. And he's arrogant enough to think he could get away with it."

"We had only just arrested him when that van clobbered me."

"But he already knew he was your prime suspect. He could have arranged it before."

"He also thought he was safe," Gage said pointedly. "Why the hell would he arrange a hit while he still thought he had an ironclad alibi?"

"Okay, maybe," Kit conceded. "Maybe the hit-and-run was just that, an accident. But he's in jail now, so he knows his alibi can't be as solid as he thought."

"But he didn't have a chance to do anything about it. He's locked up now, and his only call was to his lawyer, screaming to arrange bail faster even if he had to pay it himself. And he's the only one in lockup two, so he could hardly have ordered up a drive-by from his cell."

Kit let out a long sigh. "It just seems…too coincidental."

"Drive-bys happen every day, Kit. So do hit-and-runs."

"But shootings and hit-and-runs don't happen on consecutive days to the same person who happens to be a cop. A cop who also happens to be the main investigator in a high-profile rape case."

"You worry too much."

"And you don't worry enough, not about yourself."

"I worry," Gage said flatly, "about Diane Santos and all the others like her."

Kit sighed. "All right, all right. I'll give you a little more rope. But if you hang yourself with it, I'll never forgive you, Butler."

He smiled then, both touched at her obvious concern and relieved that she wasn't going to present her theory to the chief. He knew Ryan would never say anything unless he had to, so it seemed he'd headed off what could have been disaster. Chief de los Reyes was not the kind of man to take a threat to any of his people lightly. He was going to have enough trouble explaining his way out of this without the chief slapping him with a bodyguard, or worse. He admired de los Reyes tremendously, but he couldn't do his job handcuffed. And right now his job was putting Mitchell Martin behind bars for as long as possible.

Gage looked across the table at Laurey as she stirred her soda with her straw. She'd said little since they'd left Trinity West, and he didn't know if it was still the shock of what had happened or something else.

"Are you all right?" he finally asked.

She lifted her gaze to his face. Her eyes were wide, troubled, but no longer held the lingering fear he had seen before. He shifted uncomfortably, the restaurant chair tilting slightly beneath him, one of its legs not even with the others.

"That's not a place known for drive-by shootings," he said. "If it was, I never would have taken you there."

"I know that," she assured him.

She lapsed into silence again and stared down at her swirling soda. Gage studied her, seeing an odd sort of tension in the set of her shoulders, the posture of her long, slender body. She looked like she had when he'd walked out of the emergency room that night.

Which, he thought, reminded him of something else. Something he needed to do, to ease a mind already too wrapped up in thoughts of the woman who sat opposite him. Wondering how to start, he turned words over in his mind as he watched her, his gaze settling on the twin semicircles of her thick, dark lashes.

Then she looked up, catching him watching her, and he found himself blurting out an awkward rush of words.

"I wanted to say...I'm sorry about the other night, what I said."

He saw a faint crease appear between her brows. "The other night?"

"Before...the accident."

He saw the second's delay before what he was talking about came back to her. He wasn't surprised; he was sure what had happened today was uppermost in her mind. She had, after all, come frighteningly close to dying in one of the ugliest of ways.

"I had...no right to say those things to you," he said.

"No," she said slowly, lowering her eyes once more, "you didn't."

He took a breath and made himself add, "Especially since I was so wrong."

"You were," she agreed.

Then she lifted her gaze to his face, and he saw the trace of surprise in her expression, as if she were startled by his apology. Or perhaps, he thought wryly, by the fact that he'd felt the need to make it. But then she turned the surprise around on him.

"But it's not all your fault. It *was* the worst thing that had ever happened to me for a long time. It became...a habit to think of it that way. And that's how I acted with you."

She drew a long breath. Gage opened his mouth to speak, but then shut it again, afraid that if he interrupted her, she wouldn't finish whatever it was she wanted to say. After a moment she went on.

"I...guess I've never really...dealt with that aspect of Lisa's death. Of putting it in...perspective with other bad things that have happened."

"There's no way to put something like that in perspective," he said, his voice unexpectedly harsh, "because it's at the top of the scale. There is nothing worse than the senseless death of a good person who didn't deserve it."

Her eyes widened, and she looked about to ask him something. Instinctively he looked away, fearing that something of the rush of memory that had suddenly swamped him was showing in his face. He didn't know what it was about her that had made him betray himself like this twice now.

As if she'd sensed his moment of panicked retreat, she stayed silent, and a minute later the waiter arrived to take their order. He'd picked a nice restaurant in Marina del Mar this time, overlooking the water of the marina, hoping the peaceful setting would help Laurey put what had happened out of her mind. And figuring he owed her a decent dinner after what she'd been through.

"So," he said quickly after the waiter had gone, his bright tone sounded forced even to his own ears, "does this mean you don't hate cops anymore?"

"I never did hate cops."

His mouth twisted. "Just one specific one, right?"

She sighed. "I said I was sorry, that I should have let go of it long ago. I was young, I was foolish, maybe even stupid."

"And led astray by evil companions?" he suggested, managing a grin to take any sting out of the words.

"That, too, I suppose." She swirled her hapless soda once more. "My parents never did like Curt."

"I know."

She gave him a sideways look. "You do?"

He nodded.

"And just how did you find that out?"

"They told me when I called them a couple of days after you were picked up. I told them they were right to be wary of him, that he was big trouble."

She blinked. "You called my parents? Why?"

"To let them know the narcotics charge was being dropped, that your record would only show a minor LOPC violation."

Her mouth twisted. "I always wondered what that stood for."

"LOPC? Lack of parental control."

She drew back slightly. "Really? Boy, that must have made my father furious."

Gage grinned again. "Neither of them was happy with the inference, but it was better than you having a narcotics charge on your record."

She looked at him curiously. "Why was it dropped? I was so relieved at the time, I never really questioned why."

He shifted on the comfortably upholstered chair as if it were a hardwood bench. "Interest of justice," he muttered.

"What does that mean, exactly?"

"It means the juvie authorities were convinced that you really didn't know about the grass in Curt's car, and that you weren't...a user."

There was a long silent moment while Laurey studied his face. Then, softly, she asked, "Convinced by who?" When he didn't answer, she spoke the guess he knew she'd already made. "You? It was you, wasn't it? You got the charges dropped."

He shrugged. "I knew you weren't one of them, not really. That you were just caught up with the wrong crowd."

"I wish you'd told *me* that," she exclaimed.

He gave her a crooked grin. "The object lesson would have lost some of its impact then. You needed to be shaken up a bit, before you wound up too far down that path to get back. I told your folks to watch out who you were hanging with, so you didn't wind up in some real trouble."

"No wonder my parents wanted to send you a thank-you," she said, sounding very odd.

"They did. After your record was sealed."

Her eyes widened then. "Was it you who...told my parents about that? I heard them talking, and they said the police had told them how to go about it."

"I mentioned it, when I called that first time. Told your mother it would be fairly easy, if the LOPC was the only thing on it. She called me about a year later and asked how to do it," he said, remembering the day rather clearly; he'd finally reached the point where he'd put the young Laurey out of his mind, and then her mother had called and brought it all back. "She told me you were in college and doing well, that you had really gotten things together."

Laurey looked astonished. "I had no idea. She never mentioned it at all. Not even that she'd spoken to you, let alone...all your help."

"I'm not surprised. I'd say she knew I wasn't your favorite person."

Laurey colored, the added pinkness making her smoky eyes even more striking. "I suppose...I should thank you, too."

"Not if it hurts too much," he said solemnly. "I realize that's too much of a turnaround to expect in such a short time."

"Don't remind me," she said with a sigh. "I hate even thinking about how I yelled at you in front of Caitlin."

"It was what's left of that mixed-up kid who was yelling," he said. "And if there's anybody who understands mixed-up kids, it's Caitlin."

She gave him a grateful look, and by the time their food arrived—they shared a taste for swordfish, it appeared—they were able to talk civilly, even companionably. She told him of her job in the advertising department of the magazine in Seattle, and how just before she'd left for her vacation she'd been working twelve-hour days to put the huge preholiday issue together. He was fascinated by the vast array of people she dealt with, people from all over the world, yet with one goal in common; attracting consumers with ready cash to their product or service.

"I love it," she said with clearly honest enthusiasm. "Even when it's that busy. I get to do some ad designing, as well, and that's always been my first love. Someday I hope to move over to that side completely."

What must it be like, Gage thought, to work in a world where you dealt with beauty every day, not ugliness? *You'll never know,* he muttered silently.

"So," he said hastily, in an effort to battle the thoughts, "why are you here by yourself?"

She gave him a sideways look. "Why not?"

"Er, I just wondered if you'd left a husband or boyfriend behind, someone who isn't going to like the idea of you down here getting nearly..."

His voice trailed off, and he wished he'd never started it.

After a moment, she answered simply, "No."

Silence spun out between them. Laurey stirred the glass that now held only ice. Gage stared at his plate.

"Why did you become a cop?"

Her question came out of the blue and startled him into answering honestly.

"Because it's all I've ever wanted to do, ever since my...since I was ten."

She seemed to notice the hesitation but didn't push about it. "Boyhood dream come true?" was all she asked.

"Sort of."

"Was your father a cop? I've heard it tends to run in families."

He grimaced. "You say that like it's some hereditary flaw."

She smiled. "I didn't mean it that way, really. I just don't understand why anyone would want the job."

"Sometimes I don't understand it, either," he said wryly.

"Caitlin says you're the most dedicated cop she knows, including Quisto."

He smiled; Caitlin's praise meant a great deal to him. "She does as much for kids as I do, probably more."

"She told me you were working on a case involving one of her kids who was...raped," Laurey said. "She wouldn't say anything more about it, only that she knew you would get him. That nobody cares more than you do."

He thought of Martin, of his swaggering arrogance, his confidence that he would never pay for what he'd done, and the anger that was never far below the surface churned anew.

"Men who rape aren't animals," he said, unable to control the fierceness in his voice. "They're worse than any creature who walks the planet. They use the worst weapon to make up for their feelings of powerlessness. They're cowards, attacking those smaller and weaker than themselves. They—"

He heard his own voice rising and made himself stop. Laurey was looking at him, wide-eyed.

"Sorry," he muttered. "I tend to get...carried away."

"No," she said quickly. "Don't apologize. Not for that. I was just...surprised. I thought the police didn't really—"

At her sudden halt, his mouth twisted.

"Care? Give a damn?"

"I did wonder if they were...maybe disinterested," she admitted. "But at the least I always thought of them as detached. From the...emotional aspects of that kind of crime, I mean."

"There are enough bogus claims of rape to make some cops skeptical. And that's how some deal with it. They have to remain detached, or go crazy."

"But you...you really care, don't you?" she said, looking at him intently.

"I hate it. I hate those who do it," he said, his tone utterly flat. "They should be put away for life, no mercy."

Laurey didn't seem repelled by his coldness, in fact, she looked merely thoughtful.

When the waiter returned, they agreed to share a slice of the restaurant's famous mud pie for dessert, and it was after savoring several bites of the ice cream, chocolate and whipped cream confection that Laurey mentioned being impressed with Chief Miguel de los Reyes, after just the few minutes she'd spent with him that afternoon.

"Ryan said he's the best, and I get the impression he's not a man who's easily impressed."

"No," Gage agreed, scooping up a piece of the chocolate crumb crust. "Ryan is probably harder to impress than anyone. And he's right. De los Reyes is the best. He came up the hard way, through the ranks. And he's had his share of grief, too."

"He was shot when the former chief was killed, wasn't he?"

Gage nodded. "And damn near died. Lost his wife, too, a few years back. Breast cancer. He nearly lost it afterward, he was so crazy about her."

"He never remarried?"

"No. Most of Trinity West doesn't think he ever will."

"Too busy being chief?"

"Partly. He gives a hundred and ten percent. He's a great administrator, and he can play the political game, too, but he remembers what it's like on the street. He takes care of his people, and there's not a one of them who wouldn't follow him into hell if he asked."

"Except maybe...your charming lieutenant?"

Gage grimaced. "Yeah, except for him. One of these days

de los Reyes is going to take him down, and hard. We've known that from the day he told de los Reyes that he wasn't going to take orders from any greaser.''

Laurey's eyes widened. ''He said that? To his face?''

Gage nodded grimly. ''He and the chief had a closed-door session that went on for a long time. Nobody knows what de los Reyes said, only that Robards has kept his mouth shut about him since. That alone got the respect of most of Trinity West.''

''Why hasn't the chief already done it, if he's so bad?''

''Robards has been around for thirty years. You don't just fire a guy with that kind of seniority without having a hell of a lot of backup. And even though he's an arrogant, obnoxious, sexist bigot, Robards is shrewd, knows how to cover his tracks.''

She lifted a brow at him. ''Isn't it…against some kind of code for one cop to talk about another like that?''

''Robards,'' he said flatly, ''is outside any code. He gave up his right to anyone's respect when he tried to get Ryan caught in the cross fire the day we took down The Pack. If it hadn't been for Lacey, Ryan could have been killed.''

Laurey stared at him. ''He tried to get Ryan killed? One of his own men?''

''We can't prove it, but we know he did. And so does de los Reyes.'' He smiled then. ''But I'll tell you, if the chief decides to up and quit, and go clean up city politics the way he cleaned up Trinity West, you can bet he'll take care of the dinosaur before he goes.''

''I'd vote for him,'' Laurey said. ''There's something about him that just makes you think of…backbone and integrity.''

Gage refrained from teasing her about voting for a cop; they seemed to have put that behind them—for the moment, at least—and he wanted to keep it that way.

''We'd hate to see him go, but if there's such a thing as a decent politician in the world, he'd be it.''

She looked at him for a long, silent moment. ''You said he takes care of his people,'' she said finally.

''He does. Anything happens, anybody gets hurt, he's always there, no matter when, no matter where. One of our dispatchers was in a boat accident over near Catalina, on vacation. When he found out, he flew over there to make sure she was being taken care of right. And arranged to fly her back to the mainland.''

''And what would he do if he thought the life of one of his officers was in danger?''

Gage's breath caught as the quiet, unexpected and very pointed question came at him.

''Kit seemed awfully serious,'' she said when he didn't answer. ''And I don't think she panics easily.''

''No. She doesn't.''

''But you think she's wrong.''

''I think…''

He stopped, set down the spoon he'd been carving the side of the mud pie with, and pushed the plate toward Laurey. She shook her head and pushed it toward the edge of the table, to indicate they'd eaten as much as they wanted—or could—of the rich dessert.

''You think what?'' she prompted a moment later as they gathered up their things to leave.

''I think I can't afford for her to be right,'' Gage said shortly, a little amazed that he'd admitted even that much. But then, he was constantly being amazed at what he admitted to Laurey Templeton.

He refused to let her pry any more out of him; he'd already said too much. They walked outside into the brisk fall evening, toward the parking lot where he'd left the department vehicle the chief had told him to take until he made other arrangements.

They walked down the row of parked cars. Gage took a deep breath of the crisp air; he loved this time of year and sometimes wished he lived in a place that actually had seasons, beyond the four California seasons in the old joke: fire, flood, drought and earthquake. But he knew he would probably never leave here. Too much of him was rooted here; here was the only place he could keep trying to make things right—

"Oh!" Laurey jumped sideways, bumping into him, and he automatically reached out to steady her.

"You okay? What happened?"

"I...was just startled. I didn't see the man in that white car, he must have been lying down on the seat, and all of a sudden he sat up."

Gage slowed his steps, but Laurey shook her head. "It's all right, I just didn't know anyone was in the car, and when he moved..."

She shrugged, giving an embarrassed little laugh. After a moment Gage nodded, and they walked on. He heard an engine start and guessed the car's occupant had just bent over to pick something up prior to leaving.

He had his hand on the passenger door to open it for Laurey when, for the second time in less than eight hours, the air exploded again.

Gunfire.

Chapter 10

Laurey was amazed she could hear anything over the pounding of her heart.

She was jammed up against the side of the car. Gage's body was curled over her. Protectively, she realized. *To protect and serve,* she thought inanely.

She gasped at the sound of another shot. Closer. Louder. Much closer. Much louder. She thought she must have screamed. But she couldn't be sure, not over the pulse beating in her ears. Not over the roar of a racing engine, and the screech of tires on asphalt. Another shot, just as close. And finally she realized why. It was Gage. Firing back at the car that had just speeded past them.

"Damn!"

The oath burst from him as sharply as the shots he'd fired. Laurey shivered at the icy edge in his voice. She heard a rustling, then a scraping sound she didn't recognize. Then she felt his hands on her shoulders, gripping tightly, turning her toward him, but never moving away. She could feel his heat, his strength and, given what had just happened, she felt amazingly protected.

"You're all right?"

As quickly as that the ice in his voice was gone, replaced by a husky tone Laurey, even in her shaken state, recognized as concern.

"I...I'm not hurt," she said, not certain she wanted to go so far as to say she was really all right.

"You're sure?"

He sounded urgent, and she raised her face to try to reassure him. He was close, so close, looking down at her with fear in those vivid green eyes.

Fear for her, she realized with a little jolt of shock.

She didn't know when he'd moved, but his hands were cupping her face, tilting her head back as if to convince himself that she truly wasn't hurt. His eyes searched her face, and she saw in the green depths the fear she'd heard in his voice.

"Laurey? You're sure you're not hurt?"

"I'm...fine," she managed to reply.

For a long moment she crouched there, staring as something changed in his expression, as heat flared in his eyes, burning away the last of the fear.

"Gage—"

His mouth came down on hers, cutting her off before she could say any more. And an instant later she forgot what she'd been about to say anyway, forgot it in the sudden wave of heat and sensation that radiated through her.

His lips were warm, firm, and his kiss was urgent, compelling, and she could do nothing less than respond in the same way. The adrenaline that had begun to ebb began surging through her blood anew, her heart beginning to hammer in her chest all over again. Not from fear, but from excitement. From sweet response. From the pure joy of being alive.

And suddenly she understood, understood the need for this, understood more than she ever had before. And in understanding, she wanted more. And she wanted it now, from this man.

She slipped her hands around his neck, pulling him closer. She heard a breath escape him, brushing hotly over her lips. He tasted her, probing tentatively with his tongue, and she let him in, welcoming the hot intrusion, savoring the pounding, pulsing life of it.

Crouched there in a dark parking lot, her back braced against the car, she kissed him back, eagerly, ardently. And she saw no irony in it, no oddness; it seemed utterly, perfectly right. Later, perhaps, she would wonder what had come over her, but now, now all she could do was feel. And feel she did, electric, rippling sensation and the hot, male taste of him as she threaded her fingers through pale hair that felt as silky as it looked, indulging at last in the urge she'd always felt to brush it back from his brow just so she could watch it fall forward again.

The kiss went on and on, Laurey clinging to his shoulders partly for balance, but mostly out of the need to keep him close. She needed him there, needed to feel his strength, needed to savor his heat.

With a low, deep groan he wrenched his mouth away, leaving her feeling bereft, her lips cold in the chill night. For a moment all she could hear was her own heart and his quickened breathing. He tilted his head, resting his forehead against hers, for a long silent moment.

Laurey held her breath, afraid to speak, afraid to even look at him, for fear what she would say or see would shatter the moment. And afraid that he would speak and do the same.

But he said nothing. She felt a tremor ripple through him, and then he lifted his head. As if it were a tangible effort, she sensed him steadying himself.

After a moment Gage stood, slowly, carefully. She doubted the care was for himself, and when he reached down to help her rise, she knew it; his hand was solid, steady and strong. An echo of the heat that had flooded her rippled through her again, and she tried to suppress a faint shudder of response, focusing on the hand he held out to her. His right hand, she realized as she took it and stood on legs that were none too steady. The hand he'd been shooting with, no doubt.

It hit her then, that the noises she'd heard, including the odd scraping, must have been him putting his gun away.

She looked at his face then and saw the rigid set of his jaw as he stared off in the direction the car had gone. She fought the shiver that rippled through her; this was not a man she would want to fight. This was not the boy she'd known; this was a cop who'd seen eight years of the ugliness, who'd seen people at their worst, who'd fought a battle it must sometimes have seemed impossible to win.

This was not even the man who had just kissed her with a heat and passion that had stolen what was left of her breath and sent her heart on another racing rampage.

She felt a little dazed, more even than in the instant after the shots. She'd known her feelings had changed, and in those moments when he'd betrayed that passionate hatred for the animals who sexually abused women, she'd known she'd been wrong about him, no matter what her reasons.

She didn't even wonder at her surprising empathy now; her negative feelings had always been more personal than anything else. And she hoped she'd let go of them, that she'd put away those childish feelings.

She'd better have, she thought, fighting another shiver as she instinctively dusted herself off. She'd better have, because not only had he kissed her with a fierceness that both astonished her and set her imagination soaring, but twice now this man had put himself between her and flying bullets.

She was amazed that he'd been able to move so quickly, after the accident last night.

Her breath caught. Her head came up, her gaze shooting back to his face. He turned to look at her. His forehead creased.

"My God," she whispered. "Someone really *is* trying to kill you."

"The decision is mine, Gage. And it's final. You go to the safe house."

Laurey looked from Gage's troubled face to the tall, lean man in the lightweight overcoat whose own expression was both grim and solemn as he paced the conference room outside his office, where they were all gathered. She barely knew the man, this was only the second time she'd seen him, but she had no doubts that Miguel de los Reyes's decision was just that, final. And that Gage, no matter how he obviously hated it, would abide by it. He had that much respect for the man.

She could see why. As she'd told Gage earlier—God, an eternity ago, it seemed now—there was something about the man that spoke of backbone and integrity. Tall, lean, with patrician features, dark hair silvered at the temples, he was an impressive man in his forties, with gray eyes much lighter than her own, oddly light eyes that seemed to peer into you, probing far past the surface.

This was a man to be reckoned with, and judging from the way everyone acted around him, a man who commanded— and had earned—total respect.

De los Reyes is the best, Gage had said.

It was clear he was not alone in that opinion. Everyone seated around this room obviously shared it. She thought of what Gage had told her about him, about his own near-fatal injury in a similar incident, and wondered what memories were stirring behind those cool, light eyes.

And wondered what it must have been like for his wife to be married to such a man. She must have been quite a woman, to have had this quietly strong man so in love with her that he'd almost given up when she died.

"We're already running one safe house for the family—"

"Also necessary," de los Reyes said firmly, interrupting Gage. "The girl has to be kept safe, and we don't want her family feeling any more threatened than they already do."

"But we don't have the money for a second one."

"You let me worry about the funding," the chief said.

"But the case," Gage began, stopping when de los Reyes shook his head.

"We'll work around it. You can take copies of whatever you need to prepare with you. You'll have," the chief added in a wry tone, "more than enough time."

"Right," Gage muttered.

Kit, who was on the telephone that sat on the credenza along one wall, glanced over at him, then went back to her quiet conversation. The others exchanged glances, then apparently decided to ignore Gage's disgruntlement.

"When will the house be ready?" de los Reyes asked with a glance at Ryan Buckhart, who was lolling back in one of the chairs, his long legs stretched out straight before him, a red bandanna tied around his forehead, holding his long, raven hair neatly. Even on this late Saturday night he had reappeared within an hour of their return to Trinity West, along with Cruz and Kit, and what Laurey thought had to be most of the entire detective division—minus the unwelcome Robards. Even Quisto had come by, although since he was working patrol on the streets and was quite recognizable to many people in the area, he wasn't going to be much use to them undercover, so he'd merely made sure Gage was all right, done the same with Laurey, and left to reassure Caitlin, who was worrying despite their efforts.

She was a little stunned at how quickly things had happened and at how tightly the brotherhood of the cops of Trinity West had drawn in to protect one of their own. One of their own, who had finally had to admit that he wasn't just having bad luck, a run of being in the wrong place at the wrong time. He'd been forced to agree that the string of events was beyond coincidence.

"A couple more hours," Ryan said, answering the question about the house. "The electronics guys are there now, setting up the security and scrambler radios."

Laurey glanced from Ryan back to de los Reyes in time to see the chief nod. She had noticed, after a while, that the question of who was behind the attempts on Gage's life never came up. Even when she had given her statement and done what the officer had called an Identikit, which produced a good likeness of the man she'd seen in the white car, it had seemed almost incidental, as if they knew that man wasn't the real culprit. When she'd heard the shell casings were the same size as in the first shooting, she'd asked about a direct connection, but they'd avoided a direct answer. She supposed it could be that they were reluctant to talk about it in front of her, a civilian, but the impression she got was that it didn't come up because they all knew who was behind it. They all knew who wanted him dead, and probably why.

That it was so apparent to them without discussion made her realize that they must live with this kind of thing every day, that they went through every hour of their lives knowing that there was probably somebody out there who would just as soon see them dead.

And sometimes, it seemed, discovering that there was somebody out there unwilling to wait, somebody ready to hasten things along.

She stifled a shiver, glad that Chief de los Reyes was a strong-willed man.

"That'll work out," Kit put in as she hung up the phone and walked back to her chair, dropping a yellow legal pad on the table in front of her. "The newspaper will have a truck parked and ready by then."

Laurey blinked. A newspaper truck? Whatever for?

"We'll pick it up at Fourth and Ventura at zero four hundred," Kit went on, tapping her pencil on the pad. "Cruz, you'll be driving." She grinned. "You'll be less conspicuous than Ryan would be."

"What," Ryan said, feigning hurt feelings, "you think Indians can't throw newspapers?"

"I think you'd give everybody on the route heart failure, for one reason or another," Kit said, her grin widening. "Especially the ladies."

Ryan scowled at her, but Laurey saw the corners of his mouth twitching. Amazing, she thought, how they could joke. They were obviously all intensely worried about Gage, but still the humor was there. She remembered what Gage had said, that they had to joke or it would eat them alive. She was seeing that in action, now.

"They'll have the route written out, Cruz, so you can keep to the normal schedule as much as possible. You'll just stop a bit longer than usual in one place, while your...passengers depart. But hopefully, when they hear the papers hitting, nobody will even look, knowing it's just the paperboy," she ended with a wink. "Hope your throwing arm's in good shape."

"Great," Cruz grinned. "My family used to joke about my blue eyes coming from the paperboy. Never figured I'd actually be one."

Laurey found herself smiling; Cruz's bright blue eyes were an unusual contrast to his nearly black hair and the slight bronze tint of his skin.

"You're sick, Gregerson," Gage muttered, clearly still unhappy with the proceedings. She wondered why, when it was obvious the threat had become more immediate, and more dangerous. And after all, getting killed would stop his work completely. And permanently.

Cruz's grin widened. "You'll need a pet for company," he said. "And I just happen to know where you can get one. Quiet, clean, doesn't need to be walked—"

"Oh, no," Gage said. "You're not palming off that snake of Sam's on me."

Cruz shrugged, still grinning. He was clearly teasing, and Laurey knew he wouldn't take even that hated pet away from his beloved little girl.

"Can't blame a guy for trying." Cruz glanced at Laurey and winked. "Besides, Laurey's going to need someone to talk to, for when you get in one of your moods."

Laurey blinked. "What?"

"He gets that way, sometimes," Kit said in a confiding tone that was—obviously intentionally—loud enough for all to hear. "Moody. Hard to talk to. The snake would be easier, trust me."

Laurey shook her head, thinking that somewhere along the line she'd missed something crucial. Her gaze flicked from Kit to Ryan to Cruz to Gage. At last she glanced at de los Reyes, wondering if her expression was as confused as she felt at the moment.

"It won't be for long, Ms. Templeton," the chief said kindly. "We'll put an end to the immediate threat as soon as possible, so you can get on with your life. And in the meantime, we'll make you as comfortable as we can."

"Me?" she nearly yelped.

They all looked puzzled, but no more so than she felt.

"Ms. Templeton," de los Reyes said quietly, "you're a witness. A crucial one."

"But—"

"You saw him, Laurey," Ryan said. "Well enough to give a full, thorough description."

"I know I said I could recognize him again, but—"

"That's just it," Kit said, reaching out to put a gentle hand on her shoulder.

"But nobody's trying to kill me!"

"Nobody *was*," Gage said grimly.

Laurey's gaze shifted to him. He was sitting in the chair opposite her, his elbows on the arms, his hands clasped in front of him. The nails of one hand were digging into the flesh of the other, the only outward measure of the extent of his inner tension.

"What does that mean?"

"You got a good enough look at him to recognize him again." Gage's voice was tight, and there was an undertone to it that she couldn't name. "That means the opposite is true, too."

"The oppo—" It hit her then, and her eyes widened. "You mean...he can recognize me?"

She saw the answer in his eyes. Or, rather, in the way he looked away from hers.

"It won't be for long," Kit promised her. "Really."

Laurey sank back in her chair, stunned.

"You're the only one who really saw him, Laurey," Ryan said, his deep voice a rumble that would have been comforting were it not for what he was saying. "Gage only got a glimpse as he drove by."

"It's for your own protection," Cruz said. "Just until we get this wound up."

Her? In a safe house? Like on TV, locked away, with guards, unable to leave?

"Laurey," Kit said, something in her tone making Laurey

realize she'd unknowingly begun to shake her head, "I know it sounds scary, but really, it's necessary."

The irony of it struck her then. Mere days ago she'd bristled at the very thought of Gage Butler. And now she was going to be locked up in a house with him. Then, it would have infuriated her. Now...

Now she wasn't sure how it made her feel. A lot had changed since then, including, she admitted, her view of Gage. She no longer thought of him as the ogre of her senior year of high school, even conceded that he was a rather admirable person. She no longer blamed him, not really, for what he'd done. Although she doubted she would ever approve of the tactics, she was also willing to concede that he hadn't had a lot of choice. So she knew how she didn't feel. What she didn't know was how she *did*.

Especially after that unexpected—and unexpectedly hot—kiss they had shared.

The memory made her cheeks flush. And suddenly the idea of being locked up in a house with Gage took on a whole new and different intensity.

She stole a glance at him. He was still staring down at the wood grain table in front of him, his jaw set, his forehead furrowed beneath the fall of hair that kicked forward to his brow. He was *not* happy about this. Not at all.

That Gage seemed as resistant to the idea as she was, maybe even more, somehow didn't alleviate her nervousness. She couldn't believe he didn't see the necessity of this—never mind that she didn't quite see it for herself—so that left only one explanation: It wasn't that he didn't want to be locked up, it was that he didn't want to be locked up with *her*.

She supposed she couldn't blame him, she hadn't been the nicest of people to him. But she'd hoped they had put most of that behind them. Especially now that she'd discovered how much he'd helped her, getting the charges dropped, helping with the record sealing process, and she'd never known. But perhaps she'd been...naive to think that.

But then, it was a long jump from simple forgive and forget to what had passed between them. She couldn't help thinking he regretted what happened, regretted that hot, startlingly passionate kiss. She wasn't sure how she felt about it herself, but the idea that he wished it hadn't happened, even though he had instigated it, rankled.

Was he afraid it would happen again?

Or was he afraid she would expect it to happen again?

Neither explanation comforted her much.

Chapter 11

"This is not," Laurey said emphatically, "how I'd planned to spend my vacation."

Gage sighed. She'd been pacing since she'd awakened this afternoon, when Kit had arrived with her belongings, packed up from her hotel room. And she showed no sign of slowing any time soon. He thought of telling her to stop and sit, relax, but he had a feeling he knew exactly what kind of answer he would get.

They'd both fallen into bed, exhausted, just as the sun was coming up, Laurey in the larger master bedroom at the back of the house, Gage in a smaller one closer to the front door. He'd been grateful then for how tired he'd been; it had kept him from lying awake thinking about things he shouldn't be thinking about. Like whatever had possessed him to kiss Laurey Templeton.

He knew all about adrenaline. He'd lived with it for years, and occasionally run on it for days on end; sometimes it had been all that had kept him going. He knew about the crash afterward, and how it sometimes affected your thinking.

He knew all about brushes with death, too. Knew more than

he cared to know, and had known for longer than he cared to remember. He knew how crazily people sometimes acted as a result, even those to whom it was, if not usual, at least not uncommon.

Either one would be a nice, tidy explanation.

If he believed either one.

As it was, he didn't know what he believed. Right now, what he didn't know far outweighed what he did. Like why he kept on in this crazy job. Why he kept trying when it seemed like such a hopeless battle. But most especially, why Laurey hadn't slapped him for that kiss.

Unless, of course, one of those nicely logical and convenient explanations did apply in her case. Which made, he told himself, a lot more sense than thinking she hadn't slapped him because she had enjoyed it.

He nearly laughed aloud at that idea. She'd been caught off guard, that was all, and she'd been too scared to think of anything other than the fact that she was still alive. How many times had he heard or read about such instances? How many times had he actually been involved in them? He remembered more than once when a frightened but grateful female citizen he'd saved in one way or another had thrown her arms around him and kissed him. Hell, he'd had rough, tough, grown men hug him, crying on his shoulder.

But never, ever, had he been the instigator. It was a line he knew you didn't cross, and he never had.

Until now.

And he'd done it with a woman who just days ago had attacked him at first sight. If that alone wasn't a sign that something was out of whack, he didn't know what was.

True, she had apologized for that. And rather nicely, too. And while holding a grudge this long was a bit silly, he couldn't deny she'd had reason to develop that grudge in the first place; he'd never been completely comfortable with the assignment himself. Fooling adults who'd made the choice to walk on the wrong side of the law was one thing; fooling kids who might be just victims of adolescent confusion was something else. True, it often worked—Laurey herself was proof of that—straightening out a kid who had just taken a wrong turn or two, but that didn't quite erase the memory of the looks of betrayal he'd seen.

And that memory only reminded him of that other little problem. That little matter of intense guilt regarding Laurey. If she hadn't been with him last night, she wouldn't be here with him now. If he'd taken this more seriously and thought about her instead of focusing only on the fact that he didn't want his ability to keep working up until the last moment on the Martin case compromised, she wouldn't be facing spending her vacation under house arrest.

Not to mention that she'd twice come too damned close to being shot by bullets intended for him.

He watched her pace the length of the living room one more time before he finally said, "It won't be long. The best people are working on it, and they'll have this guy wrapped up in no time."

"Anybody at Trinity West being the best?" she said, still sounding a bit sour.

"They *are* the best," Gage said simply.

"Maybe," she said, glancing at the room, which was sparsely furnished with a single, rather garish sofa, a scarred table, a couple of lamps, and a TV/VCR combination next to a CD player in a wall unit, "But they're not going to get themselves in *House and Garden*."

Gage grinned, glad to hear even a sarcastic joke from her. "Probably not. The Trinity West budget doesn't run to luxury. Most of this stuff came out of unclaimed or appropriated property, anyway."

She looked toward the window at the sound of a lawn mower starting up. She glanced back at Gage. He shrugged.

"Beresford's trying to blend in," he said, referring to their guard for the evening shift, a one-year-past-rookie patrol officer who wanted the overtime. "He's taking Ryan's shifts, so Ryan can be home with Lacey. She's due any second, I think."

Seeming diverted for a moment, Laurey nodded. "She told me at the shower that the doctor said this weekend."

Gage nodded. "And Ryan's a wreck."

"And rightfully so," she said, stopping and sitting at last, to his relief. Even if she did sit carefully on the other end of the sofa, leaning forward as if she wanted to be ready to leap up at any moment. "Caitlin told me what happened when they lost their first baby."

"He was pretty strung out. To look at them today, you'd never believe how far apart they were after that."

"Second chances," Laurey murmured, apparently staring at nothing while idly tracing the rather garish flowers of the sofa's fabric with one long, slender finger.

Gage had no idea what that meant and decided not to press his luck; she was, after all, finally sitting down instead of pacing like a caged tigress. One he was responsible for caging.

When she turned on him then, eyes narrowed, expression intent, he thought the analogy rather more apt than he was comfortable with.

"Why am I here, Gage?"

He took some small—very small—comfort in the fact that he hadn't been relegated back to "Butler," but her words struck close enough to his earlier thoughts to be very uncomfortable.

"I'm sorry, Laurey. I never meant for this to happen. I should have thought about what might happen after the first time, but all I could think about was that I couldn't keep the heat on Martin if I was under house arrest."

She gave him a rather odd look, then said, "That wasn't what I was talking about. I don't blame you for what happened. But what do you mean? Didn't Kit say he was already in jail?"

"That's just the first step. He's going to do his best to buy his way out of everything. He's already tried."

"He has?"

"He tried to bribe me, several weeks ago. To stop the investigation."

"He did?" Laurey said, eyebrows raised in surprise.

"Not personally, of course. He hired some street punk go-between. He never gets his own hands dirty."

"But you kept going."

"Of course. But I'm sure the judge, the DA and the jury will be next on his shopping list. His kind just don't believe there isn't somebody they can't buy. And too often they're right. So I have to make damn sure it won't do him any good. A tight case isn't enough, not with slime like him. It has to be perfect. It's the only way to be sure he goes down, and hard."

She looked at him consideringly, and as his words—and his vehemence—seemed to echo in the room, he wished he could take them back. But before he could dwell on it, she made the logical jump he'd been afraid she would make.

"Is he the one who wants you dead?"

He thought of saying he didn't know for sure, which was in fact true, but he didn't think it would go over particularly well.

"Maybe."

Even that didn't go over very well; Laurey's chin came up swiftly, and her tone became more than a little sarcastic. "Maybe? I gather a lot of the case is going to depend on your testimony, and your answer is 'maybe'?"

"Okay, probably."

"Why? Doesn't he know he'd be the logical suspect? And isn't it a little late, now that he's already in jail? And isn't killing a cop just going to make things even worse? And won't it just make him look even more guilty if—"

She stopped when he threw up his hands in a halting gesture. "I can't discuss a pending case," he said.

That, he realized instantly, went over worst of all; she leapt to her feet and glared down at him from her not inconsiderable height. The sound of the lawn mower outside seemed an appropriate backdrop for her obvious fury.

"Excuse me? I've been shot at twice, spent the night in a police station, and now I'm spending a vacation I've been waiting for for two years in involuntary confinement, and all you can say is you can't discuss it?"

Gage opened his mouth to answer. Then he shut it again, because there was no answer. It was a violation of procedure to involve any civilian beyond what was necessary for the success of a case. But she was also absolutely right, and he knew it as well as she did. Her entire life had been disrupted and threatened; she had the right to know why.

Besides, he had the distinct feeling that if he didn't tell her, she would walk out of here, and neither he nor the young cop outside would be able to stop her short of throwing a rope around her and tying her down.

"I...it's hard to explain," he began, stopping when her brows lowered.

"Then let's start with something simple," she said, far too sweetly. "What's he in jail for?"

He sighed. "Rape."

The dark, delicately arched brows came up, and a thoughtful expression crossed her face. "Is this...Caitlin's case? The one she told me about?"

In for a penny, he thought. "Yes."

"She's...just a kid?"

He nodded. "Sixteen. She's a juvenile, so I can't say any more about her. Except that she's a sweet, good kid, bright...and a little too trusting. That's what got her into trouble."

"Did she have...a boyfriend?"

He looked at her for a moment. "If that's your way of asking if she was...untouched..."

"That doesn't matter," she said hastily. "It never should. I just wondered where he was when this happened."

"She doesn't have one. Never has. She's very...religious. Works a lot at her church. And volunteers at charities."

Laurey shivered. "But I still don't understand. If he's in jail, how could he do this, try to have you killed?"

"A man with his kind of power can easily arrange things if he's got people crooked enough to do it for him. Which I don't doubt he does. Or he could have started it before we picked him up. It was hardly a secret that he was my primary suspect."

"But...murder?"

He sighed. "There's a chance he may have found out about

the warrant coming down. We're checking on it. That might have spooked him.''

''But…he was already in jail.''

''He could have set it up before and only given the go-ahead when the arrest was made.''

She still looked puzzled. ''But my original questions still stand. Why would he try to kill you, when he'd be the logical suspect? And if—''

Gage held up a hand. ''You have to understand Mitchell Martin. He's…beyond arrogant. He's never had to work a day in his life. He's rich. He was born to it, raised thinking the world was his playground and everybody in it subject to his whim. Including the police. Laws are meant for the peons, not royalty. And he considers himself no less than that. If he wanted, he took. And he never, ever paid.''

''Until now,'' she said softly.

''Until now,'' he agreed, not caring that grim triumph echoed in his voice.

''Did he…hurt her?''

''Physically? Some. But that's not the worst.'' He gave her a sideways look. ''Ever hear of gamma hydroxybutyrate?'' She looked startled. ''GHB,'' he said. ''Also known as liquid X, or scoop.''

She looked thoughtful for a moment. ''I don't think so.''

''How about roofies? Roachies?''

''Roofies…'' she said slowly. ''Isn't that a…drug?''

He nodded. ''Rohypnol. It's a similar thing. Hypnotic, sedative drugs.''

''The…date-rape drugs,'' she said slowly. ''Oh, God, is that what he did?''

''Yes.'' He felt the familiar burning in his gut as the memories stirred. He stood up, abruptly. ''GHB is a little different than Rohypnol. It acts a little bit faster, in fifteen to twenty minutes, and wears off sooner. But it's more dangerous, too. If the dosage is too large, it can kill. In lower doses, it makes you giddy, makes you drop your guard. By the time you realize something's wrong, it's too late, you're already in trouble. Or you may even realize something's wrong, but you just don't care.'' His mouth twisted into a bitter smile. ''It also has the advantage of being fairly easily manufactured. At home, even.''

Her eyes widened. ''You mean…somebody could just make up a batch in the kitchen?''

''If they know how, yes.''

Laurey shivered. ''That's awful. Is it true, they just dissolve in a drink, and you can't taste them at all?''

''Rohypnol, yes. GHB is sometimes bitter, but in a drink it's pretty undetectable. Until it's too late. Both of them hit fast and progress just as quickly. In this case, it was lemonade.''

''Lemonade?''

''Safer that way. Mixed with alcohol, the stuff can sometimes be dangerous, and he doesn't want them dead. Just…unable to fight.''

''Lemonade,'' Laurey said again, still sounding stunned.

He understood; it was such an…innocent drink.

''At a church carnival yet.'' At Laurey's expression, he nodded. ''Yeah. A kids' fund-raising carnival. Nice, huh? He goes in the guise of the benevolent benefactor, donating a nice bit of cash to the cause. Figures that donation should earn him something, so he picks her out of the crowd as his payment. She's a very pretty girl.''

''My God,'' Laurey whispered.

He got up and began to pace; he was never able to think about this case calmly. Only now did he realize the lawn mower had stopped. The silence seemed loud somehow. A stupid thought.

''He sweet-talks her,'' he explained. ''Gives her money to play some of the games, buys her food…all part of his charitable act. Then he slips the GHB into her lemonade, and as soon as she's wobbly enough, he leads her off as if he's concerned that she's ill, and stuffs her into the trunk of his car. She wakes up a couple of hours later…handcuffed to a bed. He…uses her most of the night, then takes her home to her parents.''

"Takes her home?" Laurey said, clearly astonished. "In person?"

Gage smiled humorlessly. "You still don't quite see it, Laurey. He picked her out specifically because she met all his criteria. She's young, innocent, pretty, Hispanic and poor."

"I don't...understand."

"Young, innocent and pretty is what he gets off on. That she's Hispanic is how he justifies it to himself. She's less than he is, so he has the right to take her if he wants."

Laurey's eyes were wide with horror as she stared at him.

"And the poor part, that's how he stays out of jail. He takes her home and offers the family, who are scraping along at poverty level, enough money to take care of them for a year. Or longer. More money than they'll ever see from honest work. Just to keep quiet."

Laurey swallowed, and he could see how this was affecting her. But she'd insisted on knowing; he couldn't help it if the reality of the answer wasn't to her liking.

"You..." She swallowed again. "You say that like he's done this...before."

"He has. I've found at least two other girls I know were his victims. But they won't come forward, and I can't prove it."

"You mean...the other families...took the money?"

"I have to assume so."

"But...this girl's didn't?"

"No, they didn't. They told him to take his filthy money and leave." His voice rang with as much pride as if it was his own family he spoke of. "Her father warned him that if he saw him near his daughter again he'd kill him. Scared Martin off with a shotgun, apparently. And then he called me."

"You? Personally?"

He nodded. "Jorge Cordero, he told her father I was...all right. That I'd do right by them."

"Is he the old man who came out the night of the acci—"

She broke off, obviously realizing that term was no longer accurate; there had been nothing accidental about what had happened that night.

"Yes," he said, letting it go. "He's helped me out a lot, putting some kids to work at the store, sometimes even kids he'd caught stealing from him in the past."

She looked at him for a silent moment. "That's a lot of trust," she said at last.

"Yes," he agreed.

"You seem to...inspire that in a lot of people."

He shrugged, not saying anything. He knew that to a certain extent it was true, but he couldn't help wondering what it would take for him to inspire that kind of feeling in her.

She looked at him for a moment, silently, intently. "Will Martin really go to prison?"

"I hope so. We broke his alibi when we finally found a reliable, independent witness who saw the man Martin claimed to be with somewhere else on the night in question. Through that we came up with a waitress who also saw him. That was the last bit we needed to get the warrant."

"What if he isn't...found guilty?"

"If he isn't," Gage said grimly, "I may hand in my badge."

"You're really determined he won't get away with this, aren't you?"

Gage pulled at the cheese to free another piece of the huge sausage pizza Cruz had brought over when he'd relieved Beresford for a dinner break. They'd invited him to stay, but Cruz had demurred, saying he had to get home as soon as Beresford got back; he'd been informed that Sam had fixed dinner tonight, and he was under strict orders to be there, and on time.

"I wouldn't argue with Samantha Jayne Gregerson," Gage had said teasingly. "She's liable to turn her zoo loose on you."

"I can deal with the regular zoo," Cruz had retorted. "It's that damned Slither."

"I thought you two had declared a truce?" Gage said. "After he helped you round up that crazy doper that had Sam."

"Let's just say we've agreed to peacefully coexist."

It wasn't until after Cruz had gone that Laurey had turned to Gage and said merely, "Slither?"

"Sam's king snake."

"The 'pet' Cruz was talking about, the one he wanted you to take?"

He nodded. "Cruz *hates* snakes."

"Then why...?"

"He hates snakes, but he loves his little girl."

"Oh." Laurey had smiled. "That's sweet."

"Careful, girl," he warned. "That's a cop you're talking about. A man might think you were starting to like them."

Instead of the rejoinder he'd expected, her usual response about it only being one cop she didn't like, she'd only given him an oddly intent look and said cryptically, "A man might."

That had silenced him until now, when Laurey had made her observation about his determination that Martin would not get away with what he'd done this time.

"I am," he admitted. "He represents everything that's wrong with the justice system, the utter and complete belief that with enough money you can buy your way out of anything. He couldn't believe it when we arrested him. He really thought he was untouchable, that we wouldn't dare."

"But you did."

"Yes. And as long as the girl and her family hang in there, we'll put him away."

"Will they?"

"I think so. They have more integrity than Martin's ever even been introduced to. And they love their daughter, something else outside Martin's comprehension. I think they'll stick it out."

He grimaced, staring at the remainder of the slice of pizza. It seemed to have lost its flavor. He'd only eaten in the first place because he knew he needed some kind of fuel to keep going. He'd never found it so hard before to do that simple thing, to just keep going. He remembered what Kit had said about hitting the wall and wondered if this was it. But it couldn't be. Not now. He couldn't afford it. The Santos family couldn't afford it.

"All I have to do is make sure the damn system works. To show them it really does level the field, that the law is for the rich and the poor alike, and that what's supposed to be true is, that all people really are equal before the law. That's the part they don't quite believe, and I can't blame them. It sure as hell seems to work that way too often."

"Do you believe it?"

He sighed. "No. Not anymore. The ideal works, but we've gotten so far away from it, so concerned with protecting the criminal that the victim gets lost.... It's no wonder they don't trust in it." Determination crept back into his voice. "But they trust me, and I'll be damned if I'll let them down."

He finished the slice, wiped his fingers, took a sip out of his bottle of soda, set it down...and only then became aware that Laurey was looking at him. Silently. Steadily.

And he could swear there was at least a trace of approval in her smoky eyes.

Chapter 12

She had finally stopped pacing, had taken a seat on the sofa. Somehow, it didn't make Gage feel much better; there was a tightly wound tension in her that seemed worse when she was still. It was late, very late, but they'd slept so long into the afternoon that neither one of them was sleepy. But they both, it seemed, were antsy as hell.

But still, he thought, it was better than watching her move back and forth across the living room with that long, leggy stride that had him thinking things he shouldn't be thinking. And remembering things better forgotten. Like that explosive, unexpectedly hot kiss last night by the car.

He'd never meant to do it. He knew it was a mistake. He knew it was a violation of, if not formal regulations, then certainly ethical police conduct. She was a witness in a felony case; you didn't mess with that.

Of course, he hadn't realized that at the time; he'd only been so damned glad she hadn't been hurt, that his failure to take seriously enough the threat on his life hadn't caused her injury or worse. But that was no excuse. She'd been frightened, and he'd taken advantage of that. That he'd been damned near scared to death himself was no excuse, either.

And even then, even knowing all that, he couldn't manage to regret it. Not when that kiss, despite its quickness, despite the ludicrous circumstances, had shocked to life nerves he'd never known he had and sensations he'd thought long dead.

"Want to send out for another movie?" he asked quickly, before he could dwell too long on thoughts that had a tendency to make his jeans a bit too snug.

"No."

He tried again. "Kelsey offered to send over some more books. Want to call her with a list?"

"No."

He sighed and asked with wry humor, "Want Ryan to stop by so you can gape at him a while?"

She looked at him then. For an instant he thought he saw the corners of her mouth twitch, but he wasn't sure. "Thanks for the offer. He's lovely, but not my type."

"I thought tall, dark and handsome was every woman's type."

"Men who are taken," she said, "are not my type. And Ryan is very much taken."

"That he is," Gage said softly, liking the quiet respect with which she'd said it. Then, before he could stop himself, he added, "I, on the other hand, am not."

She gave him a long, sideways look. "Aren't you?"

There was a wealth of innuendo in her tone, and Gage wondered just what can of worms he'd inadvertently opened. "No," he said slowly.

"Aren't you?" she repeated. "Aren't you taken, lock, stock and barrel? Aren't you owned? Isn't there something that holds you more than any mere woman ever could?"

He drew back, seeing now where she was headed and not liking it much.

"What happened with your wife, Gage?"

"She couldn't hack being married to a police officer. We were divorced five years ago."

He knew it was a cop-out, but he resorted to it anyway. And

Laurey was looking at him as if she knew it was just that, as if she knew much more than he was saying. He did a hasty revision of his assumptions about her naiveté. She might be naive, but she wasn't stupid, which was what he would be if he mistook the one with the other.

"Was it the cop she couldn't handle? Or the man who put his work before her?"

Gage fought down the heat he felt rising. How many times had Trish said it? How many times had she told him one day he was going to have to choose? And then she had chosen for him, walking out of the small house, leaving only a note behind, saying she would have told him in person, but she hadn't felt like staging a crime to grab his interest long enough to get it said.

"I…" He couldn't think of a damned thing to say. What could he say, when she was right?

"Both, huh?" Laurey said.

He lowered his gaze, staring at the toes of his worn running shoes, wishing he could put them to use now. "Just drop it, will you?"

"Oh, sure," Laurey said, her tone falsely bright. "I'm very good at not talking about—or to—workaholics. I've had lots of practice."

His gaze shot to her face. "What's that supposed to mean?"

"Nothing." She sounded suddenly weary. "It doesn't matter."

"Look, it takes time and concentration to do this damned job. To build cases against guys like Martin, to—"

"I know," she said. "I'm sorry. At least your job is…worthwhile. Does somebody some good."

As quickly as that, she'd defused his defensiveness and left him wondering just who she was comparing him to. But before he could think of a way to ask, she was looking at him, her expression very different.

"I know…from Caitlin, and Kelsey and Lacey, too, that it's not easy being married to a cop."

Glad—at least, he thought so—for the change of subject, he

shook his head. "No. No, it's not. They're tough ladies, stronger than just about anyone I know, and it's still tough."

For a long time she was silent. And when she did speak again, her voice was very low and oddly strained.

"Dealing with this kind of thing, people like this Martin, seeing such horrible things..." She paused, shaking her head, and when she looked at him again there was honest bewilderment in her eyes. "Why, Gage? Why do you do it? I know you said it was all you ever wanted to do since you were ten, but...why? And why do you remember so specifically when?"

He hesitated, but something about that look in her eyes made him speak. "I... Something...terrible happened in my family when I was ten. The police...they took care of me."

It came out awkwardly, choppily, but it was more than he'd said about it in years. And it was all he could manage, never mind that Laurey was looking at him as if he'd said much more.

"'At least then the world can't take them away from you.'"

She said it softly, as if quoting. The words sounded familiar to him. Had he said that to her sometime during the chaos of the past few days?

"Who was taken away from you, Gage?" she asked, taking his breath away with the perceptive jump she'd made.

He turned his back on her, unable to look at her and deal with the memories her simple words had set free at the same time. He walked over to the window and stared, as if he could see something through the miniblinds that were tilted to allow in light during the day while preventing any line of sight into the house. But all he saw was darkness, the distant halo of a streetlight the only illumination.

"What happened, Gage?" she asked in that same quiet, gentle voice. "What made you believe it's better not to have a family than to have one and lose it?"

She'd leapt past his guard by guessing more than most people even wondered about. The rest of the reason he'd become a cop. And then, with more quiet words, more perceptive guessing, she ripped away the last of his defenses.

"It was your sister, wasn't it? You said you'd lost a sister, too...."

"She was murdered," he said, the words ripped out of him in a voice he didn't even recognize as his own. "She was raped and murdered within twenty feet of me, and I never did a damn thing to help her."

Laurey stifled a gasp. Something Caitlin had said hit her with the force of a blow. *He takes on the worst rape cases, the ones no one else has the stomach for, even though it tears him apart inside.* Was this why? Instinctively she knew it was.

He moved suddenly, sharply, grabbing his jacket, which was tossed over the back of the couch. He held it so that she could see the mended spot on one sleeve. "She fought him. She yanked this jacket off him."

Laurey looked at him as if she felt suddenly queasy, then as if she understood too well the reason he wore the jacket of his sister's killer.

"Dear God," she whispered. "I've heard of hair shirts before, but this?"

"I should have helped her," he said, almost numbly.

"Could you have?" Laurey asked, her voice a bit shaky, as if she were fighting for calm. "Could you have helped her, if you were only ten?"

"I...should have tried. But she told me to hide. In the closet. And not to come out no matter what happened, no matter what I heard. I had to do what she said. My mother always said that, that when we were home alone, she was in charge. That I had to do exactly as she said, because she was older. She was fifteen, old enough to boss me. So I hid. Like she told me. And I didn't come out. Even when...she screamed."

He could hear himself, knew he was sounding like the child he'd been then, but he couldn't help it any more than he could seem to stop the ugly words from pouring out at the gentle probing of this woman who had turned his life into such turmoil so quickly.

"What was her name?" Laurey asked, her tone never changing.

"Debby. She was almost grown-up, she always said, especially when she wanted to do something Mom or Dad didn't want her to do. She was even starting to look grown-up, and she—"

He broke off as something cracked. The sharp sound seemed to echo in the room. He looked down at his hand, only then realizing he'd been holding the plastic rod that controlled the angle of the blinds, and that it had snapped under the force of his grip. He stared at the broken piece of plastic rather stupidly, not sure what to do with it. In that moment he came back to himself, managing to put some distance between himself and the child he could never quite leave completely behind.

And he realized Laurey had risen and crossed the room to stand close behind him.

"What happened to her, Gage?"

God, couldn't she let it be? "Haven't you heard enough ugliness for one day?"

"Yes," she said honestly. "But I...need to hear the rest." Then she reached out and gently lifted the broken piece of plastic from his hand. "And I think you need to tell it."

He drew a long breath. He opened his mouth to tell her to forget it. To tell her to forget what he'd already said, because he wasn't about to say any more. To tell her that he wasn't going to talk about it, because he never talked about it. Ever. To anyone.

Instead, other words came tumbling out, as if they'd been lined up behind a dam that had suddenly been breached.

"As far as we know it was a random daytime burglary. Debby had just picked me up from school. I always stayed after in the library until she got out. She'd come get me, and we'd walk home together." A faint smile flickered across his lips, but faded so quickly he was barely aware of it. "She never seemed to mind her little brother hanging around. When we got home, she was going to make a cake. To celebrate our mother's first day at a new job. She was putting it in the oven when...it happened."

"The burglar broke in while you were in the house?"

He nodded, still not looking at her. "The kitchen was at the back of the house. He broke in at the front, into the living room. We heard the glass break. He was grabbing stuff, the silver, my dad's coin collection. That's when she made me go hide. She said she was going to call the police. And that as soon as she did, she'd come hide with me until they got there."

His jaw tightened, and he nearly trembled at the strength of the memories he'd fought for so long.

"I…heard her screaming. Heard a man laughing. Low and ugly. I wanted to go to her, but she'd made me promise to stay there, no matter what. Then…it got quiet."

He stopped, literally unable to go on. He had to get out of here, had to get outside.

But he couldn't. He couldn't leave this house. He was trapped, as much a prisoner as Martin. More so; Martin would be out sooner than he would, no doubt.

His body was screaming with the need to move, reacting to the desperate signals from his mind to get away from what could never be left behind. To save him from the brutal memories he couldn't flee, because they were carried with him always.

He shivered, realizing it was but the latest of many, that he'd been shaking for he didn't know how long. Countering the vicious chill was a creeping, soothing warmth, a comfort he'd never felt before. It took him a moment to realize it came from Laurey, from her arms around him, holding him, hugging him tightly, so tightly it almost stopped the trembling.

"You couldn't have done anything, Gage. You were just a little boy. You would have died, too. Do you think your sister would have wanted that?"

He heard her words, heard the quiver in her voice, felt the unexpected strength of her arms as they held him. She fit him neatly, he thought a little wildly, and the feel of her head against him, her cheek pressed against his shoulder, was comforting in a way he didn't quite understand.

"That's…that's what the cop said," he managed to get out

after a moment. "Officer Sorensen. The first one there. He kind of...took care of me for a few days, after..."

"You know he was right," she said. "You couldn't have stopped it. You would only have gotten killed, too." She didn't speak for a moment, until his trembling had lessened. Then, "You said he took care of you?"

The question she didn't ask was implicit, and he answered what he guessed she really wanted to know. "My folks...sort of fell apart. Mom never quite got over the shock, and my father...he was so angry he could barely function. I think they...forgot about me for a while. That cop was the only one who..."

"Realized what *you'd* been through?" she prompted gently when he couldn't go on.

He nodded. "He came back to the house several times. When he saw my mother was so...out of it, and my dad wasn't able to deal with it all, he...took care of me. Took me out, away from the house and them, let me talk about it, like they never would. He even took me to a psychologist who specialized in trauma in children. I didn't realize until later that he'd paid for it himself, because my parents didn't..."

"Care?" she asked softly.

He let out a long, shuddering breath. "They did, I think. They just couldn't deal with what had happened. I was one thing too many for them then. It didn't get much better. Mom started drinking a lot, and so did Dad, and they both just got angrier and angrier."

"Is that why...you don't drink?"

"Mostly." He closed his eyes. "They split up a couple of years later. It wasn't even very ugly, the divorce. They just wanted to get rid of all the reminders."

Laurey went very still against him. "Including you?"

"Apparently. I haven't seen either of them in years."

"God, I am so sorry, Gage. For your sister, your parents, but most of all for you. You really...slipped through the cracks, didn't you?"

There was so much pure sincerity in her tone that, to his amazement, it was like salve on an old wound that had never healed. He opened his eyes, and when he went on, his voice was steadier, and he thought he had the shakes under control. But he didn't tell her that he was all right now; if she wasn't inclined to let go of him, he wasn't about to suggest it.

"Not really." He shrugged, not wanting her to feel sorry for him. "It wasn't like they just…dumped me. I ended up with my aunt Jenny. They gave her the house in return for her taking custody of me. She did her best, even though I…wasn't the easiest kid to deal with by then. But we did okay. And Ray—Officer Sorensen—always checked up on us, to make sure we didn't need anything."

"So…he's really why you decided to join the force?"

He nodded. "I was determined to be the kind of cop he'd been. Sort of…to pay him back, since he would never take anything else."

"Where is he now?"

"Retired, living the good life in Arizona, by the river."

"And your aunt?"

He smiled then. "She just got married. For the first time. She's off living in London with her new husband, who's ten years younger than she is, and they're having a great time."

Laurey leaned back to peer up into his face, as if she didn't quite believe him.

"It's true," he insisted. "He's a BBC exec of some kind, and he was out here for some international communications conference or something. Aunt Jenny worked for one of the sponsoring companies, and the rest, as they say, is history."

Laurey smiled, a soft curving of her mouth that made Gage all too aware of just how close she was, too aware that she was pressed against him from knee to cheek, that he could feel every womanly curve of her, that he could smell the faint scent of peaches from her recently shampooed hair, that her arms were still around him, offering a comfort he'd never expected nor thought possible.

A comfort that was rapidly shifting, changing to something else, changing to slow growing heat that was radiating through him as he looked down at her.

"Laurey," he murmured.

"What?"

He shook his head, slowly.

She gave him a quizzical look. "Just Laurey?"

"Not *just*," he said softly.

And then, all his fine warnings forgotten, he was kissing her. Gently, almost tenderly, silent thanks for the kindness she'd offered, for the quiet understanding, for the compassionate listening to the story that had haunted him for nineteen years.

But however the kiss started, it soon became something else. Something less gentle than urgent, something less warm than hot. And the moment he knew she was with him, the moment her fingers tangled in the thick hair at his nape, the moment she exerted the slightest pressure at the back of his head as if to hold his mouth to hers, he was lost.

He didn't think about how long it had been, about adrenaline, violations of ethics or brushes with death. He didn't think of any of it, because he couldn't think at all. None of it mattered anyway, not here, not now, not with this woman in his arms, not with her lips so soft and warm and sweet under his, not when she was welcoming him, making him shudder as violently as he had when the horror had nearly overcome him.

Nothing had ever matched the power of the nightmare. Nothing had ever been able to take him out of the brutal memories, he'd always had to simply ride them out.

Until now.

Now there was nothing in his mind of ugliness, nothing of blood and pain and harsh remembrance. There was only Laurey and the sweet, giving, honeyed taste of her mouth, the feel of her long, slender body in his arms.

His tongue brushed hers, and he felt her shiver slightly. Just that tiny response set up an echo in him, and he felt his muscles tighten. Then, tentatively, her tongue returned the favor, sliding over his own, sending a jolt through him that seemed to explode somewhere low and deep, hardening him in a rush. He groaned under the assault of his senses; it had been a long time, and maybe his memory wasn't that sharp right now, but he couldn't recall ever having gotten so hot so fast.

His hands slid down her back, tracing the arrow straightness of her spine, stopping at her waist, his fingers spreading as his thumbs rested above her hipbones. He deepened the kiss, probing, driving, needing. And when he withdrew, she returned the favor, tasting him almost hungrily, in a way that was about to drive him out of his mind.

His hands tightened at her waist, and he pulled her hips closer, needing the heat and pressure of her against his swelling flesh more than he needed to breathe. She didn't resist; in fact, she moved sinuously against him, as if she wanted to caress him with the gentle curve of her lower belly. He tore his mouth away, her name breaking from his lips, sharply, as a flash of heated sensation ripped through him.

He heard her murmur something, maybe his name, maybe not. It didn't matter. Nothing mattered, except that he had to kiss her again, had to taste that—

"Butler! Get on the damn radio, will you?"

The yelp from the entryway came from Beresford who was approaching the end of his lengthy shift. Laurey went very still, even as color flooded her face, and Gage realized she'd forgotten they had a potential audience just outside.

"Copy," Gage managed to say, although he wasn't sure what he sounded like. Of course, he wasn't sure he cared, either.

He looked back at Laurey, who refused to meet his gaze, lifting her hands to her cheeks as if trying to cool them. He released her and walked over to the brown Formica bar, which held the special scrambler pacset. It wasn't perfect, but it was safer than a cellular phone, or even a regular wired phone, from being monitored or tapped. Clearly Beresford had gotten the prearranged coded page that meant there was information Gage needed.

He picked the pacset up out of the charger and turned it on, turning the scrambler to the decided upon setting.

"Gage, you there? How do you copy?"

"You're ten-two, Kit," he said; clearly the radio was working fine. "What's up?"

"Just thought you should know, Martin made bail."

"Damn. When?"

"About an hour ago."

"Bondsman?"

"Yep. Not one of the regulars, though. Seems most of them turned him down for some reason. You didn't have anything to do with that, did you?"

"Moi?" he asked innocently. "Of course not. All I did was ask them to let me know if one of them decided to go for it."

There was a moment of radio silence, and Gage could almost hear Kit chuckling. Then her voice came through the small speaker again.

"Anyway, guess this one figures he's good for it, one way or another. Or maybe Martin harangued his lawyer into putting up the money. But I thought you should know he's out. Happy Sunday."

"You'll be watching him?"

"As much as we can without getting slapped with harassment charges," Kit promised. Then, with a grin he could almost hear, "Maybe a little more."

"Thanks. I'd just as soon he didn't have another chance at me."

"Anytime, pal. I kind of like working with you."

"Ditto," he said.

"And I like that lady of yours, too," Kit said.

Gage froze. Why did people persist in saying that? He knew Laurey must have heard it, but he didn't dare look at her. He knew she would be embarrassed. And he was afraid the sudden wish that it was true would be showing in his face.

"Just get us out of here," he told Kit.

Before I try to make it the truth, he added silently.

He slammed the small radio back in the charger with a lot more force than was necessary.

Chapter 13

I was determined to be the kind of cop he'd been.

What he'd said echoed in Laurey's weary mind, and she wondered if he had any idea how well he had succeeded at that goal. He was exactly the kind of cop the man who'd helped him had been.

She'd finally had to admit that he probably helped as many kids as he arrested, perhaps more. And that he got slime off the streets for the protection of people who sometimes—as she had—disliked cops for no good reason. And sometimes risked his life for those same people.

All in all, an admirable man. Beyond admirable, really. Perhaps it wasn't so awful after all, that the attraction she'd felt for him eight years ago was apparently still alive and well....

She shivered inwardly. The memory of that kiss last night had a power to shake her that astounded her. Neither of them had mentioned it; in fact, neither had ever even acknowledged that it had happened at all. Just as they hadn't acknowledged the first one, the one she'd determinedly written off as a reaction to nearly being killed. She knew what her reasons were—sheer terror of her own response and what it might mean—but she doubted his reasons were anything more complex than wanting to forget something that shouldn't have happened.

Laurey shook her head once, sharply. She'd always thought herself open to new ideas, never thought herself so set in her ways that she couldn't change her mind, so why was this change causing her so much inner turmoil?

Because this time her heart was at stake.

She answered her own question with a truth that nearly took her breath away. The attraction she'd felt years ago for the young Gage *was* still alive. It might have lain dormant, hidden under layers of resentment and anger for all those years, but clearly it had required only a little attention to spring back to life.

Attention in the form of being confronted with evidence proving him to be the kind of man she admired, not the traitor she'd once thought him. Attention in the form of his concern for her emotional state while he was bleeding from physical injuries of his own. Attention in the form of his putting himself in the path of gunfire to keep her safe.

Attention in the form of hot, pulse-pounding kisses that roused a response that stunned her. In her entire twenty-six years she'd never felt anything like the humming, crackling sensations that had rippled through her when Gage kissed her. Smothering a gasp she feared would be audible, she lifted her head to look at him across the kitchen table.

Head down, thick, shiny blond hair kicking forward over his forehead, he was reading a newspaper Ryan had brought by late last night. Of all the detectives, they'd decided Ryan, for all his distinctive appearance, was the one who would be least likely to betray the real purpose of the house; not many would suspect the big man with the long, flowing dark hair and Native American face to be a cop.

He hadn't stayed long. He wouldn't say so, but Laurey guessed he was worried about Lacey. She had been due this weekend, but there had been no sign of impending labor. She felt fine, he said. In fact, he said it repeatedly. So often that Laurey knew he was trying desperately to convince himself.

It gave her the oddest feeling inside, to see this big, powerful man so rattled at the prospect of something—anything—happening to the woman he loved. Just the idea that a man like that could love so very much, so deeply, made her wonder....

When she realized what she really meant, that just the idea that a dedicated cop could still put a woman above his job made her start thinking crazy things, she had retreated to her room, certain her ridiculous and chaotic thoughts would be showing on her face.

Unfortunately the night that followed hadn't been any less chaotic. The chaos was of a different, more disturbing kind, though; every time she fell asleep she seemed subject to vivid dreams of what would have happened had Kit not called on the radio and interrupted them.

And every time she woke, her heart hammering in her chest, her body flooded with a sapping, languorous longing she barely recognized as desire, she fought the same battle. Even if she had set aside her childish resentments, even if she did admit that she was as much attracted to him now as she had been eight years ago, that still left a final, undeniable fact. Gage Butler was a man obsessed with his work. And she'd sworn that if she never did anything else right in her life, she would never, ever get involved with a man like that. She would never, ever set herself up for the kind of life her mother had led, grateful for the tiniest crumb of attention while she kept a house and family going virtually on her own, because her husband had no time for anything that took time away from his work.

At least your job is worthwhile. Does somebody some good.

Her own words came back to her now, in the light of morning. Did it really matter? Did it make any difference that what Gage was doing was so unlike her father's single-minded financial dealings, his concern only with accumulating more wealth and status?

She knew it did. She knew that it would be wrong to really compare the two men, they were so vastly different both in temperament and approach. As different as the motivations behind their obsessions. Gage was driven by a compulsion based in memories so grim they even haunted her own thoughts. The fact that he still lived in the house where his sister had died, that he wore the jacket she'd torn from her murderer as if it were some sort of talisman, only confused her further; she didn't know whether to be sorry or horrified.

But the basic difference was evident. Gage was driven by the memory of a sister he loved, something Laurey was intimately familiar with. Her father, on the other hand, had a much simpler motivation: greed.

Not that there was anything wrong with wanting to be a business success, but her father's drive was not just for money, it was for position, to feed his already sizable ego. His sole goal in life had been to one day move out of Marina Heights and into the more elite Marina del Mar, both physically and socially. And he'd been willing to sacrifice anything—including his wife and children—for the furtherance of that goal.

While Gage was equally determined to help people—and willing to sacrifice his life to do it.

She stifled a shiver at the memory of him crouched over her, at the realization of how easily one of those bullets he'd been shielding her from could have hit him.

"You all right?"

She snapped back to the present to find he'd looked up from the newspaper spread out on the table and was watching her with some concern.

More, she thought wryly, than her mother had ever gotten out of her father at the breakfast table.

"You were looking...pretty intense," he said, when she didn't speak.

"I was...thinking about my father," she said, thinking it was the safest part of the truth she could give him.

He seemed to hesitate for a moment, then asked, "What about him?"

She could hardly tell him that she'd been comparing them, so she quickly grabbed at the last thing she'd been thinking. "About how mad he was at me for wanting to stay at Marina Heights High after we'd moved to Marina del Mar."

Gage looked puzzled. "Why? You moved right before your

senior year, right?'' At her look of surprise, he shrugged. ''Your mother mentioned it, that since you were about to graduate, you'd gotten permission to finish there, with your class, instead of transferring. It's not that unusual to get an out-of-district exception under those circumstances.''

''I wasn't surprised that you knew, just that you remembered after all this time,'' she said. And was gratified to see him look at first startled, then almost embarrassed, by the obvious implications.

''So why was he mad?'' The question came quickly, as if he wanted to avoid any further inadvertent admissions about just how much he knew and remembered about her, and why.

Telling herself that she was being foolish to think such things, to read anything at all into his reactions, Laurey explained. ''His entire life was centered around 'making it,' which in his eyes was getting out of Marina Heights.''

''But you lived in Trinity West. That's not exactly a slum.''

''I know.'' The west side of Marina Heights was a transitional neighborhood, where the area changed from the poorer east side and headed down to the ocean and the wealthier communities. ''But to him, nothing less than Marina del Mar would do. And when he finally made it, it infuriated him that I didn't want to transfer to Marina del Mar High School.''

''It's…a nice school,'' he said noncommittally.

''I know. Lisa went there for a year when Marina Heights High was being rebuilt, right before I started. That's where she met Caitlin. But when they finished, Marina Heights was nice, too. And all my friends were there. I didn't want to leave and graduate with a bunch of strangers.''

Gage looked down at the paper, fiddling with a corner of it. ''Maybe…your father was worried.''

''Worried?''

''About who…some of your friends were. Maybe he wanted to get you away from them.''

She laughed. ''My father? He barely remembered my name. He had no idea who my friends were, and he didn't care.''

Gage's head came up. She didn't think she'd sounded particularly bitter, but he looked at her as if he could see every bit of the pain hidden by her purposely light tone. Maybe he could, she thought. He'd obviously had enough experience doing the same thing, hiding remembered pain beneath an unruffled exterior.

"The only reason," she said carefully, "that he was angry was that it embarrassed him among his *new* friends to say that his daughter went to Marina Heights. He wanted to give the impression he'd always been wealthy, that he'd moved here from some other wealthy town, not just moved 'up' from Marina Heights."

"Ah," Gage said. "One of those." She looked at him, startled by his knowing tone. He shrugged. "Quisto says they run into a lot of those in Marina del Mar. They tend to…stand out. Flashy cars, Armani suits, Rolexes. When the real old money tends to run around in cutoffs and old dock shoes."

Laurey laughed, and it was genuine this time. "You just described my father to a T. At least, the last time I saw him."

"Which was?"

He'd earned it, she supposed. He'd certainly told her enough about himself, although she doubted he would have had it not all come boiling to the surface so abruptly.

"A couple of years ago, on his way to a business meeting in Seattle, he called me to meet him at the airport for coffee."

Gage blinked. "Coffee at the airport?"

"It was all the time he could spare." The bitterness crept through that time, although she suspected he would have guessed even if it hadn't. "He had business to attend to."

"I gather this was a regular thing?"

"My father has his priorities. I accepted long ago that his family was way down on the list."

"I…see."

She wondered exactly what he saw, and why it was making him look so pensive. Then, suddenly, his brows furrowed.

"You said you last saw him a couple of years ago?" She nodded. "But what about…?" He hesitated before going on gently, "Your sister? Her funeral?"

Laurey felt her face stiffen. "He couldn't…make it. He was in New York. On business."

Gage swore, low and harsh under his breath. And Laurey felt a stab of pleasure at the sound of it. She truly didn't care for her own sake, not anymore, but the way he'd deserted her sister, even in death, had destroyed any lingering hope she'd ever had that anything would ever change.

"I'm sorry, Laurey. People just…shouldn't be parents if they're not willing to…do what it takes."

And what about you, Gage? she wondered. *Will anything ever be as important to you as your work? Will you ever ease up, admit that you can't do it all? Or will the work own you forever, just as it owns my father?*

"You should be proud," he said, his voice quiet now. "A lot of kids with…parents like that end up really messed up. I know, I deal with them every day."

"I deal with them, too," she said, looking at him very steadily. "And the most painful thing I've had to learn from working at the rehab center is that I can't help them all. No one can."

She saw his jaw tighten, knew she'd struck home. He quickly shifted his gaze back to the newspaper spread out on the table before him. After a moment, when it became clear he wasn't about to explore that topic, she sighed and fished out a piece of the paper to read.

It was the front page, and Mitchell Martin's arrest was headline news.

Gage photographed well, she observed, thinking for a moment with a magazine advertiser's eye. If he'd ever wanted to go into modeling, he could have been rich. For a moment she pondered the striking possibilities of an ad featuring Gage's bright blondness flanked by Quisto's aristocratic features and Ryan's exotic darkness, then quashed the thought with an inward chuckle; three more unlikely choices would be hard to come up with. None of the three men was particularly impressed with his own looks, something she found rather refreshing.

But when she looked at the face of the handcuffed man Gage was leading into the city jail, a chill swept over her. The grim story of what he'd done came back to her in a rush. He looked like the people Gage had spoken of, with his fancy clothes and jewelry, but not like a man with a twisted mind, a man who would drug and rape a virginal young girl, then offer her family money, as if she were no more than a prostitute to be paid for and then forgotten.

But at the moment this photo had been taken, he looked quite capable of murder.

"He looks outraged," she murmured. "As if you were in the wrong and he was utterly righteous."

"That's exactly how he feels," Gage said. "And I'm sure he feels killing me to get me out of his way is merely...a necessity."

She looked up at him and saw the glow of determination in his eyes again, and knew that if it were humanly possible, Gage Butler would see that this man would pay for what he'd done. And in that moment she understood; if there was ever something it could be right to be obsessed about, it would be the kind of justice Gage was dedicated to.

"How do people get like that?" she asked, more rhetorically than anything.

"You'll have to ask Kit. She's the one who figures out that kind of thing."

"Kit?"

"She's taken a lot of classes, psychology, criminal profiles, that kind of thing. She can pull motives out of thin air, it seems like sometimes. She's the one who figured Martin out, why he feels so...invulnerable."

"I'll bet he doesn't now," Laurey said, looking back at the photo of Martin in handcuffs with some satisfaction.

"According to Kit, now he's just mad."

She shifted her gaze back to his face. "At you?"

Gage shrugged. "Probably. I popped him. He isn't the type to forgive public humiliation."

"So...he'll be after you more than ever?"

He looked uncomfortable, as if he hadn't wanted her to realize that. "Maybe."

"So we're back to that? You won't discuss it?"

"It doesn't matter. We'll be safe as long as we're here."

"And just how long will that be?" she asked, her voice rising. "Days? Weeks? Months?"

"They'll find the guy he hired, Laurey."

"But now that he's out, won't he just hire somebody else?"

"He may try, but we're on to him now, and we can turn the heat up pretty high. He'll have trouble finding anybody willing to take it on."

"But he could find someone."

"Eventually, maybe. But with any luck, he'll be in prison first."

"And what's to stop him from keeping after you, even if he does go to prison?"

He let out a long sigh as he shoved back his hair with one hand, and she watched with a fascination she didn't want to feel as it slid silkily back over his forehead. "You're determined to make the worst of this, aren't you?"

She was yanked out of her silly contemplation of his hair.

"Pardon me!" She stood up so abruptly that she nearly knocked over her chair. "I'm just not able to dismiss the idea of hired killers so easily."

She turned on her heel and walked out of the kitchen.

Gage watched her stalk off, knowing with a sinking in the pit of his stomach that she had every right to be angry. He'd tried to reassure her, but she'd clearly thought he was making light of her fears. Fears that were valid, very much founded in reality. He should go after her, apologize, do something.

You should sit right here on your butt and let her go, he told himself sternly. *Didn't you learn anything last night?*

He'd spent most of the night lying awake wondering where the hell his head was at. Wondering why he hadn't been relieved that they'd been interrupted by Kit's news, since he had no time for a relationship in his life, no time for anything that would take away from his work.

Apparently he hadn't learned anything, because he wasn't relieved now, either. Wasn't relieved that she had walked away from him, angry again. Wasn't listening to his own good advice to leave well enough alone, to be glad she was angry, and hope she was upset enough to just stay away. To take temptation out of his path and leave him to get on with life as usual.

You're using your job to hide from life. You just keep on like you always have, nothing in your life but your work.

What Kit had said a few days ago echoed in his mind. Was she right? Was he using his work to hide from life? Was he over the edge?

You've got to find some balance. You're bordering on obsession here.

Kit clearly thought he was far too close to that edge. Kit was very, very perceptive. And she had training to back up her perceptions. Could she be right? He'd always known he was intense about his work, but he'd always told himself he just had different priorities than—

My father has his priorities. I accepted long ago that his family was way down on the list.

This time it was Laurey's words that came back to him, as clearly as if she had just spoken them. He hadn't cared much for the portrait she'd painted of her father. He liked even less that he'd subconsciously connected himself with the man.

He wondered if Laurey had done the same. Perhaps even consciously.

And before he realized he was moving, he was headed down the narrow hall to the room she was using. He knocked before he could talk himself out of it.

Her muffled response could have been "Come in" or "Go away." He chose to think it was the former and opened the door. She was sitting cross-legged on the double bed, a glossy magazine balanced open across her knees. She was looking at him, her expression unreadable.

"Checking out the competition?" he asked, hating how forced he sounded in his effort to be upbeat.

She glanced at the magazine, then back at him. "Did you want something?" she asked formally, ignoring his obvious conversational gambit. She wasn't going to make this easy. But then, he supposed he didn't deserve for it to be easy.

"About what I said... You have every right to be upset. I

know your...whole life has been disrupted. I was...out of line to belittle what you were feeling.''

She said nothing, and he rammed his fingers through his hair, shoving it back.

''I...overreacted. Probably because I know you're right. Maybe because I'm supposed to protect civilians from...this kind of thing. But that's no excuse, either.'' He took a deep breath, thinking he should give up; he didn't appear to be getting anywhere. ''Must be cabin fever, I guess,'' he ended lamely.

''After a day and a half? That's not promising.''

His mouth twitched at the corners, but he stopped the threatening smile; he wasn't positive she was joking. ''No. It's not. I'm not used to...being cooped up.''

''Neither am I,'' she said pointedly.

''I know. I don't like this any more than you do.'' Then his mouth did twist into a very wry smile. ''Well, most of it,'' he amended. *In for a penny,* he thought, and added, ''Some of it I liked a lot.''

Her eyes widened and searched his face, as if looking for some hint that he really meant what it seemed he was referring to. He knew perfectly well why; they'd avoided the topic, had talked about everything but, had dug into painful pasts deeper than either of them probably had in a long time...but this, by a seeming tacit agreement, had been off-limits. He wasn't even sure why he'd brought it up.

He wasn't sure he'd had a choice.

''I...shouldn't have kissed you.'' His voice was tight, and he heard her suck in a quick breath, as if his words had hurt. ''It's in violation of more ethical and moral standards than I can list right now. I should feel guiltier than sin, and I do, but...''

She started to speak, stopped, and he saw her swallow before she forced the word out. ''But?''

''I'm not sorry,'' he said, sounding a little reckless, just as he felt. ''I should be, but I'm not.''

''You're...not?''

He shook his head. "I'm...a lot of things. Guilty. Worried. Scared. But not sorry."

There was a silent moment, and he stood there wondering just how big a fool he'd made of himself.

When she finally did speak, she asked the last thing he'd expected.

"Scared?"

He nodded slowly.

"Of what?"

He hesitated. He wasn't sure why, but he had the oddest feeling that he was at some kind of turning point. And that he didn't have any idea how significant it might be.

"I'm...not sure," he said, honestly enough. "Maybe I'm afraid Kit's right."

"Kit?"

"She told me...I was using the job to hide."

Laurey closed the magazine. For whatever reason, he had her attention now. "From what?"

"Life, she said." He gave her a rueful look. "What she *meant* was from..."

"From?" Laurey prompted.

He sighed. "I've...never been much good at...maintaining any kind of relationship. Not just...with a woman, but... anything. Anything that..."

"Interfered?"

Her voice was quiet, and he saw in her face what he'd guessed at earlier; her father had taught her well about men who let their jobs control them. She clearly suspected he was one of them.

And he wasn't at all sure she was wrong.

He looked at her for a moment, seeing the troubled concern in her eyes, the soft, gentle set of her mouth, the slightest of lines between her brows as she concentrated on him. Solely on him. Her intentness warmed him in a way he'd never known before, perhaps had never allowed before. How could her father have thrown this away?

"I don't...want to be like your father, Laurey," he said suddenly, wondering where the hell it had come from.

"You're not like him. Not really." Her certainty startled him. "You may be…as driven, as obsessed with your work, but it's for entirely different reasons. Better reasons."

"Does that really make…a difference?"

"It does." She took a long breath. "It might be just as hard to…live with, but at least…it's understandable."

"I…thank you. I think."

"You're…a special kind of man, Gage Butler. I'm sorry it took me so long to see that."

He nearly gasped aloud; he'd never expected to hear such a thing from her. "Watch it, lady," he said, his tone teasing but his voice impossibly husky. "You're going to end up getting kissed again."

She looked up at him steadily for a long, silent moment during which he could swear his heartbeat was echoing in the small room. His muscles tensed, he told himself it was in preparation to run, but he feared it was simply to keep from dropping to his knees right beside the bed she sat on.

"Oh, I hope so," she said softly.

He did go to his knees then. She didn't have to hope twice.

Chapter 14

In some still functioning part of her mind, Laurey recognized the foolishness of it, the foolishness of caring for a man whose job was his life. But she'd also learned well the uncertainty of life itself, remembering how her sister had postponed so many things she wanted to do, thinking she had all the time in the world. But no one had all the time in the world.

And she knew deep down that if she didn't take advantage of this moment, she would always wonder, through whatever time she did have, what she had missed. Whether it was the belated fulfillment of some childish fantasy, she didn't know. And at this point, she didn't care. She couldn't, not when he was kissing her so deeply, not when he was holding her so tightly. Not when, as close as he was, stretched out on the bed beside her, she wanted him even closer.

She'd dreamed of this, eight years ago. Well, not exactly this; she hadn't known enough to picture this at a virginal eighteen. She'd known what she'd heard from her girlfriends' gossip since she'd been about fifteen, but most of it had been couched in terms she hadn't really understood until much later, when she'd found out for herself during her single relationship that had become serious. On her side, at least.

And even if she had understood, she knew deep down it wouldn't have mattered, because nothing could have prepared her for this. Nothing could have prepared her for the onslaught of sensation that Gage unleashed in her with the lightest of kisses, the slightest of touches.

She found his fumbling with her clothes oddly moving; when he muttered an apology for his clumsiness, because it had been so long for him, she nearly wept. And nearly wept again at the sight of the bruises that marked him, a stark reminder of the fragility of life. Particularly a cop's life.

When at last they were naked together, and he'd looked at her with a touch of awe and whispered that he'd known eight years ago that she would someday blossom into this lovely woman, she did weep.

"I knew," he insisted, his voice so soft and husky it sent a shiver down her spine. "I knew someday you'd be this beautiful. I knew you'd grow into your height, and that someday all the guys who only saw how much taller you were than them would kick themselves."

"I...wasn't taller than you," she said, knowing it was inane, wishing she could think of something to say that would make him feel the way he was making her feel.

"No. But I couldn't do anything about it."

Because he'd been married at the time. And he would not betray those vows, no matter what shape the marriage was in. She was sure of that; it just wasn't in his makeup.

She ran her hands over his shoulders, down the muscled length of his arms. She looked at the soft thickness of his hair, gleaming in the afternoon light. She let her gaze drift down over his bare chest, not daring to let herself look any farther.

"You," she said softly, "were the most beautiful thing I'd ever seen." He went still. "I know," she said ruefully. "I know you've been told that before. Probably often."

"Maybe," he agreed, and she silently thanked him for not denying what she knew was true. "But not often by someone I...wanted to hear it from."

Her breath caught; he was looking at her so intently, with such heat in his eyes, that there was no doubting his meaning.

"Gage," she said, then stopped. There was nothing more to say, really. But something in her voice must have hinted at the emotions behind that utterance of his name, because he moved quickly to gather her into his arms.

She nearly gasped at the erotic shock of it, her skin against his as he pressed their bodies together. His mouth came down on hers, swallowing the tiny sound she made as his hands slid up and down her back from shoulder blades to waist in a long, slow stroking that made every inch of her tingle. He kissed her deeply, hungrily, with an urgency that matched the stroking of his hands.

No one had ever kissed her like this, with such need. No one had ever started such an answering fire in her, a fire that made her want to taste him just as thoroughly, to touch him just as much—no, more, much more. She wanted to explore every masculine inch of him, from the thick silk of his hair to the slightly darker gold thatch that surrounded the most masculine inches.

She'd always wondered what was missing in the kisses she'd known before, or if she just had foolish ideas about what could happen with a kiss. Now she knew what had been missing. It had been this man. This man who had set her heart racing at eighteen, and set it hammering now. Had she known, then, even in her youth and innocence, that he was the one who would do this? Had she somehow sensed it, that he was the one whose touch could send her flying? And had it been that more than anything that had drawn her to him? More than his golden looks, more than the edge of danger, the secret side she had sensed in him, even then?

She didn't know. And right now she didn't care, because he had slid his hands down to her hips and was pulling her tight against him. She heard him make a low sound, and in a rush she realized that he was fully aroused and pressing against her belly. Instinctively she moved, savoring the feel of that hard, male flesh in a way she'd never done before, had never wanted to before. He made that sound again, deep in his throat, and it sent the blood pulsing through her in hot, heavy beats.

She wanted to hear that sound again and again, and more, she wanted something more, something to tell her he was feeling as she was, hot, reckless, and rapidly heading out of control.

He rolled on top of her, and she nearly cried out herself at the feel of his weight, shocked that it felt so good, so right. Then he wrenched his mouth from hers and gave her exactly what she had needed to hear.

"Laurey," he said, his voice raspy, "if you want to stop, say so now. Please. Because if you wait much longer, it'll just about kill me."

She stared up at him. He wasn't giving her an ultimatum, he wasn't saying stopping was now or never. He *would* stop, anytime she said so. It would just cost him more if she let things go on and then called a halt.

Of course he would stop, she thought rather dazedly through the haze that had seemed to envelop her the moment she'd felt herself pressed down by his body on hers. Gage would never force this. His life was dedicated to making sure no woman ever had to do this unwillingly or under duress. And in that instant she knew that, while it might not change the fact that he was dedicated to the point of obsession with his work, what that work was *did* make a difference. To her.

"I don't want to stop," she whispered.

He muttered something under his breath that sounded like an oath or a prayer, she couldn't be sure. Then, his voice even more strained, he asked, "Are you...on anything? Pills?"

The question jolted her; she hadn't even thought about it. That it had been Gage who had asked, that it had been he who had thought to ask, made her feel...she wasn't sure what it made her feel. Tenderness, perhaps.

Added to frustration, it was an odd mix. Because she wasn't on anything.

"Laurey?"

"I...no," she said. "I...there was no reason. I haven't... I mean, it's been a long time for me, too."

"I...guessed."

Then he moved, rolling off her and standing up. She shivered at the sudden chill, but it faded as she watched him walk into the bathroom that opened off the master bedroom, watched the long, easy stride, watched the muscles flex beneath golden skin. Even the bruises added to the effect, silent testimony to the strength of a man who kept going through the pain, who didn't let it even slow him down.

It was an odd sensation, almost dispassionately admiring the naked beauty of him at the same time that she was longing for him to come back to her, to let her bear his weight again, to let his skin heat hers to tingling awareness, to touch her, kiss her and, finally, fill that empty place within her that had begun to ache in a way she'd never known before.

And then he was back, something in his hand as he stopped beside the bed. She stared at him, her eyes wide, her breathing rapid. He *was* beautiful, golden hair, golden skin, strong body, with that most male part of him full and ready. For her. Just the thought made her feel a strange melting sensation inside that she only vaguely realized was her body responding to the sight of his, readying itself.

"God," he muttered, "don't look at me like that or I'm going to lose it right here."

"I can't help it," she said simply.

He was fiddling with the small foil packet in his hand. When she realized what it was, her gaze shot back to his face. He explained helplessly.

"Laurey, don't think I...planned on this. Last time we used this house, it was for a couple, and the guys who set up safe houses...they try to think of everything that might be...necessary."

"Oh."

She saw his broad chest expand as he drew a deep breath. "Changed your mind?" he asked.

She wasn't fooled by his light tone; the rigid set of his jaw told her what it would cost him to walk away now. But he would do it, if that was her decision. She knew that with a bone-deep certainty she'd had few times in her life. And it was that certainty that told her she would be a fool to turn away from this. Life was too uncertain. She could die tomorrow, never knowing what was possible.

Her throat was suddenly too tight to speak, so she answered in the only way she could—she held her arms out to him in welcome.

With a strangled groan Gage came back to her, stroking her body, placing swift, hot kisses over her like sweet rain. She felt the heat of his hands and lips lingering in each spot long after he'd moved, until she thought there wasn't a single bit of her skin he hadn't tasted or touched.

He cupped her breasts and lifted them, and she sucked in her breath as her nipples contracted as if he'd touched them. And then he did, and that breath came out in a rush. His fingers teased her flesh into taut peaks, and she couldn't help her body's reaction; she arched against his hands helplessly. He groaned, low and guttural, as if her movement had been a caress returned. And then he caught her nipples, one after the other, between his lips and flicked them with his tongue.

She cried out his name, sharply, almost desperately. He stopped. She felt the coolness of air on flesh hot and wet from his mouth. She shook her head mutely; she hadn't wanted him to stop. She tried to tell him, but she couldn't speak, couldn't seem to find enough breath. But she could move, and she did, slipping one hand behind his head and pressing him to her breast in a silent plea.

He waited a moment, a moment that seemed like an eon to her. And then he moved again, quickly, capturing her nipple and suckling it long and hard in nearly the same instant. Fire shot through her, swift and fierce, careening around like a wild thing, turning on itself until her body was writhing under the sensation. He shifted to her other nipple and did it again, wringing a cry of his name from her.

Then he shifted his weight, and she parted her legs for him without hesitation or thought. After sheathing himself to protect her, he slipped between them, and she moved convulsively, rubbing herself against hot, rigid male flesh. Gage said her name, low, deep, heartfelt, and pleasure of a different kind rippled through Laurey as he rubbed himself against her in turn; she found herself savoring every sign that this was more than some blind easing of need, every bit of proof that Gage wanted *her*, not just someone to break a long stretch of celibacy.

And then he lifted his head and looked at her, and any thought of that vanished; this was not a man who would seek solace with any handy female. She could see in his eyes, so vividly green in the afternoon sunlight, that he knew exactly who he held, and that this was exactly where he wanted to be.

Her last doubts vanquished, Laurey slid her hands down his back, loving the feel of skin over fit muscle. She hesitated just above the swell of his buttocks, uncertain. Then she felt him shift, just slightly, lifting himself against her hands in silent invitation. With a sigh she moved downward, cupping that taut flesh, urging him, inviting him in turn.

As if he'd been waiting only for that, he moved his hips, slowly, easing himself inside her. She gasped at the first blunt probing. He stopped, as if afraid he'd hurt her.

"No." It came out on a single, harsh breath. She tightened her hands on his hips, urging him forward. "Don't stop. Please, don't stop."

With a sound that was half laugh, half groan, he slipped his hands beneath her and curled his fingers back around her shoulders, bracing her. Then he moved, quickly, sheathing himself in her to the hilt. His head lolled back, his eyes closed, his lips parted for a long exhalation that echoed with sheer pleasure. Laurey quivered at the sound of it, even as her body tightened in welcome around his. It felt so right, so completely right, that she nearly wept once more.

And then he began to move, to thrust into her in long, measured strokes, making her cry out with growing urgency when he drove deep and with loss when he drew back. Soon she was moving with him, lifting her hips to take him even deeper, only accepting his withdrawal for the pleasure of feeling him slide into her all over again.

She heard him say something, almost pleading. But she lost it in the torrent of sensation that flooded her when he slipped his hand between their bodies and began to caress that tiny knot of nerves that his touch had already awakened to exquisite sensitivity.

She could barely breathe from the feel of him pushing in and out of her, of his fingers circling ever more rapidly, from the sound of their union, slick, wet, from the sight of him above her, his strong, golden body moving in rhythm with hers, his face drawn taut with urgent pleasure.

And then breathing didn't matter, because she'd made the amazing discovery that you didn't need to breathe to fly. The swelling, the rising, the bursting, came so swiftly, so powerfully, that she cried out sharply in shock and wonder and astonishment as her body first gathered itself, then launched into flight. Sight, smell, hearing, touch, all seemed to coalesce into one single sense, as if in those seconds they all came together to work as they should, creating an explosion of sensation beyond imagining.

The only other thing she was aware of was Gage's sudden shuddering, his repeated moaning of her name as his body arched against hers, and the hot, sweet pulse of him inside her.

Gage stirred, aware only that some loud, steady noise had finally penetrated the haze. He wasn't happy about it. He liked this warm, floating feeling. It was a place he'd never been before. He wanted to stay. He wanted nothing more than to rest here, Laurey cuddled in his arms, the tiny echoes of sensation still tickling him like the brush of her hair over his skin.

The noise continued. Beresford and his lawn mower? No, it was the rookie's day off. But it was afternoon. Wasn't it? Who was due in? And whoever it was, they were supposed to stay mostly outside, watching under the guise of much needed yard work, a benefit the chief had been grinningly aware of.

Reluctantly Gage lifted his head. And in that moment became aware that Laurey had gone very still, barely breathing.

"Somebody's here," she whispered.

"I heard," he said. "Sounds like a damned blender or something. I think...oh, damn." He sat up abruptly.

"What?" Laurey asked. She sat up beside him, clutching the tangled sheet over her breasts.

"It's Kit. She said she'd come by Monday. It is Monday, isn't it?"

"I...think so." Laurey stared at him. "Do you think she...?"

Kit didn't miss much, but there was always a chance. And there was no point in upsetting Laurey any further. He gave her a wicked look.

"Honey, you made some noise, but you weren't *that* loud."

Color flooded her face in a rush.

"And," he went on softly, "I loved every little sound you made."

He saw a tiny tremor go through her, and she bit her lip. He hoped it was pleasure, because just remembering the tiny moans she'd made as he was burying himself into her welcoming heat was making the blood pool in flesh he would have thought exhausted.

"You made a few of your own," she said pointedly, and rather breathlessly.

"Yeah, I did, didn't I?" He gave her a lopsided grin. "There's a first time for everything."

She looked so startled, then pleased, that he couldn't resist. He leaned forward to kiss her. She went soft, pliant under his mouth, and he groaned as he fought the urge to begin all over again.

Then, with a rather grim expression, he rolled out of the bed and yanked on his jeans. Zipping them was hard going, and his jaw clenched as he willed his body to accept that it wasn't going to get what it wanted at the moment.

"I'll try to head her off," he said.

The blush—and the heat—faded from her smoky eyes. "Are you...will there be trouble? Because of—" she gestured at the bed they'd thoroughly tumbled "—this?"

He started to deny it, but somehow the words wouldn't come.

"Not for you," he finally said. "I'm the one who's broken more rules than I can count."

"Gage," she began, but he held up a hand to stop her.

"It's all right. I knew what I was doing. Sort of," he finished with a wry smile.

"Will she…report you or something?"

He glanced toward the closed door. The sound had stopped. "I don't know."

"At least…she didn't walk in on us," Laurey said shakily.

"She wouldn't. She's a class act. That noise was to let us know she was here."

"Then…maybe she won't do anything?"

He shrugged. "She's also a sergeant. She has…a duty to enforce policy."

Laurey pulled the sheet tighter in front of her. It didn't matter; he could see the soft, sweet curves of her breasts as clearly as if they were still bared to his gaze.

And if he didn't get out of here, he was going to be so aroused all over again that any chance of bluffing his way out of this with Kit was going to vanish. He hated to leave Laurey when he should be holding her, and judging from the uncertainty in her eyes, reassuring her, but he had to head Kit off before she did walk in on them.

Besides, he wasn't feeling any too certain about this himself. In fact, he was wondering if he hadn't lost his mind; he knew perfectly well there was no room for a relationship in his life, yet he'd been unable to stop himself here today. And had quite possibly landed himself in more hot water than he could get out of.

He yanked on his T-shirt and walked as quietly as he could toward the kitchen, where he guessed Kit was.

He was right. She was standing at the counter, putting coffee grounds in a paper filter. He saw a small appliance beside the coffeemaker and realized it had been a grinder he'd heard, not a blender.

"Thought you might like a little variety," she said without turning or even looking around. "Anybody who's had to drink Ryan's coffee needs an antidote."

It didn't surprise him that she'd known he was there. He walked into the room, aware of the cool linoleum under his bare feet. He heard the sound of distant running water and tried desperately not to think of Laurey in the shower, her long, slender body glistening with lucky drops.

"He does make it strong enough to bend the spoon," he said. He waited, but she seemed intent on her task. She still didn't even look at him. Not that it would have mattered; Kit didn't give much away.

"I brought that," she said, pointing to a large manila envelope. "For Laurey to look at."

In that instant he was glad she wasn't looking at him; he was sure what had happened between him and Laurey was written all over his face. Except that he wasn't sure exactly what *had* happened. It had been unlike anything he'd ever known, and judging by Laurey's expression of shock and wonder when her body had convulsed around his, it had been new to her, too.

Knock it off, he ordered himself sharply. *You keep thinking about it and you might as well hang out a sign. And you'll have a place to hang it, too.*

"So, where is our captive witness?"

As she filled the coffeepot with water, Kit's voice was bright, cheerful, without a trace of suspicion. But Gage's gut reacted as if it were an accusation. With an effort, he answered fairly evenly.

"She...was reading a magazine." Well, she had been. A couple of hours ago. Urgently needing a diversion, he asked, "What's in the envelope?"

"Take a look," Kit said, setting the pot on the hot plate and flipping the switch on the coffeemaker.

He picked it up. It wasn't sealed, only held closed with the metal fastener. He opened it and pulled out a familiar piece of doubled cardboard. There were six squares cut out of the top layer, just large enough to hold a half-dozen photographs. Right now the slots held pictures of six men who matched the general description Laurey had given of the shooter.

He looked up at Kit. "You got him?"

"We think so," she said with undisguised satisfaction. "We

need Laurey to take a look at that photo lineup and, if she hits on him, then the real thing, but we think we have him.''

''Who is he?''

''Name's Gaylord. Small-time punk who used to be on the fringe of The Pack. Still hangs out on Steele Street. He's a cokehead and heroin addict who's hit some hard times since Ryan dried up the supply down there.''

''So he needed bucks to go elsewhere?''

She nodded. ''And Martin provided them.''

''Allegedly,'' Gage said, smiling sourly as Kit grimaced at the painfully familiar word. ''All we have to do is prove it.''

''I think he'll break. He shot up recently—that's what they picked him up on—but he's already coming down pretty hard. No gun, but he may have tossed or hidden it. We're working on it.'' She smiled. ''The best part, though, is that from what we can tell, he probably didn't report back. He has fresh marks, a set about one and another about two days old. He had another hit on him, but no cash, so he probably spent all his advance money. We're guessing he's been flying high since Saturday night.''

It took a moment for the import to register. ''You mean…Martin doesn't know Laurey saw the guy?''

''Chances are pretty good.''

Gage thought swiftly. ''What's he booked on?''

''The dope. Until Laurey identifies him, the drugs are all we have on him.''

''Is he going to be able to make bail?''

''I doubt it. He's flat, and I don't think he'll be calling Martin for help, not after blowing it twice. Three times, if he was driving the van.''

''Anybody push him about the Martin connection?''

''Not yet. They only picked him up this morning, and we need Laurey's ID.''

''Good. Don't.''

''What?''

''Don't. Don't even question him about it. Don't even ask him if he's ever heard of Mitchell Martin. Hold him only on the drug charges. But keep him bogged down in the system as long as you can.''

Kit drew back, staring at him. ''The guy tries to kill you at least two, probably three, times, and you don't want us to even rattle his cage? Do I have that right?''

''Yes.''

Her astonished stare became puzzled, then thoughtful. ''You never do—or don't do—anything without a reason. Want to tell me this one?''

He didn't, not really, but he knew he had little choice. Kit would back him all the way, but only if he was straight with her.

''Just in case we can't make the connection,'' he said. ''If we do, then Laurey will have to testify. But if we can't, there's no point in officially dragging her into this.''

Kit frowned. ''Even if we can't make the connection, this guy still tried to kill you. And Laurey's a witness.''

''No,'' he said doggedly. ''If we don't push, Martin might not find out we have his man for a while. And there's no point in bringing her to Martin's attention.''

''You mean…as a loose end he might feel compelled to take care of?''

He nodded. When Kit spoke again, her voice was oddly soft. ''You'd rather see this guy walk after he does his drug time than take him down on a straight attempted murder rap? Just to keep her out of it?''

''If that's what it takes.''

It took a long time. She just looked at him for a while, then, slowly, turned and got a cup down from a cupboard. She poured a mug full of the freshly brewed coffee. Gage smelled the distinctive hazelnut flavor she preferred. He watched the steam rise from the dark blue mug. He watched her study the dark liquid as if searching for answers there. Finally she took a sip. And, at last, she looked at him again.

''All right, Gage.''

He let out a breath he hadn't been aware of holding.

''But only as long as things are stable. This guy's off the

street, and for the moment Martin's hamstrung. But that could change.''

"I know. Thanks, Kit.''

"I'll add it to your account.'' She took another sip of coffee. "But that reminds me. We owe the chief, big time.''

"Again?'' Gage asked, going for some of the tempting smelling coffee himself.

"Yes. Seems he indeed did think there was more to your... accident than met the eye.''

If nothing else, Gage thought, he liked this woman for never saying "I told you so.''

"He made sure Martin's only unmonitored visits while in our fine hotel were with a single attorney, Phillip Farrell, and Farrell has been advised of his own...liability if we prove Martin arranged for something to happen to you while Farrell was his only contact.''

Gage heard the undertone in her voice and lifted a brow at her. Kit giggled. Gage gaped at her; he'd never heard such a sound from Sergeant Katherine Walker before. She sounded inordinately pleased.

"What?'' he prodded.

"I guess the chief sort of made your welfare Farrell's responsibility. I heard from Sol in the jail that what he actually told him was that if anything happened to you, even after Martin gets out, he would personally see to it that Farrell's life and career became a living hell, so he'd better keep his client under control.''

Gage stared. "De los Reyes did that?''

She nodded. "He's something, isn't he?''

"That he is,'' Gage agreed fervently.

"He...told me I should take the next lieutenant's test,'' Kit said, sounding strangely shy.

"You should,'' Gage said quickly. "You'd be damn good at it.''

"Thanks. But I don't know....''

"I do. You're the best, Walker. Do it.''

To his amazement, the unflappable Kit blushed. "Thank you.''

"You should," he said with mock severity. "I'm making a great sacrifice here. I don't want to have to work for somebody else. It's not every sergeant who would..."

"Put up with you?" she suggested sweetly.

"Yeah," he admitted. "But Lieutenant Walker has a nice ring to it."

"Compared to Robards, anything has a nice ring," she said dryly.

"Well, that, too," he agreed, grinning.

He heard the shower stop and suddenly remembered his shoes and socks lying discarded on the bedroom floor. "I think I'll go put my shoes on," he said rather inanely.

He was almost into the hall when Kit's voice stopped him. "Butler?"

Uh-oh. He looked back over his shoulder at her. He saw her glance flick in the general direction of Laurey's room.

"When I said you needed a sex life, this wasn't exactly what I had in mind."

Chapter 15

Laurey almost wished it hadn't been so clear. Her life would be simpler, she was sure, if it hadn't been. But there was no doubt in her mind; the moment she looked at the six photographs Kit Walker had handed her, she'd known. Her gaze had caught and held on the middle photo in the bottom row, and she'd been certain beyond a doubt that this was the man she'd seen in the car.

"That's him," she said, pointing.

"You're sure?" Kit asked.

"Positive."

She saw Kit's gaze shift to Gage, who was looking at her as if for some kind of confirmation. Kit nodded once. "Gaylord," she said.

Gage let out a long breath, unmistakably of relief.

"Right answer?" Laurey asked with brows lifted.

Kit grinned. "Right answer. He's enjoying the hospitality of Trinity West as we speak."

"And," Gage put in, "he's the only one who knows you saw him."

She turned from Kit to Gage. Was that why he was so relieved? Because now she was safe?

"So," Kit said to her, "you're free."

Of course, Laurey thought. That was why he'd looked so relieved; with the assailant in jail, hiding here was no longer necessary. For her, anyway.

"You mean I can go?"

Kit nodded. "No reason to worry now. Martin doesn't even know you're involved, as far as we can tell."

Involved. What an…interesting word for her to have chosen, Laurey thought dryly. And Kit was looking at her steadily, a quietly knowing look in her hazel eyes.

Knowing? Did she? Could she? For an instant Laurey couldn't breathe as she looked at the other woman, as she tried to discern if it was truly knowledge she saw there, if somehow Kit had figured out what had happened between her and Gage. He had told her Kit didn't miss much, but at the moment she felt as if it were written in glowing letters across her forehead, not requiring any particular perceptiveness.

Kit's expression changed, and for a moment Laurey saw quiet understanding and concern there. And she realized that if Kit did know, she would do nothing. At least, unless she had to. Then Kit spoke, as if nothing had passed between them.

"At least you'll be able to salvage some of your vacation."

"I…suppose," Laurey said, her glance skating to Gage. "But…you're still stuck."

He shook his head. "I'm outta here."

"But just because he's—" she gestured at the photo lineup on the kitchen counter "—in jail doesn't mean this Martin won't hire someone else."

"I think," Gage said with a wink at Kit, "that Chief de los Reyes took care of that."

"Maybe," Kit cautioned. "But I wouldn't trust Martin not to try again anyway, eventually. He's got that kind of mentality, has himself convinced he's untouchable. He'll be more cautious now, but he may not give up."

Gage looked at Kit consideringly. "You're the expert, boss.

How long will it take for him to put his arrogance back together after being arrested, and—" he hesitated, glancing at Laurey before he went on "—*advised* by his lawyer?"

"A while, maybe. But now that he's out, and back amid his familiar surroundings of power, if the image of invincibility he's built up in his head is strong enough…" Kit shrugged, ending with, "I wouldn't stop watching your back." She turned to Laurey. "Do you feel up to going to Trinity West to do an in-person lineup?"

Gage stiffened. "I thought we agreed this wasn't going to be…official, yet."

"It isn't. I just want it on record, in case we're able to…make the connection."

Laurey had no idea what they were talking about, but she had the feeling it involved something that was not exactly standard procedure. She became more certain of it when they arrived at Trinity West and she heard Kit explaining to the jailer who was putting together the lineup that, for the moment, this was to stay downstairs, which Laurey gathered meant away from the brass upstairs.

She was as certain in person as she had been with the photos; there was no doubt in her mind that the short, wiry man with the slicked-back hair and the pointed chin was the man she'd seen in the car. Despite the knowledge that none of the six men—the same ones who had been in the photographs— could see her through the two-way mirror, it was unpleasant to be this close to a man who could easily have killed them both.

This time Kit didn't comment when she unhesitatingly pointed out the second man from the left, merely picked up a phone on the table beside them in the small observation room.

"Okay, Jack," she said into the receiver. "We got a hit. Number two."

A moment later the jailer appeared before the mirror and ushered three of the men, including the one Laurey had picked out, out of sight down a narrow hallway that Laurey assumed led to the jail cells. To her surprise, the other three men simply stood up and began to talk amiably, one of them putting on a suit coat and tie he picked up from a chair off to one side of the room.

"The one dressing up is our court liaison officer," Gage said, correctly·interpreting her puzzled expression. "The other two are Jim Kragen and Larry Newsome, our burglary detectives." He gave her a crooked smile. "We had to come up with guys you didn't know, so that let out Cruz and Ryan."

"And Robards," she said.

"Perish the thought," Kit muttered.

"Yeah," Gage agreed. "The last thing we need is him mucking things up. It's been tough enough keeping him from mouthing off and screwing up the whole investigation. If de los Reyes hadn't given him that staff report to keep him busy…"

"Out of your hair, you mean," Kit said. "Which reminds me…do you want to tell the chief what we're doing, or shall I?"

Laurey didn't miss Kit's glance at her, but before she could ask what was going on, Kit was looking back at Gage and shaking her head.

"We have to tell him," Kit said, apparently forestalling a protest she'd seen coming. "You know he'll back us as far as he can, but not if we don't play it straight with him."

Gage sighed. "I know." Then, with a grimace, "You tell him. He likes you, so maybe he'll cut us some slack."

"He respects you," Kit countered, "so he'll cut you more than he would some others." Then, at his expression, she added, "Don't look so surprised. For the results you get, he'll bend a little. He knows what your case.clearance rate is, and the kind of work you do with kids and victims. The man knows everything that goes on around here."

Her gaze flicked to Laurey for a split second, then back to Gage. "Well, almost everything." She glanced at her watch. "It's almost three. Why don't you two get out of here? Robards should be back from his two-hour lunch by now, and if he gets word about the arrest, he could be headed down here to see if he can stick his nose in."

She was gone before either Gage or Laurey could react,

leaving them both staring after her, then down at the floor; she wondered if he was as afraid to look at her as she was afraid to look at him.

"Just…how many rules *did* you break?" she finally asked.

For the first time since Kit's arrival had interrupted them this afternoon, he touched her. He lifted her chin with a gentle finger.

"More than the one you broke, I'd guess."

"Me?" She drew back a little. "What rule did I break?"

"A big one of your own, I think," he said softly.

She stared at him. "What do you mean?"

"I'd guess you made a decision a long time ago not to ever get involved with anybody like your father."

"I told you, you aren't—"

"I know. But you also said the results are the same, regardless of the reasons."

She had, she supposed, said that. And looking at it coldly, dispassionately, she knew it was true; the reasons didn't change the long hours, the neglect of any other life outside the work, the emotional abandonment of the people who loved you.

"You're probably right. Kit's probably right." A harsh, compressed breath escaped him. "But let's just forget it for now. Let's try and salvage some of what's left of your vacation, all right?"

"I… All right."

"What were you planning to do?"

What she hadn't planned to do was spend the time with a man who rattled her nerves and made her think things she'd never thought before, hot, erotic fantasies she'd never been prone to in her life. A man who had proceeded to show her that they didn't have to be fantasies at all.

A man who, as he'd astutely guessed, was the very kind she'd sworn never to get involved with.

"Laurey?"

"I…was going to do something I miss, up in Washington." God, she thought, for the first time really realizing what she'd done, getting herself tangled up like this twelve hundred miles from home. It took her a moment to steady herself enough to go on. "I miss being able to go to the beach in November."

"Your wish is my command," he said grandly. "To the beach it is."

"You don't have to...do this," she said, hearing the strain in her voice.

He went still. For a long moment he studied her. Then, in a tone so unemotional she knew he'd chosen it purposely, he asked, "You'd rather I didn't come with you?"

"It's not that," she said quickly, hurt in some way she didn't understand by the flatness of his question. "I just thought you'd have...other things to do, after be-ing...incommunicado for two days."

"I do. But I'd rather do this."

"Why?"

The question was out before she could stop it, although she'd never meant to ask it. She'd never meant to ask for some sort of declaration, of something she wasn't sure she wanted to hear even if he would say it. Which she doubted.

Sounding as wary as she felt, he answered slowly. "Look, I know this is...new. There's a lot to deal with, and none of it is easy. More crazy, with everything that's happened, on top of how you feel about...us obsessive types."

Crazy? she thought. That was about the word for it. What else could explain what had happened, when it was so out of character for her as to be unbelievable? There was no other explanation. It had definitely been temporary insanity.

Except that she wasn't at all sure it was temporary.

"I...don't know how I feel," she said, sounding, she was sure, as confused as she felt.

"Neither do I," he said.

Laurey winced inwardly, stung by his words. Then she chided herself; if she had the right to be uncertain and doubt-ful, then so did he, and it was selfish of her to resent the fact that he felt just as she did.

"We're both...a little dazed, I think. All this happened pretty fast. And under unusual circumstances. That's why it's no time to make any...decisions. Just let it go, Laurey. For now. You deserve a bit of time without the high drama." He chuckled rather grimly. "Believe me, it's not going to go away if you ignore it for a while."

It had been just that, a period fraught with tension, and she very much wanted to put it out of her mind. She didn't know how he lived like this, with this kind of thing going on all the time. It would drive her crazy.

Perhaps it already had, this afternoon, she thought wryly. But the temptation was irresistible, and at last she nodded.

It seemed like a very short time later—although her perception of time seemed out of whack at the moment—that they were parked on a bluff overlooking the Pacific.

"If you're feeling agile, we can go down the trail to the beach. It's a nice spot. Great view of Catalina Island at sunset."

"Let's go," she said, thinking a little physical exertion was just what she needed to take her mind off the other physical things she'd indulged in today.

He went first, to show her the way. And, she guessed from the way he kept a careful eye on her, to give her a hand if she needed it to get down the rocky bluff. He did it without comment, never implying that she would need his help, just being there in case she did. Her innate independence warred with an unexpected pleasure in having someone looking out for her in such a quiet yet resolute way.

There were only a few people sitting on the sand when they reached the beach, and a few others strolling along the waterline. This time of year the sun was already dropping toward the horizon, a huge, orange ball that would soon paint the streaky clouds in the vivid colors of pink and gold and orange and blue that Laurey had never forgotten. It was cool, but not cold—at least, not to her Seattle-adapted body—and she felt the peace of the place and the sunset begin to work its magic.

They walked for a while, then sat down, backs propped against a jutting rock that still held some warmth from the sun.

"Better?" Gage asked quietly.

"Much."

"I come here sometimes at sunset," he said. "It's a good place to let go of the tension, bit by bit, as the sun goes down."

He said nothing more as the sun made its plunge toward the sea, but there had been a lot of wisdom in those simple words, Laurey thought. A wisdom that she guessed was hard-earned. She thought it would be a good thing to try, to let the stress that had built up in the past few days just slip away as the sun slipped away.

She watched the sky, simply absorbing the beauty and the color as the scene changed with every moment, the brightness shifting to softer, darker shades, until the island nearly thirty miles offshore became only a black shape against the last of the faint glow. By the time the sky was dark, she felt utterly relaxed.

There had been a lot of beauty in her world today, she thought. Many kinds of it. And first and foremost, she admitted to herself, was the beauty Gage had brought to her with his kiss, his touch, and his tender loving. No matter what happened, that was a memory she would always treasure.

"Thank you," she whispered to him.

His shoulder was pressed against hers, so she felt rather than saw him shrug. "It's a favorite place of mine."

"For that, too," she said. "But I meant…for today."

She felt him go still. "You say that like…goodbye."

"I didn't mean it that way. I just wanted you to know that…no matter what…"

She was floundering, wishing she hadn't given into the impulse to speak her thoughts, not when there was so much chaos surrounding them. Then Gage moved, lifting his arm and settling it around her shoulders.

"Me, too," he said softly. "No matter what."

"…an outrage, a gross miscarriage of justice. Something is very wrong with this police department when a law-abiding, tax-paying citizen is insulted in this manner. I will not take this lying down, and you can be sure I will have the badge of the detective who has been harassing me without cause. I have already instructed my attorneys to prepare a lawsuit, and Detective Butler will be the first name on it.''

Gage flipped off the car radio. He'd heard enough of Martin's ranting to last him a lifetime.

"He even sounds arrogant," Laurey said. She'd been in the middle of a sentence as they drove, something about how different, but equally beautiful, she found the Pacific Northwest, when the news report had come on. She'd stopped, staring at the radio as if it had suddenly started spouting a foreign language. The reporter had begun with a dispassionate recap of the case, the shock of the community at the arrest of one of its more prominent citizens, the commotion caused by his arrest, and then had cut to a tape of Martin's furious comments.

"Yes," Gage agreed. "And he's more arrogant than he sounds."

Any further discussion was cut off by the shrill chirp of his beeper. He reached for it, pulling it off his belt so that he could see it and still keep his eyes on the road; racking up a city car was not what he needed to add to his life right now.

When he saw the number displayed, he wasn't sure he was in much better shape.

"What's wrong?"

He looked at her, realizing something must have shown on his face. "I don't know. Yet. But it probably ain't good news. It's the chief. Hand me that cell phone in the glove box, will you?"

"Want me to dial it?"

"Thanks," he said, accepting the offer. "The department frowns on CPI TC's. City-property-involved traffic collisions," he explained at her look. "The standing joke is you're always at fault unless the car fell off the hoist in the garage."

"Even if someone hits you?" she asked as she looked at the pager he turned toward her and dialed the number.

"Even if," he said, taking the phone. "Although I may skate on the other night, since—Rosa? Gage. You rang?"

"Yes," came the brisk, businesslike voice of Chief de los Reyes's efficient secretary. She wasted no time with niceties.

Gage knew it wasn't because she didn't care, but she would already have heard from her boss that he was all right, and she didn't believe in wasting time on redundancies. "He wants to see you."

"When?"

"Preferably now."

What the chief preferred, he generally got, and usually without complaint, after two years of proving he was fair and reasonable. A marked change from the legacy of the prior chief; Lipton had had a very different way of doing things, and it hadn't been the most pleasant for his people. It had been the kind of approach that spawned cops like Robards, which was proof enough for Gage that de los Reyes's way was better, for the department and the city.

"I'm on my way, driving time," he said.

"Is Miss Templeton with you?"

Startled at the unexpected question, Gage glanced at Laurey before saying warily, "Yes, she is."

"Good. Bring her, as well."

"Why?"

"I don't question, Detective Butler, I just deliver the message."

"Rosa," he said, his tone half warning, half teasing.

"He doesn't tell me everything."

"But you still have an idea. You always do."

He thought he heard a soft chuckle. "You know he usually has good reason for whatever he asks, Gage. But I have no idea what it is in this case."

He sighed. "All right. On my—our way, driving time from the coast."

"Have a nice afternoon at the beach, did you?"

"Yes, thanks. See you in a bit," he said politely, and hung up before she could go any further with her speculations.

He handed the phone to Laurey, who put it back in the glove box and closed it before shifting in her seat to look at him expectantly.

"The chief wants to see us," he said.

"Us?"

He nodded, then, before she could ask, said, "I don't know why you."

"And I don't get a choice?"

He lifted a brow. "Want me to let you out here?"

She made a face at him. "You know what I mean."

"Sure, you have a choice. You're a civilian. He's not your boss."

"But he's the chief of police."

"Yes. But he doesn't throw his weight around, not like that." He gave her a lopsided grin. "Me, he orders. You, he requests."

"Is this like getting called to the principal's office?"

"For me. You'll be treated like an honored guest." Her brow furrowed, and he relented. "I'm kidding. De los Reyes is a good guy. You met him. Sometimes he has to be the boss, but he's always fair."

After a moment she nodded and settled back into the passenger seat of the plain brown sedan as he made a turn onto the Marina del Mar street that would eventually become Trinity Street West.

"That reminds me," she said. "What did he do?"

"What did who do?"

"The chief. You said back at the house that he...took care of Martin hiring someone else."

"Oh." Gage had almost forgotten she'd heard that exchange. "He, er, pointed out to Martin's lawyer that we knew he was Martin's only contact."

"You mean...the lawyer could be part of it? Could have...arranged the attempts on you?"

"That's what de los Reyes let him think we're thinking."

"But you're not?"

"No. Not really. He's a big mouth, but that comes with the territory. He might have lousy taste in clients and skate around the ethical edges, but I don't think he'd let himself get caught up in a contract hit situation."

"Then why...?"

Gage coughed. "Er, I think the chief wanted to let Farrell

know that keeping his client under control—and me alive—would be in his best interest."

"Do you think Farrell will take his advice?"

"Unless he wants his life and career to become…difficult. De los Reyes gets a lot of respect in this town. He has a lot of influence, although he rarely uses it. But if he really wanted to make the guy's life miserable, don't think he couldn't do it."

"I don't think I would ever underestimate him," Laurey said seriously.

"People who do are usually sorry. It was that way on the street, and it's been that way ever since he walked into a job nobody else wanted to touch. He pulled Trinity West out of the gutter by sheer force of personality and will."

"Things were…that bad?"

He eased the car to a stop at a red light at the intersection that marked the border of Marina del Mar and Marina Heights. The sign drivers heading into Marina Heights saw was a standard metal street sign with the rather innocuous city seal stating Entering Marina Heights. Going the other way, he knew, into Marina del Mar, they saw a much more elegant—and expensive—carved wooden sign with ocean waves and a leaping porpoise below, and gold lettering above declaring you were Welcome to Marina del Mar. And therein, he'd often thought, lay the tale.

"They were a disaster waiting to happen," he said in answer to her question. "But de los Reyes took a city government that was ready to jettison the whole place and contract with the county sheriff for police, and convinced them to give him a year to pull it off. He took a department on the brink of chaos and turned it into the toughest, best run PD in the county, if not the state. He took a bunch of cops that didn't give a damn anymore and turned them around until most of us would follow him into hell if he asked."

"And what did it cost him?" Laurey asked quietly.

He glanced at her as the light changed and he accelerated through the intersection. She had come a long way, if that was her first thought. "Does it matter?" he asked, just as quietly.

"I suppose only to…anyone who cared about him."

Was there an edge to those soft words that was meant for him? Not for the first time, he wished they hadn't been interrupted by Kit's arrival this afternoon. Those quiet, intimate moments of aftermath were when they could have—should have—talked of what had happened between them, when they should have worked out where they would go from here. But they had been interrupted, and now he didn't quite know how to bring it up. He'd thought to do it at the beach, as they watched that glorious sunset, but she had been so wound-up that getting her to let go of the tension had seemed more important right then.

"He…said something about that once," Gage said at last, as he made the turn into the parking lot at Trinity West. "Back when he took the job. Said he could do it because there was nothing to distract him. That there was nothing else that mattered to him, so the work ahead would get his all. And it did."

"He sounds…lonesome."

"Maybe. Nobody's really close to him. Kit worries about him, but she worries about everyone. She doesn't like it that he doesn't seem to need anyone."

He had the car parked and turned off before she said, "Sometimes those are the ones who need someone the most."

There was no particular inflection in her voice, but something in the way she was looking at him made him wonder yet again if there wasn't some message there for him.

"Look, we need to talk," he said. "I know that. But right now…" He lifted one shoulder in a helpless shrug.

"I know. The principal's waiting. Let's go."

Chapter 16

They stood in the anteroom of the chief's office, waiting. It was after five now, and most of the daytime personnel were already gone, including Rosa, but it wasn't unusual for de los Reyes to be around after hours, as he apparently was now. He was on the phone and motioned through the open door to them, indicating he would be only a few minutes. Gage nodded and turned to Laurey, only to find she had moved away, was walking slowly down the small room, staring at the rows of photographs and plaques on the walls.

This room was normally not open to the public, but the chief made certain it was always left open for the officers of Trinity West. Gage himself had spent some time in here, whenever something rattled his faith in what he was doing. Too bad lately it hadn't helped much. He supposed it was burnout, something most cops were subject to at one time or another. But it felt much deeper than that, had to be deeper, if even this room didn't help.

To many of them, it was a sort of shrine. To the rest, a hall of fame, commemorating Trinity West officers who had been honored for valor. Some were still cops, some were not. Some were still alive. And some were not. Kit's fiancé, Bobby Allen, who had been killed during a bank robbery among them.

And one…always that one, the one where they didn't know if he was dead or alive.

He watched as Laurey stopped before the most recent of the plaques, Cruz Gregerson's, the Medal of Valor he had received just over a year ago for defusing a bomb when there'd been no time to call out the bomb squad. She didn't smile at the photo of the man she knew but rather looked very solemn. She walked on, slowly, then paused again before another plaque. He knew which one it was by her surprised expression. Ryan Buckhart looked quite different with his hair shorn short and in full dress uniform. But looks didn't change what was commemorated there; Ryan had risked his life, and had indeed nearly died of smoke inhalation after pulling three small children from a blazing house three years ago.

After a moment she continued, walking slowly, making the turn at the far end of the room and heading back toward him. He knew by the progression of emotions on her face—puzzlement, curiosity and then awe—when she had reached the place on the memorial wall most of Trinity West tried to avoid. She glanced at all three plaques, then read each one in turn. The car accident, where he'd risked horrible burns and had nearly sliced off his own arm dragging a baby out of an engulfed car. The bank robbery where he'd taken a bullet in the side protecting an elderly woman who had inadvertently walked into the line of fire. And the last, the most amazing, where he had given himself up in exchange for four children being held hostage by a crazed, barricaded suspect and had nearly died from the resultant torture.

She read them all. Then she turned to look at Gage.

"Three?" she asked.

He nodded. "And those are only the tip of the iceberg. Yeager was the best, the best of all of us. And he gave something to everyone he worked with. There's not a cop who worked with him who wouldn't say so. He gave all he had to the people he worked with and the people he served." He nodded toward the plaques. "Those are just the most spectacular of the things he did. The whole list would take a book."

"That's...amazing."

"Yeager was amazing."

"*Was?* Is he...dead?"

He looked at the photo. And spoke the painful truth. "We don't know."

Laurey blinked. "What?"

"He quit under...some pretty awful circumstances a few years back. We've...lost track of him. He might still be alive...."

"But you don't think so?"

"He...was pretty strung out when he left. And he wouldn't be the first cop to eat a bullet."

She gasped. "You think he...killed himself?" she asked, looking at him with troubled eyes full of a compassion that made him think yet again just how far she had come in such a short time. Hard to believe this was the woman who had been furious at the mere sight of him.

"I hope not," he said fervently.

She reached out and put a hand on his arm comfortingly. And it hit him that it was even harder to believe that the same woman who had been so furious had this afternoon taught him a world of things he'd never known before. The hot, sweet memories flooded him, and his body responded with a speed that took his breath away. He saw Laurey's eyes widen, as if she'd somehow known where his mind had gone.

"Thanks for coming in, Ms. Templeton." Chief de los Reyes's voice was the cooling off he needed, and he pulled himself together as the man ushered Laurey into his office and left Gage to follow on his own.

"You're both all right?" he asked, as if he'd noticed their mutual discomfiture.

They both nodded, but Gage noticed Laurey could no more meet the chief's perceptive gaze than he could.

"Good." He gestured them into the two chairs before his desk, but rather than go to his own chair, he leaned on the edge of the desk on their side. "I need to talk to both of you about our next steps. Gage, because we need to decide how we're going to protect you should Martin ignore…his attorney's advice. And you, Ms. Templeton, because you've unfortunately landed in the middle of all this."

"Laurey, please," she said, and de los Reyes smiled and nodded. She smiled back, and Gage was suddenly reminded of what a good-looking man the chief was—tall, lean, with those regal features and that touch of silver at his temples. Why it had hit him now, he didn't want to think.

"I don't think he'll try again," Gage said, rather hastily.

"But are you willing to bet your life you're right?" de los Reyes asked. Before Gage could answer, the chief shook his head. "I'm not. I don't have enough people like you that I can afford to lose one."

Gage opened his mouth, then shut it again; there was nothing he could say to that without sounding either foolish or arrogant—or both.

"I'm thinking we should go public."

"No," Gage said, instantly.

"It may be the only way. I went along with keeping it quiet at first, but now…"

"No," Gage repeated.

De los Reyes looked at him consideringly. "It makes sense, Gage. He won't be as likely to go after you if he knows we—"

"No," he said a third time. The chief's expression made him realize he had interrupted his most superior officer. Fortunately de los Reyes wasn't the kind of man to take offense at such things. "Look," Gage said, resisting the urge to glance at Laurey, who was watching with interest but obvious puzzlement, "if it was just me, then…maybe. But it isn't."

"That's why, Ms.…rather, Laurey is here."

She spoke up then. "Excuse me, but I don't quite understand. What did you mean, go public?"

"With our suspicions that Mitchell Martin is behind the attempts on Gage's life. In the hopes that his knowing we suspect him, and that it's public knowledge, will prevent him from trying again. And it may shift the winds of public opinion, make people think of Martin as a suspect instead of a wrongly accused victim.''

"Oh.'' She glanced at Gage. "That makes sense.''

"Granted,'' Gage admitted. "But my answer is still no.''

"Why?'' she asked, her tone one of obvious puzzlement.

"I believe,'' de los Reyes said quietly, when Gage didn't answer, "he is trying to protect you.''

"Me?'' She had turned to the chief when he'd spoken, but now she looked back at Gage. "Protect me? From what?''

"Right now, nobody knows you're even involved. But when the chief said 'go public,' he meant to the press. Do you have any idea what it's like when they get hold of something?''

"I've watched the news,'' she said dryly.

"Then you know they'll probe and pry until they find out everything. They'll be asking why we suspect him, even though it seems obvious to us. One of the first things they'll want to know is if there are any witnesses. And I don't want Martin finding out about you.''

"Which is, I'm told,'' de los Reyes put in mildly, "why you didn't want us to charge your shooter with anything other than the drug charges.''

"You didn't?'' Laurey asked, clearly even more confused now.

"If we charged him with the shooting,'' Gage said, meeting Laurey's gaze at last, "we'd have to use you as a witness. Which means Martin would find out you saw everything. And all for nothing, if we can't connect the two of them. I didn't see any point in dragging you into it until and unless we can prove the shooter was working for Martin.''

"But…he still tried to kill you. And *you* were a witness to that.''

"That…doesn't matter,'' he said, knowing it sounded absurd.

"It doesn't matter that he tried to kill you?'' Laurey exclaimed.

"I think what Gage is trying to say, in his rather…obscure

way," the chief said, "is that he doesn't think it's worth the price to hang an attempted murder rap on our guest."

"The price?"

"Of you being irrevocably placed in Mitchell Martin's line of fire, so to speak," de los Reyes said. He looked at Laurey in a considering way that made Gage more than a little nervous. "And that is a…departure from the norm I find very interesting."

"Can we just get on with this?" Gage said abruptly, not liking at all the turn this was taking. "Martin's a loose cannon. He may stop, or he may go crazier than ever. You can't be sure."

"All right," the chief said calmly. "You've made your position quite clear, so, Laurey, it would seem it's up to you."

"Like hell," Gage said, jerking upright to sit on the edge of his chair before remembering where he was and who he'd just sworn at. "Sir," he added rather lamely.

The chief glanced at him but didn't speak before looking back at Laurey. "I won't deny there is a slight danger in this course. We have every reason to believe that Martin does not know about you or your involvement. And although we will, of course, try to keep you out of it, Gage is right that the media may somehow ferret your involvement out and use it. Your identity and part in this could become widely known. The press are annoyingly, and sometimes dangerously, conscienceless about that kind of thing."

"And if they do?"

"Then if he is, indeed, unbalanced enough to continue down this path, there is a slight chance he may decide to go after you, as well."

"But you think if you go public," Laurey said, "then he's less likely to go after Gage again?"

"That's my assessment, yes."

"Then do it."

"Laurey, no," Gage protested.

"It's my decision, Gage."

"But you don't understand—"

"I understand enough." She looked at the chief. "Sir?"

"You're certain?"

"I am."

De los Reyes smiled. "Thank you."

Gage muttered something under his breath. Laurey frowned at him. "You're the one who says he practically walks on water. Trust him, will you?"

Gage's head came up sharply. Disconcerted, he flicked a glance at the chief, who looked startled, but rather pleased. A bit embarrassed, Gage got to his feet. "If that's all? Sir?"

"I think so," de los Reyes said. "Except for one thing. Happy birthday, Butler."

Thoroughly embarrassed now—he made a point of never letting his birthday be widely known, just to avoid most cops' penchant to use any excuse for a party—Gage mumbled a thank-you and turned toward the door, thinking he'd never been more glad to get out of this office, even on the two occasions when Chief Lipton had had him in here to chew him out.

"Oh, and Laurey?"

She'd been right behind him on the way to the door, but at the chief's words she turned back. He gestured her back toward the desk. Gage waited just outside the door; he wondered what de los Reyes wanted to tell her, but figured he'd come close enough to trouble with the man without pushing his luck by barging back in when de los Reyes clearly wanted to talk only to Laurey.

She was smiling when she came back, an odd little smile that made him uneasy. But he waited until they were outside and at the car before he asked her, "What was that about?"

"Just something he thought I should know."

"About what?"

"You."

Uh-oh. "Something…like what?"

"That's between the chief and me."

"Laurey…"

She ignored him and got into the car. Not having much choice, he pulled open the driver's door and got in himself.

Before he even had his seat belt fastened she spoke, clearly changing the subject.

"Why didn't you tell me it was your birthday?"

Diverted, he shrugged. "I…it's not something I generally announce."

"Even to the woman you're in bed with?"

Although he rarely did, he'd come close to blushing when she'd told him he was a special kind of man. Closer when she had called him beautiful. But this time she had really done it; he felt his cheeks heat, and it wasn't just from the memories of that afternoon, although just thinking of how it had felt when he'd slid into her welcoming body was enough to over-heat the entire car.

"I…haven't been in bed with a woman for several birth-days. Besides, I sort of…forgot."

"You forgot it was your birthday?"

"I was thinking of…other, much more interesting things," he said, and had the satisfaction of seeing her color in turn.

She lowered her eyes, lacing her fingers together and staring at her hands as if they belonged to a stranger. "Gage, I…"

"Regrets?" he asked, managing to keep his voice quiet, although his hands were clenching around the steering wheel, as he waited with some dread to hear her say it had been a mistake.

"No," she said. "It's just…I've never done anything like…that, and I don't know how to act now."

"Don't act at all," he said, his voice harsh. "Just feel how you feel."

"But I'm not sure how I feel."

"Then that's how you feel."

She looked at him then, her expression rueful. "That almost made sense. And that worries me."

He smiled, or tried to; he was fairly sure it was more than a little crooked. "Laurey, I know we still need to…talk. We should have this afternoon, but Kit showed up, and maybe we should have at the beach, but you were so—"

He stopped when she lifted a hand. "No. I needed…to not talk, or think."

"Sometimes you need time to just…be aware of being alive," he said.

He saw the gleam of understanding and connection in her eyes. "Yes. Exactly. Thank you."

He wasn't sure what she was thanking him for, but he would take it. Gladly.

"So…do you want to talk now?"

"Honest?"

"Preferably."

"No," she said fervently. "I want food. I'm starved."

He blinked, startled. Then he grinned. "Now that you mention it, so am I." He hadn't realized it; he was used to ignoring some of the less urgent signals his body sent him, such as hunger or sleepiness. But neither of them had eaten since that morning. "Okay, food first."

"Thank you."

"Okay if we stop by my place? I'd like to take a shower and change. You can, too, if you like, since you have your things with you."

"I'd like that," she said. "I still feel a bit windblown from the beach."

"You look…wonderful."

He meant it, but just saying the words, and noticing how strange it felt, reminded him again of just how long it had been since he'd paid a woman a simple compliment outside of work. Or had been in a position to.

"Thank you," she said, a shy note in her voice that tugged at something deep inside him; she sounded as if she wasn't used to such compliments. And he wondered if she'd ever really gotten over seeing herself as the tall, gawky girl she'd once been.

She should be used to compliments, he thought. And he just might have to make darn sure she got used to them. A lot of them. He'd—

The sound of a siren stopped his thoughts. It was a short, quick burst of sound, not the response to an emergency but most likely a wake-up call for some inattentive driver, but it woke him up, as well.

He turned his attention to starting the car. He wouldn't be doing anything, he told himself. This was his life, this place, this job, and there wasn't room for anything else. Especially not the kind of relationship Laurey would expect. And deserve. It was only the fact that he'd been forcibly removed from that job for a couple of days that had made him even begin to think it might be possible. That had made him concentrate on her, instead of his work. That had been the reason he'd even had time for such foolish ideas. That had been the reason he'd done something he'd never, ever done before; crossed a line that shouldn't be crossed.

Ironic, he supposed, as he pulled out onto Trinity Street West and headed home, that the job had put him in that position, had put him in that safe house, locked up with the only woman to tempt him in a very long time. The very thing that made it impossible had also made him want what he couldn't have.

The fact that he had taken it anyway—never mind that Laurey had been a willing participant—was something that he doubted he would ever be able to reconcile in his mind.

I've never done anything like that.

She didn't have to tell him, he knew. He'd always known. Laurey Templeton wasn't the kind of woman to have sex lightly. In fact, he thought, frowning, she wasn't the type to just have sex at all. She would never go to bed with a man just for the sake of physical release. To some extent, her heart would have to be involved.

He nearly groaned aloud. He had never meant to hurt her, but now it seemed inevitable, because there were just too many strikes against them. His dedication to his work, her feelings about that kind of dedication. The fact that he couldn't change the way he worked; he had to give it everything. Even the knowledge that it had cost him his marriage hadn't enabled him to back off. They said he was driven, and maybe they were right. But he didn't know any other way to do the job. Any other way to keep the nightmares at bay.

His mind skittering away from that subject, he thought of

the other big strike: the fact that she had her own life, her own career, and it was twelve hundred miles away.

God, he didn't want this, couldn't afford this.

But he *did* want it. He wanted *her*.

He glanced over at her. She sat quietly in the passenger seat, looking out the window, but he could see, even from here, even in the darkness, that she wasn't focused on anything outside. And he wondered if she was wrestling with thoughts like his, or simply wishing they had never complicated things by discovering that they set off some serious fireworks together.

Whichever it was, she said nothing at all, even when he pulled into his driveway. The small house was nicely lit by the streetlight, and looked quiet and peaceful, even welcoming. He got out and walked around to open her door for her; she gave him a look that made him wonder if she was going to protest the small courtesy. But she didn't, merely followed him around to the back of the car. He opened the trunk, getting out both the small duffel he'd packed to go into hiding and the larger suitcase Laurey had brought for her entire trip.

"Guess I'll have to get my hotel room back," she said.

Gage nearly bit his tongue stopping himself from saying she could stay here. They had too much to work out before he could make such an offer, and he had the numbing feeling in the pit of his stomach that, after they did, it would be a moot point.

"Or maybe," she said wearily, "I should just go home."

The stark words clawed at a place in him he'd never known was there, some vulnerable place he'd always managed to keep hidden until now. He wanted to shout "No!" but how could he? What was he going to do, ask her to stay? Stay and...what?

"Don't—" He stopped, afraid the next word was going to be "go." He swallowed and tried again. "Don't think about it now. You're tired and hungry. You can decide what you're going to do later."

He grabbed both bags before she could say any more and headed toward the front door. He heard her behind him and wished that things were different, normal, that they could be a normal couple coming home, that their entire relationship hadn't been haunted by the kind of adrenaline producing situations that threw your perceptions out of kilter, that—

Stop it, he ordered himself.

He set the bags down on the porch. He dug into his pocket for his house keys while Laurey, still looking a bit grim, paused to look at the hedgelike bush, festooned with orange and yellow flowers, that grew beside the steps. Lantana, he thought Tim, his gardener, had called it.

He unlocked the front door and gave it a shove. Out of the corner of his eye, he saw Laurey move. He turned to look as she bent to pick up a broken stem, the colors of the flowers muted in the glow of the streetlight. Then she started up the steps toward him.

Three things hit him with the rapid-fire swiftness of machine-gunfire. And just about as hard.

A large footprint, nearly hidden under the bush, in the soft dirt where she had found the broken stem.

The door, instead of swinging open easily as usual, moving slowly.

The sound of something dragging across wood.

"Get down!"

He yelled it as he flung himself off the porch at Laurey. He hit her hard, and she cried out.

And then the world exploded around them.

Chapter 17

She was putting up a good front, but Gage sensed that underneath the brisk efficiency, Laurey was still shaken. And why shouldn't she be? Three times in as many days, she'd nearly been killed. All because she was with him.

She sat on the edge of the bed in the one room she'd quietly told the desk was all they would need, wrapped in a hotel robe, a hotel towel wrapped around her freshly washed hair. She had little other than the guest package the hotel had provided and some items Kit had picked up for her at a drugstore. Her bag had been blown to pieces, along with his, and all she had of her own was what had been in her purse. He had less; he'd showered and sent his own jeans to the hotel laundry, and put on a pair Cruz had lent him, leaving the shirt off out of deference to the gouge some flying piece of shrapnel had left over his collarbone. He was hurting in more places than he could count; the aches from the crash had just begun to ease up, and now he had a whole new set. He tried to ignore them, but he knew he was moving a bit stiffly.

Even after the fire department had extinguished the initial blaze, the bomb and arson investigators wouldn't let him look for anything salvageable, not until they were done. He hadn't fought them over it, had just stared at the oddity of his own home marked off with yellow crime scene tape for the second time in his life. Maybe there was something about the house, something that drew tragedy in some way.

But he hadn't really cared that they wouldn't let him inside; he'd been more worried about Laurey than about seeing what was left of his possessions.

She reached up and pulled away the towel, moving rather stiffly. He knew she had to be bruised from the impact when he'd hit her, but Dr. Cutler had said they would both be fine, although she'd told Gage that if he didn't stop using up so much of her time, she was going to start billing him personally rather than the city.

They'd been lucky. He knew that. The bomb squad had told him that if he hadn't jumped when he had, getting them both below the level of the porch as the blast went off, they could have been killed. But he had, and most of the blast had gone over them instead of into them. And from the initial reports, he might even have something of a house left. The bomb squad expert had told them the way it had been set up, the blast had been directed outward.

"It was a simple mercury switch. All it took was the pull of this cord attached to the doorknob to unbalance it. This thing was meant to kill whoever opened that door, not blow up the house. And if you didn't have the reflexes of a cat, Butler, it would have. And the lady along with you."

And the lady along with you.... He stifled a shiver.

She began to try to untangle her hair with the small comb the hotel had provided. They'd come back here after the bomb squad had said they were fairly certain the bomb had been set and waiting for at least thirty-six hours, which put it before Martin got out on bail. With that information, Gage had talked the chief out of tossing him right back into the safe house, since it was probably one of Martin's initial attempts; Gage just hadn't been home to set it off.

But obviously that sense of being followed hadn't been his imagination. Whoever had set this—Gaylord didn't look smart enough, but then, Gage had thought he would have cracked and given Martin up by now, too, and he hadn't—had probably followed him, had maybe seen him leave the house with his duffel bag late Saturday night, figured he was gone for the weekend, then come in and rigged the door, not trusting any more futile shooting attempts.

Laurey twisted around as she tried to get the comb through a particularly tangled lock of hair. The movement made her wince, and she lowered the comb with a weary sigh. Gage moved without thinking, sitting behind her on the bed and taking the comb from fingers that he noticed were trembling slightly.

"Let me," he said.

She said nothing, but she didn't move away, so he began to work his way methodically through her wet, disheveled hair. And patiently. Every tiny tremor that rippled through her made him move more gently, more carefully. At last he had the dark mass free of tangles. But he kept running the comb through it in long, slow strokes, because she had let her head loll back and seemed to be relishing what he was doing.

Finally, with a little sigh, she reached back and stopped his hand. He thought she would move away then, but instead she leaned back toward him. He felt the coolness of the damp strands of her hair, then the softness of the thick, terry-cloth robe. And after a moment, he felt the heat of her body penetrating the cloth, warming the skin of his chest.

He cradled her there, his emotions as tangled as her mane of hair had been. He wanted to say a hundred things; he didn't want to say anything. He wanted to touch her everywhere; he didn't dare touch her at all. He wanted to run like hell; he wanted to stay like this forever.

And underlying all of it was that nagging guilt; if she hadn't been with him, none of this would have happened.

"Thank you," she whispered, startling him.

"I…you're welcome. You have beautiful hair. Even wet."

She turned her head slightly, and he saw just the corner of a smile. "Thank you. But I meant…for saving my life. Again."

He stiffened. "What?"

"That's three times you've put yourself between me and disaster."

He opened his mouth, but no words would come, no words could get past the sudden tightness in his throat. Here he'd been feeling guilty at putting her into harm's way, and she was thanking him for saving her life?

"That's a bit…above and beyond the call, isn't it?" she said. "Not that I'm not grateful, but—"

"Grateful?" It burst past the lump in his throat. "Did you ever stop to think that you wouldn't even have been in those situations if not for me?"

She twisted her head around then and gave him a rather puzzled look. "That doesn't change what you did."

"But if you… If I hadn't… It was my fault, damn it!"

She stared at him. "Your fault that some evil, sick mind with a power complex is trying to kill you for showing the world what he really is, a twisted man who'd drug and rape a child?"

"No," he said. "But if you hadn't been with me, he wouldn't have nearly killed you, too."

"Oh, no, you don't," Laurey said, turning completely around now to face him, sitting back on her heels. "You're not taking on that responsibility, too."

"I…what?"

"I'm a grown-up, Gage. I make my own decisions." Her mouth quirked. "Except, of course, when I'm ordered into protective custody."

"Exactly," Gage said, thinking she'd just proved his point. "You haven't had any choice."

"No," she said, shaking her head. "As much as I disliked being ordered, once I thought about it, I did see the sense of it. If I hadn't, I wouldn't have gone, orders or not."

"But the shootings, and the bomb… Damn it, I should have realized something like that might happen. Hell, I should have admitted what was going on before. You never should have been with me, when they took those shots, or at the house."

She smiled, and he felt his pulse give a little leap. "If you'd arrested me, forced me to go with you and all this happened, you might have a right to this guilt thing. But you didn't, so you don't.''

He stared at her as she absolved him of all responsibility. He knew there were a thousand things they needed to talk about, not the least of which were all the reasons this thing that had flared to life between them could never work, but right now, looking at her, all he could think of was touching her, holding her, tasting her sweetness once more.

He tried to rein in the heat that rushed through him, wondering where the hell it was coming from, when he'd developed this volcanic ability to overheat in a matter of seconds. He'd never been one for useless trips down dead-end roads, but he seemed to be rushing headlong down this one at about ninety miles an hour. He had no place in his life for what this should be, so why was he torturing himself?

Then Laurey lifted one slim hand and cupped his cheek, and he knew why. Because even a brief, fleeting taste of this was more than he could resist. And even knowing that it would only make the time after she was gone, after she'd gone back to her life and left him to his, even harder to get through, he couldn't bring himself to pull away.

"Gage," she whispered, and the sound of his name in that tone that made him remember with vivid, body-tightening clarity just how hot, fierce and sweetly consuming their loving had been, shattered what little remained of his common sense and restraint. Desperately he hung on to one small piece, knowing he had to give her the option, even as his body hated him for doing it.

"Are you sure you want this? It's not just…reaction?"

"Trying to take responsibility for my decisions again?"

"No. But things haven't exactly been…ordinary lately. And sometimes that can affect your judgment."

She laughed, a soft, wondering sound that brushed over him like feathers, sending a tingle racing along his spine. "Somehow I don't think you and 'ordinary' go together very often."

She slid her hand down his neck until her fingers were next

to the small bandage that covered the cut he'd sustained in the blast.

"For instance, there was nothing ordinary about what you did tonight. You saved both of us, Gage."

"I—"

She moved her hand again, putting a finger to his lips to hush him. The lightest of touches, it nevertheless sent a tiny jolt through him that made him forget to breathe for a moment.

"And there was nothing ordinary about how you put yourself between me and those bullets on Saturday."

"Just doing—"

She stopped him before he could get the words "my job" out.

"There's nothing ordinary about the way you do your job, either. And," she said, her voice going husky, "there was certainly nothing ordinary about the way you...made love to me."

Her words and the way she said them hit him as hard as any blow to the gut ever had. "God, Laurey..."

"I never knew," she said in that same husky tone. "I'd often thought something was missing, but I never knew just how much."

She leaned forward then, kissing his lips softly. In the same moment her hands slid over his chest. Her fingertips lingered gently over the long bruise that had been left by the seat belt, so gently that he felt no pain, only a touch that was almost healing. And then she moved, brushing over his nipples, and he sucked in a harsh breath. Not missing his reaction, she repeated the caress of flesh he'd never known could be so sensitive. And then she did it again, until the spark she'd created caught and began to burn. Low and deep it burned, a growing heat that forced him to shift his body to relieve the sudden, fierce pressure.

"Laurey," he whispered, cupping her face and tilting her head back. She parted her lips, wet them with her tongue. He knew it wasn't a calculated move to entice, just an instinctive invitation that she doubted she was even aware of giving.

But he was. And his body was; he was as hard now as if

this afternoon had never occurred. As if the hot, fierce coupling had never happened. As if he hadn't spent himself in her so thoroughly that he'd felt as if there was nothing left.

He felt as if he'd been waiting his entire life, not merely hours, and when she looked up at him with longing and need so clearly in her eyes, he wondered crazily if she felt the same.

And then the lure of her moistened lips was too powerful to resist. He lowered his mouth to hers, and discovered that knowing to expect the electric shock didn't lessen its impact. The fire already begun within him blazed, sending hot tentacles along what seemed like every nerve, yet they all ended in one place, that part of him that wanted nothing more out of life than to be deep inside her once more. At the same time, he wanted to hold her, just hold her, to let her know how much he admired her and what she'd done with her life, to tell her how bravely he thought she'd dealt with things she never should have had to deal with.

He'd felt need before, he'd experienced desire, but never had he felt anything like this. Never had he felt such a tangled mass of emotions, so many at once. During the burglary that had resulted in Debby's death, he'd felt pure fear. After, rage and guilt. When his parents had finally given up on their marriage—and him—he'd felt abandoned.

And he'd also decided he would never, ever let himself be hurt like that again. It had seemed obvious to his twelve-year-old mind that if you cared too much for any one person, it hurt when they inevitably left you, in one way or another.

And now all his rules were shattered, made useless by the confusion within him, by the force of his need for this woman, and, oddly, by the gentleness of her touch. But right now he didn't, couldn't, care. Not when she was kissing him as if she'd hungered for him as much as he had for her. He forgot every bruise, every ache except the one growing unbearably in his groin.

He kissed her deeply, savoring the honeyed sweetness of her mouth. Slowly, languorously, he probed and searched for every bit of that enticing taste. But the ability to go slowly vanished in a split second when she copied him, nibbling at his lower lip, tracing the even ridge of his teeth, then probing beyond until her tongue brushed his. He shivered, unable to stop himself or the erotic jolt that tiny invasion gave him.

His hands went to her shoulders, slipping beneath the thick terry cloth to slide over her skin. She made no move to stop him as he gently urged the robe back. It slipped downward, baring her to the waist, and still she didn't protest; instead, she freed her arms from the sleeves and raised them around his neck.

The movement brought her closer, close enough so that the soft, warm curves of her breasts pressed against his naked chest. He smothered a groan, but it escaped anyway when she slowly moved, rubbing herself over him sinuously. He felt her nipples harden against him, and her name broke from him on a rush of breath. Seemingly encouraged by the sound, she rose, turning on her knees on the bed and moving until she was straddling him.

"You're killing me," he muttered, meaning it; he could feel her heat, hovering over flesh so rigid with the need for that same heat that he thought he would explode if she so much as touched him.

Then she did touch him, gently, caressingly, through the denim of his jeans. "Oh, I hope not. Not on your birthday. I don't have a gift for you, so this will just have to do."

He sucked in a breath and held it, fighting his body's urgent demand for release. "Laurey, I borrowed these jeans," he said hoarsely, warningly.

"Then perhaps you should get out of them," she suggested, her voice as silky as her skin. Before he could gather enough breath to speak, she had pushed him flat on his back and unzipped him. He'd drawn the line at borrowing underwear, so in the space of a hissing breath her hands were on him.

He swore, low and harsh, as she traced his swollen length. Her touch was gentle, wondering, and he arched his body toward her in a silent plea for more. She stopped, looking at him in equally silent query. He opened his mouth, willing to beg, but no words would form. So instead he put his hand over hers and curled her fingers around him, showing her what he couldn't tell her.

"So hard?" she said.

"Yeah," he gasped as his entire body tightened under her tentative caress.

"It doesn't…hurt?"

Only then did he realize her other words had been a question about her hold on him, not an observation about his condition. "Oh, it hurts," he agreed with a strained, rueful chuckle. "It hurts so damn good I'm about to lose it right now."

"Should I…stop?"

"Only if you're going to take me right now."

Her eyes widened, turned dark and smoky gray. "Like…this?"

It took him a moment to figure out what she meant. "Yes, like this. You do it. You take me, you decide how hard, how fast, how deep.…"

His words trailed away, partly because they were too arousing even to himself, and partly because of the hot, fierce look of pleasure that had come over her face. Laurey rose on her knees and began to undo the belt of the robe. Gage moved quickly then, shoving the jeans down and off, mostly with his legs and feet, because he didn't want her to leave him, to move. He wanted her on top of him just as she was now, only with him buried deep inside her.

At the last second he snagged a foil packet out of his pocket; he'd grabbed a handful of condoms from the safe house, and they'd been in his pocket when he'd pulled off his worse-for-wear jeans and given them to the hotel laundry.

Before he could deal with it, Laurey had taken it. She opened it and pulled out the contents. Then she proceeded to sheath him with a long, slow, rolling motion that nearly drove him out of his mind. He was fairly sure he was whimpering by the time she was done; he was completely sure he didn't care. He'd never thought he could die of anticipation, but he wouldn't lay odds on his taking another breath if she didn't move soon.

When at last she eased herself down onto him, slowly, almost hesitantly, he closed his eyes against the fierce pleasure of it, thinking the anticipation was nothing against the reality of her closing around him, hot, slick and ready. She wanted this, wanted him. The readiness of her body fairly shouted it, and the knowledge licked at him like tiny flames, adding to the inferno already blazing inside him.

Her head lolling back, baring the lovely line of her throat, she began to move, just a slow, gentle rocking that never should have had the effect it did. But he couldn't deny the need gripping him like red-hot talons, clawing deeper with every slight adjustment of angle, tightening with every tiny sound of pleasure she made. He reached up and cupped her breasts, his body clenching as her nipples drew up tight, as if in anticipation. It was a temptation he could not resist, and his fingers caught and gently twisted the taut nubs. She cried out, arching her back to thrust her breasts toward him, at the same time grinding her hips hard against his, driving him so deep he echoed her urgent cry.

And then she changed the motion, lifting up, then easing back down, slowly, voluptuously, as if she were using him to stroke herself. Her head came forward, and she looked at him. Her lips were parted, her eyes heavy-lidded with pleasure, lashes half-lowered, but not enough to mask the heat glowing there.

He moved a hand to the place where they were joined, suppressing the violent urge to let go the instant his eyes focused on the spot where dark curls tangled with pale blond as she rode him close and tight. She began to move in rhythm with his touch, and it took every ounce of his restraint to resist the coaxing of her body as it grew hotter and tighter around him.

And then she went utterly still for an instant. He felt the first ripple go through her, felt it in the most intimate way possible, from deep inside her body. Her thighs gripped him as she moaned.

"Gage...oh, Gage..."

He barely had time to savor the sound of his name spoken in those tones of awe and wonder. Her body clenched tightly, gripping him in a way that made his effort to wait hopeless.

He gave it up, knowing she was there with him. His shoulders came up off the bed, and he clutched her, forcing her down harder against him. He let the tide surge through him, boiling up with a hot fierceness that made him cry out as the explosion took him, then left him shivering and weak when it was over. Too weak to move, too weak even to think.

He could focus on only one thing: that she had burned through every defense he had, that she had somehow slipped past every roadblock he'd ever built, that she had reached a part of him that had never been reached before. She'd said she didn't have a gift for him, and then had proceeded to give him the most incredible gift he'd received in his life.

It wasn't until he lay back, his body drained, his pulse at last slowing, it wasn't until he was drifting softly in some peaceful place he'd never known until she had come into his life, that it hit him. It was the thought that he wished this could go on and on, that he could spend every day like this, with her in his arms, that brought it on. That made him realize what he'd done. Something he'd sworn long ago he would never, ever do.

On top of everything else, he'd given the world a lever to use against him.

The winds of change had shifted.

"He was right," Laurey said as she read the newspaper Gage had stopped to pick up in the hotel lobby.

"Chief de los Reyes usually is."

He sounded odd, his tone one of resigned admiration, yet still edgy. Very edgy, as he had been all morning.

He'd been dodging the subject she knew was uppermost in both their minds. After a night spent in a passion that had surpassed even their first encounter in the safe house, Laurey knew there were things they needed to—things they *had* to—discuss. Like where they went from here.

"The whole slant of this article has changed," she said. "Listen to this. 'While Marina Heights Police are not saying that the attempts on the life of the case's lead investigator and a civilian witness are the responsibility of accused rapist

Mitchell Martin, they are saying he is a primary suspect in the hit-and-run, two shootings and last night's bombing.'" She looked over at him. "At least he's an 'accused rapist' now, not 'a leading businessman.'"

"Reporters know how to say the same thing five different ways to get five different reactions," he said wryly.

"I noticed. This makes it sound like he was trying to kill me, too, when he didn't even know about me."

"But he does now." Gage's voice had gone flat; clearly he still wasn't happy with that.

"They didn't identify me," she said pointedly.

"That's only a matter of time."

"By then, maybe it won't matter. If this works, and the public he's trying to impress starts to think he might be guilty, then maybe he won't risk any more attempts. The chief told me it looked like the bomb had been set up before, not after he got out on bail, so maybe—"

"Maybe, maybe, maybe," Gage growled. "You want to trust your life to a maybe?"

"Why not?" she asked simply. "You do."

"That's different."

"Uh-huh."

With that brilliant retort she figured she'd said all there was to say on the subject and lapsed into silence. They were nearly at Gage's house, on their way to find out how much was left of it. He hadn't wanted her to come, fearing, she was sure, another attempt of some kind, but he couldn't push the point without admitting he shouldn't go, either. Besides, even Gage had had to admit that it was probably the safest place in town at the moment, with cops still all over and the arson/bomb squad still poring over the scene.

It looked both worse and better than she'd expected. Worse because the front of the house was a charred skeleton, with piles of unrecognizable debris still smoking in places, better because the back of the house still stood, and looked intact.

This time they were let through, with a warning to go carefully. She was going to have to buy more clothes, Laurey thought glumly as she picked her way through the wreckage of what had once been Gage's living room; she would be coated in soot and wet ashes before long. Gage had told her that she should wait outside, but she'd insisted on going with him, to help him salvage whatever he could. She almost wished now that she'd done as he'd said; there was something unbearably grim about this process. It reminded her too much of looking at the twisted mass of metal that had been Lisa's car, of going through the items that had been retrieved from it: cassette tapes, garage door opener and most heartbreakingly, the flashlight key chain Laurey had given her sister several years before. That small item, and the fact that Lisa had kept and used it all that time, had destroyed what little composure Laurey had managed to hang on to; the full impact of her sister's death had come rushing in.

This is different. Nobody died here, she told herself as she tried to concentrate on the task before her. Thanks to Gage and his quick reaction, neither of them had even been badly hurt.

She glanced over at him; he'd walked around a heap of charred timbers to the far wall. Or, rather, where the wall had been, where, she recalled from her peek through the sliding glass door, the stereo and television had been. Had it really only been four days ago? It seemed impossible. But she supposed, when you lived in the course of a week more than most people lived in a month, time seemed to compress. And Lord knew, she had—

She stopped as her toe hit something hard amid a pile of soft, wet ashes. She looked down and saw the glint of something metallic. She bent to look and realized it was a strip of brass.

Tentatively she reached out and touched it, having some vague idea that it might still be hot. Instead it was cold, and she nudged it gently out of the ashes, glad for once that they were still damp enough to keep from flying up into her face.

It was a picture frame, looking blackened but almost intact. She looked at it sadly; these were the things that were the most tragic loss: pictures, memories of those loved, the irreplaceable things. Almost reluctantly, she turned it over.

The glass had shattered and was black in places. The photograph it held was burned at the edges and scorched across the center. But she could still see the subject. Too well.

A young girl looked out at her from amid the ruins. A pretty girl, maybe fourteen, with a pale shade of blond hair Laurey had seen before, and a pair of green eyes she knew too well. Except these eyes were different. They were clear and bright, unhaunted, unshadowed, and she knew that in the face of his sister she was getting a glimpse of what Gage must once have been like, before Fate had brought on that darkness he carried.

And it was this girl's awful, painful, ugly death that had done it. Emotion welled in her, sorrow for the ordeal of this girl she'd never known tangling with the pain of the contrast between open, innocent youth and the wounded, shadowed look in her brother's eyes.

He looks like my animals do when they're hurt. They can't say it, so it shows in their eyes.

Little Samantha Gregerson's wise words had never seemed so true. A deep, unrelieved ache grew inside Laurey, an ache to see Gage looking like this, free of the darkness. And in that moment, kneeling in the wreckage of what had been his home, looking at the sister whose murder had haunted him with guilt for nearly two decades, she finally admitted why.

She had fallen in love with Gage Butler all over again. Not with the same childish naiveté as she had eight years ago, but with all her adult heart, and despite her own vow never to love a man who loved his job more than anything else. And there was little doubt that nothing was more important to Gage than his work. And understanding why, that he was driven by the memory of what had happened to this sister who looked so like him, would not make it any easier to live with.

"I'm sorry," she whispered to the girl in the photograph. "You were so young. But can't you let him go? He's never had the chance to be young, because of what happened to you. Please, let him go. Make him see—"

"Just what is it you'd like me to see?"

Laurey sucked in a swift, audibly startled breath. "God, you scared me."

She looked up at him and saw that he was staring intently, his brows lowered ominously, at the picture she held. "Gage," she began, but something in his eyes, something hard and cold, stopped her.

"Go ahead," he instructed. "What is it I'm supposed to see?"

She steadied herself. "That it's time to let go of the past. You couldn't save her. And saving the entire planet won't make up for it."

His eyes went even harder, and she hated having them turned on her. There was no sign of pain or shadow in the green depths now, only anger. Directed at her. But somehow she sensed more was at stake here, more even than her newly admitted love for him. It felt as if his very soul was the prize here, and she was terrified that he was losing more of it every day he kept on this way.

"She wouldn't have wanted this, Gage," she said, not even caring that he had to hear the pleading note in her voice. "Can't you see that? It's gone beyond dedication, way beyond. You work too long, too hard, to the exclusion of everything else. You wear that jacket like a hair shirt. And as if that wasn't enough to keep your guilt close, you live in the house where she died, so every day you're reminded that you couldn't save her. So you're reminded that the best you can do is kill yourself trying to save all the rest. That's not dedication, Gage, that's obsession."

"You know," he said, his casual tone at odds with that stony glint in his eyes, "I'm getting real tired of everybody telling me I'm obsessed. I wish you'd all just leave me the hell alone and let me do my job."

It took most of what nerve she had left after the past week to do it, but she held that stormy gaze. "You should be glad people care enough to worry about you. You certainly don't make it easy."

She saw him shift his attention to the photo she held. For a long moment he just looked at the image of his dead sister. "I didn't ask anyone to care," he muttered, barely loud enough for her to hear. "That's a fool's game."

Laurey's hands trembled suddenly. She set the scorched photo down with care and slowly stood up, wiping her sooty hands on the jeans she'd bought this morning. Caitlin, Kelsey and Lacey had all offered clothing, but she was too tall to wear anything of theirs. She turned away and began to make her way out of the wreckage. She moved cautiously, picking each place she put her feet with care. She concentrated on walking out of that pile of ashes as if every step could be her last. She felt as if it were the truth.

She knew why she was making the simple act of walking so all consuming. She knew it was to keep from thinking about the ludicrous fact that in the space of less than a minute she had admitted she loved Gage Butler and had that love, albeit undeclared, thrown back in her face. She'd given it her best shot, tried desperately to reach him through the guilt that drove him, and she'd failed. No one could care more than she did, but she'd failed.

That's a fool's game.

She could hardly deny that, not when she'd been the biggest fool of all. Fool enough to think that he wasn't like her father. Fool enough to believe that the reason for being obsessed with his work made a difference. Fool enough to believe that any man like that could, or would, make room in his life for her. There was no more room in Gage's life and heart for her than there had been in her father's.

He might care about the victims he helped, about the kids he was dedicated to saving, but just as her father had used his work as an excuse to stay remote from his own family, Gage was using his to keep his caring impersonal, detached from himself. Oh, he cared, probably more than any cop around. But always from a distance. A safe distance.

That's a fool's game.

If that was how he felt about simply caring for another human being, then it was fairly clear how he would feel about love. There was no room in his life for any one person to be that important to him.

Don't ever give the world a lever to use against you....

Ryan Buckhart's words rang in her now aching head. He'd

been right, perhaps more so than he'd known. Gage would never give the world the lever of loving someone.

She reached the grass, stepping across a small branch from the lantana bush that had been destroyed. It was oddly intact, the bright flowers a vivid contrast to the destruction. But cut off from any chance of survival, they, too, would die. Quickly. No doubt much more quickly than the love she'd finally admitted to. It would take time for that to die. A very long time.

She shivered and rubbed her arms as she kept walking. She wasn't sure where she was going, only that she had to keep moving. His house wasn't the only thing in ashes, she thought morosely. She was sadly thankful that at least she had not told him she loved him. She supposed the only thing left for her to do was to go home and remind herself how many times she had sworn never to get involved with a man who placed his work above all.

Some pleading part of her mind was trying to be heard, to tell her that she was reacting too strongly to what had been a comment made by a man who had just had his house blown up. But nothing could change how he'd reacted when she'd almost involuntarily spoken to the image of his dead sister. Nothing could change the coldness in his eyes, as if she'd trespassed unforgivably on some sacred ground. Nothing could change that icy declaration that caring was a fool's game. She kept walking.

Nothing could change the simple fact that he didn't come after her.

Chapter 18

He hadn't slept in days. And he knew better than to think it was because of being in a strange bed. Kelsey's Oak Tree Inn was peaceful, restful. It was he himself who was not at peace, not at rest.

He was also under a microscope, or so it seemed. Everyone at Trinity West seemed to be watching him intently, with either wariness or concern. It had taken him a while to notice; in the two weeks since Laurey had left, he hadn't been aware of much. He'd kept going, sticking to the routine of long hours, of complete immersion in his work, because he could do it without thought; the routine was second nature to him, and it was the only thing that could distract him from the hole Laurey's departure had left. Even the fact that Martin was back in jail, after Gaylord had broken and confessed who had hired him to kill Gage, brought only a minor ripple of satisfaction.

As had his confrontation with the man, who wasn't quite as arrogant anymore, now that his attorney had threatened to quit over his stupidity in trying to murder the cop investigating him and hiring an idiot to do it.

"We've broken your alibi," he'd told Martin matter-offactly, while lolling back in his chair. "We've traced the purchase of several of the ingredients to make the drug to you. And when that girl gets on the stand, looking as sweet and innocent as she was before you put your filthy hands on her, and when we have her priest testify she was considering joining a convent, you're going to look like the slime that you are."

His coolness affected the man where his anger never had. And Gage had smiled as Martin shifted uneasily in the small, hard chair.

"I guess I should thank you," Gage told him. Martin's brows, so sparse they looked almost plucked, rose in surprise over his reptile-cold eyes. Gage got up and, still smiling, leaned over the interview table. "You gave me more to hang you with. Drugs, rape, kidnapping…all gift wrapped with attempted murder. Thanks for my birthday present, Martin."

Martin had still been angry, still a blowhard, but Gage could see it was hollow now, and even the man's tirade against him as he'd walked out had had little effect.

Or maybe he just didn't care anymore. He didn't seem to care about much of anything anymore.

It was for the best, he told himself yet again as he went down the hall to the coffee room for yet another cup of the questionably consumable but caffeine-laced station brew. It had to be this way, he knew that, and better she should leave angry at him than hurt. He'd had no business letting it go so far anyway, not when he'd known what the inevitable end would be. For a while, when she was near and having that chaotic effect on him, he'd forgotten that there was no room in his life for such things, had even begun to wonder if maybe there was.

He'd come to care a great deal for Laurey, enough to question one of the basic rules he lived by, and that had scared him. Caring, letting people get close, was what got you hurt. Because they left. They always left, and you ended up sitting there with the pain of all your caring drowning you.

That's a fool's game.

His own words echoed in his head. And called up the vivid

memory of Laurey's pale face, her eyes wide with pain as she turned away from him, accepting the blow he hadn't meant to deliver then, but couldn't find the words to take back once it had been done.

His hands shook, and he had to set down the pot of coffee. A half cup would have to do, he thought. He wasn't going to risk getting scalded by trying it again. He turned and headed back toward the detective division office.

It was better this way, he told himself once more. A clean break, now, before either of them was irrevocably involved or irreparably hurt. Or at least, before she was; he wasn't so sure about himself anymore.

He snapped out of his unpleasant reverie when he nearly collided with somebody in the hall. He barely managed to keep from drenching the other man with hot coffee and was more than thankful for the fact when he realized it was Chief de los Reyes.

"Sorry, sir," he said.

"No harm done." De los Reyes stopped, and studied him for a moment, frowning. "I retract that," he said. "Step into my office."

Gage blinked, startled, as the man gestured toward the door at the end of the hall. "Sir?"

"I want to talk to you."

"Now? I have some work I need to—"

"The world won't collapse if it waits a few minutes. Now, Detective Butler."

Moments later he was in the chair he'd sat in the last time he was here. With Laurey. Determinedly he shoved the image out of his mind, tried not to think about the quiet courage with which she had told the chief to go ahead and make her existence public if it would keep Martin from trying to kill him. And it had worked; his life had been, if nothing else, uneventful since the day de los Reyes had held his press conference.

The chief sat in his chair behind the big desk, setting the tone. Gage knew it meant this was going to be something more formal than just a friendly chat. He braced himself inwardly.

"Kit came to me about you the other day. I told her I'd

look into it as soon as I got back from the chiefs' meeting tomorrow. But I see now that it can't wait."

"Kit…came to you?" Damn, Gage thought.

"This is not about Kit," de los Reyes said, heading him off with surprising force. "She did what she felt she had to. And she was right." He leaned back in his chair. "You look like hell, Gage."

"I…haven't been sleeping too well."

"You're staying at the Gregersons', right?"

"Yes. They had room, and Kelsey offered…." He ended with a shrug.

"A nice, quiet place, from what I've heard. Conducive to relaxation." Gage studied his hands, not having an answer to that. "But you're not relaxing."

"Maybe I'm still a little…rattled."

"Hmm," de los Reyes said, steepling his hands in front of him. "Martin has backed off since his arraignment and the addition of attempted murder charges. And the DA says our case is rock solid. Martin has apparently decided killing you is not the way out of his troubles, so you're out of protective custody. The clerk in the judge's office who leaked word on the warrant is on suspension pending an investigation. Your home is being repaired, your car being replaced, with help from the city. Everything's being put back the way it was."

Not quite everything, Gage thought grimly.

"And unofficially," de los Reyes said, "should we be so fortunate as to toss Mitchell Martin into state prison, I'm sure I can find someone who will explain to him how easily a man can be reached, even in prison."

Gage stared at the man across the desk. He knew what was behind the carefully chosen words, that he'd just been given a promise that Martin would know that if anything happened to Gage, he would be presumed responsible. And that he wouldn't be safe from retribution just because he was in prison. It wasn't politically correct, he supposed, but it was the reason anybody at Trinity West would go to the wall for this man.

"Thank you," he said, rubbing his gritty eyes with the heels of his hands. "I'll...breathe easier now."

"Will you?" de los Reyes said. "I've seen people where you are, Gage. Some come out of it. Some don't. This isn't a lifetime career for everybody. And you've put in a lifetime in eight years."

Gage's hands came down. What did that mean? he wondered, and looked at de los Reyes, searching for an answer in his face. He remembered Kit's statement that the man knew everything that went on under his command, and now, looking into gray eyes that were unusually light, lighter than Laurey's smoky gray, he didn't doubt it. And he knew that nothing would get him in more trouble with Miguel de los Reyes than to lie.

"I'm tired," he admitted. "And lately I've been wondering a lot about...whether it's worth it."

The chief was silent for a long moment. Then, with his gaze fastened intently, almost unnervingly, on Gage, he said with quiet resoluteness, "I hesitated to do this, Gage, but I see no choice in the matter now. You've been pushing too hard for too long. I know why—" Gage's head came up again, and he saw both knowledge and compassion in the pale eyes; he *did* know. Gage lowered his gaze again as the man went on "—but that doesn't change what I have to do. I'd hoped that now, with this case stabilized, you would do it yourself. But now it's an order, Gage. You're on leave until the Martin trial begins."

"What?" Gage exclaimed. It wasn't the order that startled him; he'd been half expecting it, knowing Kit wouldn't have forgotten his promise to take time off, a promise he hadn't yet kept. It was the amount of time that had shocked him. "They set the trial date for three months from now!"

"Exactly." De los Reyes smiled, an odd combination of amusement and concern. "Contrary to what you might think, as good as you are, Gage, we *can* survive without you."

"But—"

"You need to find some balance, Gage. You're walking too

close to an edge that could crumble out from under you, and I like and respect you too much to want that to happen.''

"Okay, I'll take some time," Gage said, almost desperately. "But not three months!"

"It's not negotiable, Gage."

"But—"

"See you next year," de los Reyes said. And his tone left no doubt that the subject was closed.

He was going, Gage thought wearily, out of his mind. He should be relaxing, with all this free time, but instead he felt more wound up, more tense and more confused than he ever had on the job. He'd never realized until now how much of an outlet it had been. He'd never realized until now exactly how much of his life it had been.

Face it, Butler, he muttered silently, sourly, *it is your life. And it has been for a long time.*

He was going to have to do something—anything—to take the edge off, before he flew apart into a million pieces. At first he'd tried to expend some of his edgy energy in repairing his house, but the work was coming along quickly, and the foreman of the crew had tossed him out the third day he'd shown up.

Maybe he should move, find somewhere else to stay until the house was done. Sometimes being around Kelsey and Cruz was a bit...much. They were so crazy in love it almost hurt to watch them. And when Quisto and Caitlin had arrived for Thanksgiving dinner tonight, it had been even worse; Caitlin was radiantly pregnant and, watching her, Gage felt a pang he didn't completely understand. But it wasn't until Ryan and Lacey had arrived, bringing the new baby, that Gage had broken and run for it.

He knew he would never forget the night little Amanda had been born. It had been one of the few things that had stirred him out of the lethargy that had overtaken him. Lacey had a rough labor, and when it was over, big, strong Ryan Buckhart had broken down and cried. And Gage had no sooner convinced himself, with some relief, that this was the kind of pain not caring let you avoid than Ryan had shown them his tiny daughter, smiling with pure, glowing joy, and Gage realized that not caring kept that away, as well.

He'd escaped to the quiet of the pond just above the house, welcoming the chill of the November air. And trying not to wonder what Laurey was doing on this holiday that focused on the togetherness of families, a togetherness he'd not known since he was ten. He could ask Caitlin, he supposed; he knew they'd kept in touch. It was how he had known she'd gone back to Seattle.

His mind veered off that course. He didn't want to think about her being gone, and he wanted to think even less about her coming back to testify at the trial; he didn't know how he would survive that.

He stared at the still water of the pond, wondering idly if it was deep enough to drown in. His mouth twisted at one corner; three inches of water was enough to drown in, if you were determined enough.

A light came on below, near the house, drawing his gaze. Sam, he thought, checking on her zoo. The child was amazingly dedicated to the small creatures she rescued; no holidays for her. While Kelsey and Cruz had been more than kind, it was Cruz's little girl who had astounded him with her youthful wisdom and understanding. More than once she'd hugged him, or climbed up on his lap to snuggle, for no apparent reason. She was always bringing him things, leaving him little notes and drawings in an apparent effort to cheer him. He didn't quite know why she did it, and sometimes her attempts caused more pain than they eased, but he hadn't been able to ask her to stop.

He would go down there now, he thought. Some of the feed she used for her critters was stored up out of reach of some of the local marauders who were capable of foraging on their own, and Samantha clambering up the ladder to get at it made him a bit nervous.

He heard her quiet, soothing humming as he neared the garage tool room that had been remodeled into a habitat for the menagerie of injured animals; the girl was a premier veterinarian in the making, Gage thought.

He stopped in the doorway when he realized this wasn't a regular feeding but a holiday one: fresh lettuce and scrubbed carrots for the two rabbits, tiny pieces of fruit for the birds…he didn't want to even speculate about Slither, or what a king snake would eat for Thanksgiving. Sam was unaware of his presence, and he took the chance to watch her, a smile curving his mouth despite his mood.

But then something about her gentle, careful tending of her charges struck a familiar note, and the smile faded. He suddenly understood her attention to him; she approached him the same way, as if he were some wounded creature she was trying to heal. Somehow she had sensed it, that he was torn apart inside, and was trying the only way she knew how to help. A wave of sudden emotion swamped him. Tangled, confused emotions, the kind he'd been battering down for two weeks.

He backed away before she saw him, because he wasn't at all sure he wasn't going to crack right here and now.

In fact, he wasn't sure he hadn't cracked already; voices kept echoing in his mind. Wasn't that one of the first signs? He'd been able to keep them at bay while working, but now…now nothing seemed able to quiet them. Kit, Ryan, the chief, their words hammered at him.

It can't go on, Gage. Do I have to go to the chief and have him make it an order before you get some help?

I've been there, buddy. I grew up without having a human being in the world who gave a damn about me. And I'll tell you, it's a damn cold way to live.

You're walking too close to an edge that could crumble out from under you, and I like and respect you too much to want that to happen.

And Laurey, the most painful of all…

It's time to let go of the past. You couldn't save her. And saving the entire planet won't make up for it…. It's gone beyond dedication, way beyond. You work too long, too hard, to the exclusion of all else. You wear that jacket like a hair shirt. And as if that wasn't enough to keep your guilt close, you live

*in the house where she died, so every day you're reminded
that you couldn't save her. So you're reminded that the best
you can do is kill yourself trying to save all the rest. That's
not dedication, Gage, that's obsession.*

Obsession.

Obsession.

The word spun in his mind like an endless loop, and he saw
Laurey, looking at him with such pain, such compassion,
such…love.

It *had* been love. He saw it now, so clearly, what she'd
been trying to do that day in the ashes of his house. She'd
been trying to break through, trying to make him see. And he
saw why. She loved him.

She loved him, and he'd killed it, unthinkingly crushed it
as surely as that explosion had destroyed the pitiful vestiges
of an isolated life.

He was running, and he didn't know to where. In fact, he
wasn't even sure where he was; somehow he'd left the Inn
behind and was on a narrow road he didn't recognize. He
slowed, then stopped. He looked around, but all was darkness.
There was no moon, and even the stars seemed faint. Shaking,
he sank to the ground on the edge of the gravel road. The
silence seemed to descend around him; even the distant hum
of traffic seemed to vanish. There was nothing to distract him,
nothing to see, nothing to hear, nothing to turn to to fight off
the tide of memories.

They came at him, battering him, in all their ugly fury.
Relentlessly, until he was rocking back and forth, moaning
under his breath. But his desperate "No, no, no," was useless
in this silent, dark place, and he knew that he was seeing the
essence of where his soul had been living, in this hell of his
own making.

Laurey was right. Debby would not have wanted this. She
had lived her short life joyously, in the sunlight, not in darkness, and he knew, with a gut-level certainty that he'd fought
against for nearly twenty years, that she would hate what he'd
done to himself in her name. She would have told him to let
go of the grief. She would have told him that he had to find

the most joy in life he could, because he would have to do it for both of them. Debby had loved him. She would not have wanted this.

He sat there, still shaking under the impact of those revelations. And for the first time ever he cried for his sister.

Laurey shook off her umbrella before she tossed it into the back seat of her car. The area around the Madison Street office of the magazine was quiet, nearly deserted on this Christmas Eve. She wouldn't be here herself if she hadn't spent the night with a girlfriend whose apartment was within walking distance. After the rather rowdy office party, where for one of the few times in her life she'd downed enough alcohol to take her beyond a buzz and all the way into tipsiness, it had seemed the thing to do rather than risk the drive to her apartment in the University of Washington district, locally known as U-Dub. Now she drove carefully on the slick streets, thankful it was only water and not the treacherous black ice she had to deal with. With the minimal traffic, she was quickly onto the freeway and headed north.

Of course, she thought as she drove, many things seemed rowdy to her these days. Not just that party, but the people all over town, the traffic in the streets, even the people in the office seemed unduly cheerful. The gaily decorated stores were as bad, and the seasonally enthusiastic Pike Place Market, usually one of her favorite places, was unbearable.

But then, almost everything was unbearable to her now, and had been for every minute of every day of the six weeks since she'd left Gage standing in the ruins of his house. The Thanksgiving spent with her parents had been excruciating; every sign of holiday cheer only probed a wound that had yet to heal. She wondered if it ever would, or if she would be forever doomed to regret that he hadn't loved her back, that he hadn't even wanted her love, that she hadn't been enough for him when measured against his beloved badge. But most of all she regretted that she hadn't been able to reach him, that Gage would go on and on in that endless cycle of guilt and punishment, that he would drive himself harder and harder until it killed him. Or some other slime like Martin did it for him.

The only thing she didn't regret was loving him in the first place. No matter what had happened, she wouldn't give up those memories for anything. He'd taught her more about love and passion than she'd ever known, and that was a lesson she couldn't feel sorry about, even if it made her current pain worse.

She only wished he could have learned it, as well, could have learned that although there was risk involved in caring, and even more in loving, the gain was worth the cost. She wished—

Stop it, she ordered herself. Wishes were useless things, even at this time of year, when they were supposed to be granted. She concentrated on the last of the drive and parked with care when she reached home, one quarter of an older house that had been divided into apartments. She gathered up the gag gift she'd acquired in the office exchange—a rather garish, plastic bird of paradise plant, complete with a bright orange-and-yellow flower that reminded her painfully of the flowers in front of Gage's house—her briefcase and umbrella, and walked to her door.

There was a loud scraping noise from the small private patio beside her door. She spun around. The bird of paradise hit the wet cement at her feet. And at the sight of the soaking wet man who stood there, her hand shot to her mouth, pressing hard against her lips to stop a cry.

"Hello, Laurey," Gage said.

Chapter 19

He was still shivering, but he shook his head at her offer of anything more than hot coffee, a towel for his sopping hair and the chance to take off his wet jacket and shoes. The bruises were gone, she noticed, then chided herself; of course they would be, it had been six weeks. It was just that he'd been battered in one way or another half the time she'd known him, it seemed.

And then it hit her; for the first time since she'd known him, he was wearing a different jacket. Not the leather one his sister's murderer had worn. She shivered in turn, then steadied herself, forcing herself not to read any great significance in the absence of the haunted garment.

"How...long were you waiting?" she asked, eyeing his towel-tousled hair.

"I..." He stopped for a particularly harsh shiver. She ignored his earlier refusal and draped the blanket throw from the back of her couch over him. He let her, as he managed to ask, "This time?"

She stepped back, then sat on the chair opposite the couch. "You were here before?"

"I...got in yesterday. I came straight here, but...you didn't come home." There could have been a world of implication in those words, but there wasn't; he was speaking simply, tiredly. "I finally went and slept in the rental car for a while, but I couldn't see the door from there, so this afternoon I came back and waited here."

"In the rain?"

His mouth quirked. "This time of year, I gather it's pretty tough not to do everything in the rain around here."

"We reap the benefits," she said.

"I know. It's...beautiful. I never realized how beautiful."

Were they just going to sit here discussing the weather and the beauty of this place? she wondered.

"Why are you here?" she asked, not caring if she sounded abrupt; she'd been too shocked by his unexpected appearance. "And on Christmas Eve?"

He looked uncomfortable. "I sort of...forgot about that. I...needed to see you. To talk to you."

"If it's about the case, I already let Kit know where to reach me if they need me to testify."

He looked startled. "You...did?"

"Yes. Didn't she tell you?"

"No." He grimaced slightly, lowering his eyes to his feet; his socks were wet, too, but he'd kept them on. "But I haven't been to the station in a while."

It was her turn to be startled. She would have figured he'd have to be on his deathbed to stay away, and while he was wet and cold, he certainly didn't appear ill. "You haven't?"

"I was...on a leave of absence."

She gaped at him. "Why?"

"Chief's orders."

"Oh." What should she say to that? Offer condolences, she supposed. "I'm sorry."

His head came up, and he looked at her then. And she saw something in his eyes that nearly took her breath away. Something warm and alive that looked heartrendingly like hope.

"I'm not," he said softly. "It was the best thing that ever happened to me. All that time off...I had nothing to do but think. About what everyone had been telling me for so long. About what you told me. And…about what you didn't tell me."

Laurey's breath caught. He couldn't know, he couldn't possibly. Could he?

"I realized, when I didn't have the work to hide behind anymore, that that was just what I'd been doing. You were right, Laurey. I passed dedication a long way back. My work had become an obsession. Maybe the motivation was different, maybe even worthwhile, like you said, but…the result was the same as if it weren't. I shut out everything and everyone, and I told myself I preferred it that way. That if I didn't care, I could never hurt again like I did that night. The night my sister died."

"Oh, Gage," Laurey murmured, not knowing what else to say.

"But one night I finally realized you'd been right. Debby never would have wanted this, not for her sake. She wasn't like that. She would have hated…what I'd become. So I…finally got some help. One of the department shrinks. I've been going…for the past month, trying to work some things out. He finally made me see that my way hurt just as much in the end. And had none of the benefits."

He took a deep shuddering breath, and Laurey could only guess at the pain coming face-to-face with all this had cost him.

"All the people who tried to get in, people who wanted to help, good people…Kit, Ryan, Cruz…even the chief. But I wouldn't let them. I didn't want anybody to get close, because when they left, or…died, it would hurt too much. And I shut you out most of all, because I knew when you left, it would…kill me."

"Gage," she began, but he held up a hand to stop her.

"Please. Let me just…get this out. I've spent a lot of days trying to figure out what I could possibly say to make you understand, to make you forgive me for being the…cold bastard I was to you."

She made a tiny sound of protest; she'd always known he

wasn't intentionally the way he was, that it had been self-protection. But he shook his head.

"No. I had no right to treat you that way when all you'd ever done was give to me."

"And scream at you like a shrew," she reminded him.

A ghost of a smile flitted across his lips. "After that, I mean." But he seemed to take courage in her small joke and went on. "I finally realized there was only one thing to say that matters. I don't expect you to accept it, or even believe it, but I have to tell you. I love you, Laurey."

Her eyes widened, and she nearly gasped aloud. She'd never expected to hear it, let alone so unadorned and forthright.

"I could tell you about all the confusion I went through, explain why it took me so long to realize it, but I doubt it would make any difference. I know that…whatever you may have felt for me I probably…killed that day at my house. I understand that."

"You've…come to understand a lot in a month."

"And I haven't liked much of it," he said quietly. "I've wasted a lot of years. I've hurt a lot of people along the way, people who didn't just leave but were shoved away. I have so much to regret…but there's nothing I'll mourn deeper or longer than losing you."

Laurey stared at him, saw the stark, unvarnished truth of his words—and the emotions behind them—in his eyes. He'd come such a long way; this was not the man who had stood amid the wreckage of his home and told her coldly that caring was a fool's game.

"Just…" His voice cracked, and he tried again. "I don't know if it will make it better or worse, but just tell me… You did care…didn't you?"

All the emotion she'd tried so hard to crush in the past month bubbled up inside her. "No," she whispered.

Gage paled. "Then I guess I was wrong. About that, too, along with—"

"No, I didn't just 'care,' Gage. The word is 'love.'"

"Oh, God." A visible shudder rippled through him. He

lowered his eyes again. "Did I, Laurey? Did I kill it that day?"

"You...hurt me," she said, unwilling to give him a direct answer. "A great deal."

"I know I did. I've thought about that more than anything. And I thought of a dozen ways to try to persuade you to give me another chance. I wouldn't buy any of them, if I was in your place. But when it came down to it...there's really only one. One thing to prove to you I mean what I said, and that...things would be different."

She saw him draw a deep breath. Then he let it out. He swallowed. His lips tightened. And Laurey was holding her own breath, wondering what on earth could be so very hard to say. Instinctively she got up, walked to the sofa and sat down beside him. And then he told her.

"I quit."

She gasped. "What?"

"I quit," he repeated.

"You're not serious!"

"I handed in my resignation the day before I left."

She stared at him, utterly stunned. He might as well have said he'd cut off an arm or a leg.

"Funny," he said, as if speaking of nothing more important than the weather they'd been talking of before, "nobody seemed surprised. Not happy, but not surprised. De los Reyes even seemed to have expected it."

"Gage, why?"

"I told you. It's the only way you could be sure."

"But you love your work. You live for it."

"I lived for it and nothing else for far too long."

"But to *quit*," she said, still stunned.

"I have to," he said. "It's like an addiction, Laurey. If I do it at all, I can only do it one way, the way I've always done it. The all-consuming, destructive way I've always done it. There's no middle ground for me. If I don't stop... eventually it will destroy me. One way or another. I won't lie. It hurt so much to quit...but it would kill me to stay."

It was so close to what she'd just thought that she nearly shivered herself. "I...you're not doing this...for me, are you? I don't want that, Gage. I could never live with the thought that you'd given up what you love, because you thought I—"

"No." He cut her off gently. "Not *just* for you, although that's a big part of it." And then he looked at her, directly, unwaveringly, and she did shiver at the power of what she saw in those vivid green eyes. "It's a simple choice, Laurey. As a cop, I can only be...who I was. I don't know any other way to do the job. And it was eating me alive. I'm quitting, even if you...throw me out that door. But it was you who gave me the strength to see, to look at myself and see what I'd turned into."

He reached out then, touching her for the first time, his palm gently cupping her cheek, his thumb tracing her lips. She heard his breath catch, and the tiny sound made a quiver begin somewhere deep inside her.

"You gave me a taste of what my life could be," he whispered. "And I want more than a taste. I love you. I need you. I want you with me for however long we both have. I'd prefer to be married, but I'll take what I can get. And next to that, nothing else matters much."

The last of her hesitation vanished, seared to ash by the fire of his touch and the growing heat in his eyes. "You...hurt me that day, but...no matter how hard I tried to hate you again, I couldn't. I was hurting for you too much. I've thought of little else since I left. I love you, Gage."

He closed his eyes for a moment, and Laurey knew she had never seen so much welcome relief before. "Thank God," he murmured. His tone was so thankful, she decided to give him the rest.

"In fact, I've loved you since I first saw you all those years ago."

His eyes opened. "I know."

She blinked. Arrogance? From Gage Butler? It didn't fit. "You knew?"

"Not then, I didn't. I thought it was just...a crush or something. But I finally figured that out along with everything else.

I realized you're not the kind to hold a simple grudge that long, so I knew there had to be a reason you were so furious with me after all that time. That was the only thing that made sense."

"It *was* a crush. The biggest one I've ever had, before or since. I thought you were the most wonderful, beautiful, sexiest man who ever lived."

She had the extreme pleasure of seeing him blush. "Jeez, Laurey—"

"Of course, that was then, and this is now," she said.

His mouth twisted. "So now you know better, huh?"

She nodded. "I don't think that anymore." At his expression, she smiled softly. "I *know* it."

As his color deepened, Laurey leaned forward and kissed him. A warm, welcoming kiss that held all the promises for the future she could put into it.

Much later, in her curved brass bed, as he stroked her hair and she reveled in the feel of being sprawled atop him, and in the knowledge that adrenaline and near-death escapes were not what had made their passion so powerful, he asked if she would mind having the wedding in California.

"Trinity West sort of has it down to a science, after Quisto and Ryan and Cruz," he said. "And I think they'd…like to all be there. They're still my friends, and always will be."

"I'd like that. I feel like they've become my friends, too."

"They feel the same way," he assured her. He lifted his head then, giving her a quizzical look. "I'm curious, though. What did the chief say to you that day? When he called you back after he decided to go public?"

She smiled. "Only three words. That could have been taken any number of ways. I get the impression a lot of what he says is like that. But they were three very true words."

"They…were? What were they?"

She reached up and cupped his face in her hands. "He said, 'He's worth it.'"

Gage looked stunned, but the flush that rose to his face told her that he was pleased, as well. She pulled him down to her, kissed him, and sighed happily when he snuggled against her shoulder.

"I put the house up for sale," he said after a moment. Laurey went still. "It was time. Just like it was time to...get rid of that damned jacket."

"I'm glad," she whispered.

"I'll probably always wish I could have saved her," he said. "But I'm not going to...torment myself over it anymore."

She let out a small sigh of relief; he truly had rid himself of the guilt.

It was a moment before he said, sounding only half joking, "Are you sure you want to marry an unemployed ex-cop?"

"I want to marry *you*," she answered positively. "The rest is incidental."

"I'll do something," he assured her. "I'm just not sure what yet."

"I know. You're not the type to just sit around."

"I don't know," he mused in mock consideration. "The idea of being a kept man has a certain appeal."

"Okay," she said simply.

He laughed then, and at the joy in the sound, a note she'd never heard from him before, Laurey gave heartfelt thanks. Still laughing, he rolled her beneath him and rained kisses down on her any place he could reach.

"Merry Christmas," she said. "And thank you for the best present I've ever gotten."

"Thank you for my life," Gage said, so solemnly it brought tears to her eyes.

When he made love to her that time, something deep and profound happened between them and afterward they lay quietly for a long time, in silent acknowledgment.

It was Gage who at last broke the spell.

"Do you suppose we could get Sam into a dress long enough to be a flower girl?"

He'd told her about the little girl and what she'd done to foster the breakthrough that had finally reached him. "Sam can be a flower girl in whatever she darn well pleases," Laurey said fervently.

Gage smiled, a soft, loving smile that went beautifully with the joyful laugh she'd heard for the first time tonight. "Do you think someday we could...work on one of our own?"

Laurey's heart leapt at this proof of how far he'd come; she knew Gage realized more than most how much caring it took to raise a child. She knew better than anyone that he would never, ever shortchange a child. And above all, she knew just what it meant for him to offer up that most powerful of levers to the world, how much sheer courage it had taken.

"I would love that as much as I love you," she whispered. He hugged her, tightly. "Maybe we should...practice some more first, though," she said, nuzzling his ear.

"The perfect child takes a lot of practice," he agreed willingly.

That Christmas morning both Laurey and Gage agreed that the best presents were those you couldn't wrap. Then they held each other tightly, savoring the knowledge that together they had found gifts that would last a lifetime.

* * * * *

Curious to know what happens when things start heating up between Chief Miguel de los Reyes and Sergeant Kit Walker? Don't miss the next book in the TRINITY STREET WEST series from Justine Davis and Intimate Moments—coming your way in 1998!

Author Note

In 1996, the state of California passed legislation, effective January 1, 1997, making the possession of the sedative Rohypnol a felony. The drug had not previously been illegal.

Return to the Towers!

In March
New York Times bestselling author

NORA ROBERTS

brings us to the Calhouns' fabulous
Maine coast mansion and reveals the
tragic secrets hidden there for generations.

For all his degrees, Professor Max Quartermain has a
lot to learn about love—and luscious Lilah Calhoun is
just the woman to teach him. Ex-cop Holt Bradford is
as prickly as a thornbush—until Suzanna Calhoun's
special touch makes love blossom in his heart.
And all of them are caught in the race to solve
the generations-old mystery of a priceless
lost necklace…and a timeless love.

Lilah and Suzanna
THE
Calhoun Women

**A special 2-in-1 edition containing
FOR THE LOVE OF LILAH and
SUZANNA'S SURRENDER**

Available at your favorite retail outlet.

Silhouette®

Look us up on-line at: http://www.romance.net   CWVOL2

Take 4 bestselling love stories FREE

Plus get a FREE surprise gift!

Special Limited-time Offer

Mail to Silhouette Reader Service™

P.O. Box 609
Fort Erie, Ontario
L2A 5X3

YES! Please send me 4 free Silhouette Intimate Moments® novels and my free surprise gift. Then send me 6 brand-new novels every month, which I will receive months before they appear in bookstores. Bill me at the low price of $3.96 each plus 25¢ delivery and GST*. That's the complete price and a savings of over 10% off the cover prices—quite a bargain! I understand that accepting the books and gift places me under no obligation ever to buy any books. I can always return a shipment and cancel at any time. Even if I never buy another book from Silhouette, the 4 free books and the surprise gift are mine to keep forever.

345 SEN CF2W

Name	(PLEASE PRINT)	
Address		Apt. No.
City	Province	Postal Code

This offer is limited to one order per household and not valid to present Silhouette Intimate Moments® subscribers. *Terms and prices are subject to change without notice.
Canadian residents will be charged applicable provincial taxes and GST.

CMOM-696 ©1990 Harlequin Enterprises Limited

Catch more great

◆ HARLEQUIN™ Movies

featured on **the movie channel** tmc

Premiering March 14th
Treacherous Beauties
starring Emma Samms and
Bruce Greenwood based on the
novel by Cheryl Emerson

Don't miss next month's movie!
Hard to Forget
based on the novel by bestselling
Harlequin Superromance® author
Evelyn A. Crowe, premiering
April 11th!

If you are not currently a subscriber to
The Movie Channel, simply call your
local cable or satellite provider for more
details. Call today, and don't miss out
on the romance!

the movie channel tmc   ◆ **HARLEQUIN™**

100% pure movies.   ™ *Makes any time special.™*
100% pure fun.

**Look for these titles—
available at your favorite retail outlet!**

January 1998
Renegade Son by Lisa Jackson

Danielle Summers had problems: a rebellious child
and unscrupulous enemies. In addition, her Montana
ranch was slowly being sabotaged. And then there was
Chase McEnroe—who admired her land and desired her
body. But Danielle feared he would invade more than just
her property—he'd trespass on her heart.

February 1998
The Heart's Yearning by Ginna Gray

Fourteen years ago Laura gave her baby up for adoption,
and not one day had passed that she didn't think about
him and agonize over her choice—so she finally followed
her heart to Texas to see her child. But the plan to watch
her son from afar doesn't quite happen that way, once the
boy's sexy—*single*—father takes a decided interest in *her*.

March 1998
First Things Last by Dixie Browning

One look into Chandler Harrington's dark eyes and
Belinda Massey could refuse the Virginia millionaire nothing.
So how could the no-nonsense nanny believe the rumors that
he had kidnapped his nephew—an adorable, healthy little boy
who crawled as easily into her heart as he did into her lap?

**BORN IN THE USA: Love, marriage—
and the pursuit of family!**

BUSA4

ALICIA SCOTT

Continues the twelve-book series— 36 Hours—in March 1998 with Book Nine

PARTNERS IN CRIME

The storm was over, and Detective Jack Stryker finally had a prime suspect in Grand Springs' high-profile murder case. But beautiful Josie Reynolds wasn't about to admit to the crime— nor did Jack want her to. He believed in her innocence, and he teamed up with the alluring suspect to prove it. But was he playing it by the book—or merely blinded by love?

For Jack and Josie and *all* the residents of Grand Springs, Colorado, the storm-induced blackout was just the beginning of 36 Hours that changed *everything!* You won't want to miss a single book.

Available at your favorite retail outlet.

Silhouette ®
TM

SC36HRS9

DIANA PALMER
ANN MAJOR
SUSAN MALLERY

MONTANA MAVERICKS Weddings

RETURN TO WHITEHORN

In **April 1998** get ready to catch the bouquet. Join in the excitement as these bestselling authors lead us down the aisle with three heartwarming tales of love and matrimony in Big Sky country.

A very engaged lady is having second thoughts about her intended; a pregnant librarian is wooed by the town bad boy; a cowgirl meets up with her first love. Which Maverick will be the next one to get hitched?

Available in **April 1998.**

Silhouette's beloved **MONTANA MAVERICKS** returns in Special Edition and Harlequin Historicals starting in February 1998, with brand-new stories from your favorite authors.

Round up these great new stories at your favorite retail outlet.

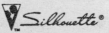

Silhouette®

Look us up on-line at: http://www.romance.net

PSMMWEDS